For my beautiful girls,
may this be a cautionary tale.

First published in England 2009
by Prospera Publishing Limited

A CIP catalogue record for this book is available from
the British Library

National Library of Australia
Cataloguing-in-Publication data:

Schmidt, Nicky

Naked in Knightsbridge.
ISBN: 978-0-9561222-7-8

Set in Palatino

Printed and bound in the UK by CPI Cox & Wyman.

Prospera Publishing Limited
Level 3, 3-5 Barrett St, London W1U 1AY.

Contact: editor@prospera.co.uk.

Naked in Knightsbridge

NICKY SCHMIDT

ACKNOWLEDGEMENTS

To Big X, Mrs S, Marsha, Yannick, Jayna and all at Prospera, many thanks for the edits. To the many friends and family members who contributed ideas for Jools' escapades, thank you and may I say to some of you, I am worried for your mental health.

Readers please note: *some of the policies mentioned regarding government benefits are fiction and liberties have been taken for the purposes of the story. Please check with any organisations mentioned for correct information should you require it.*

Chapter 1

Dear Miss Grand,

I am writing with regards to your business overdraft, which is now almost £5000 in excess of the agreed amount. As you are aware, this additional expenditure is unapproved and in breach of your contract with us. You are therefore required to bring your borrowing under the agreed limit of £20,000 immediately, in order to retain your line of credit.

Yours sincerely,

Horace Fortescue
Loans and Finance Director
Commercial Bank London

THROWING THE LETTER onto the coffee table, Jools nudged best friend Mel and pointed eastward. Outside, Hunk of No Fixed Abode was standing by the letterbox, looking seedy.

'Not him again,' Mel grumbled. 'A hobo with a strange mail fixation. What could you possibly see in someone like him?'

'I'm sure he has one or two redeemable qualities,' Jools grinned wickedly. 'Besides, I haven't had sex in eight months.' She picked a HobNob out of the packet on the window sill and bit it in half. 'I figure he won't run screaming if he claps eyes on my unshaved bits.'

Mel snorted. 'God, will you raise your standards up past your navel long enough to give a relationship a chance? You aren't half bad-looking when you put on a bit of slap and a decent skirt.' She looked Jools up and down. 'Or any skirt, for that matter. And if you don't mind me saying, you could do with a bit of exercise and a few less biscuits.'

Jools knew Mel was trying to be supportive – in truth, she *could* do with a lot less biscuits. At nearly 11 stone, with weird, fuzzy dark-blonde hair that would do any loo-brush proud, and cream-coloured teeth that had borne the brunt of ten years of double-shot espressos, she urgently needed one of those extreme makeovers. Luckily her face was passable – greenish eyes and a certain satisfying symmetry to her features – but a pretty face didn't hide the fact she was seriously lacking in finesse.

Reminding her friend of ten years that having standards was a luxury she couldn't window-shop for, let alone afford, Jools considered Hunk of No Fixed Abode again thoughtfully.

'Nice cheekbones,' she said hopefully, as she watched him caress the mailbox.

'How can you tell through all that hair? Look, it's growing out of his cheeks. Possibly out of his eyeballs, too. And why on earth does he hang out by that mailbox all day? It's not natural to molest a mailbox. I'm sure it's a violation of some sort.'

'Maybe he knows the postman?'

'Wants to mug him, more like. And if I recall, it's actually a postwoman.'

Jools swore. 'I hope she's not competition.'

Mel rolled her eyes. It was alright for Mel, Jools thought sulkily. She was gorgeous, in that pixie-like way men adored. Tidy black bob, size 8 body perfectly proportioned for her all-black feminista garb purchased exclusively from Prada. Mel was listed in Debrett's even though her father, Lord Something or Other, had almost disowned her when she'd told him that come the revolution, he and his kind would be the final guests in the Tower.

Somehow, Mel managed to overlook the fact that she was also 'that kind'. She worked tirelessly for two quid a week as an equal opportunity solicitor, sticking claim forms up the proverbials of evil bosses who dared to insult the gender, race or religion of her clients.

Why were they friends? Jools suspected Mel's curiosity about the other half – the great fat unwashed – had brought them together. When Mel spied Jools at UCL, abusing a vending machine for stealing her change, Mel decided to take her on, the same way someone adopts a wayward stray from a shelter.

Given Mel's looks and connections, the new friendship helped Jools establish herself as a dominant force of the 'it' crowd. She even managed to lose her virginity to a popular and remarkably randy little medical student named Horry, who told her he 'liked 'em chunky'.

Eager to move on from the mailbox molesting hobo, Mel asked what the latest was with the business.

'Not good.' Jools preferred to avoid thinking about the state of her small cleaning company. Dire was the best description for it now and if Jools was honest, it had never been more than a few women running around cleaning houses for a few bob.

It had all started when she couldn't get a job after university. Oddly, her arts degree with a major in bed-hopping didn't seem to excite potential employers. She'd gone round to Mel's old Knightsbridge flat (who'd since upgraded to a three-bed in Kensington) to complain about her sad state of affairs and Mel's next door neighbour, Mrs Randy, had popped in to share the disastrous news that her cleaner had quit.

'I'll do it,' Jools had said, despite being utterly useless at cleaning anything effectively – except her dinner plate, of course.

But Mrs Randy (why someone would choose to keep that unfortunate surname 'in memory of my dead husband' was beyond Jools) had seemed happy enough at her feeble attempts with a dustcloth and Dyson, and when she had extracted a crisp twenty pound note for two hours' work, Jools figured there were worse ways to make money. (Like the time she had to dress as a chicken and parade outside the takeaway place on the high street, clucking and handing out 'buy one get one free' coupons – all for the princely sum of four quid an hour.) Jools shuddered at the memory. Wiping down every toilet seat between Knightsbridge and Heathrow was better than that sort of public humiliation.

So she launched a quest for more work near Mel's, hoping to save energy and money by keeping all her clients close together. Knocking on one imposing door, she came across Mrs Pho. The woman didn't want to pay for cleaning – the richer they are, the stingier – but she would let Jools use her 30-square-foot basement studio flat as an office in return for cleaning the five-storey house every week, and her kitchen every day. She also wanted Jools to scrub down her mother-in-law on Mondays but Jools drew the line at *that!*

Slowly, over two years, her small company expanded – thanks to a large bank loan and the conditional generosity of Mrs Pho. Mel told her over and over to become a limited company, saying Jools would be personally liable if things went wrong, but somehow she never got around to it.

Then things started to unwind.

First, one of her cleaners went on a pilfering spree and redefined 'cleaning out' a bedroom by nicking £4000 worth of jewellery from the Slatterly-Walsh household on Montpellier Street. Their insurance company sued Jools for it. Bastards. It wasn't her fault, was it? Of course, not having insurance presented more than a slight problem in defending the claim. Even with Mel's pro bono aid, all of Jools' reserves went to appease the 'We Are Not Kidding We Will Send the Boys Around' insurance.

After that, Jools got business insurance, which cost her triple thanks to her business being sued for theft. But she was certain things would work themselves out, so she just called the bank, increased her overdraft, paid the insurance and carried on.

But things didn't get better. A chain of gourmet sausage shops – for which Jools had the exclusive cleaning contract – poisoned a couple of hundred people, including the local health and safety officer. They had to close, and Jools took a heavy hit – 60 per cent of her income was sausage-related. That's what you get when you rely too much on cheap meat. And they even had the nerve to blame *her* for the listeria!

Her remaining clients were the finicky kind no one else wanted – and they rarely paid on time, if at all. Like Mr Polowski, who always found 'DE FLUFF' under the sofa. Jools suspected he had a jar full of 'DE FLUFF' he'd gathered, placing it strategically throughout the flat to test her. And he was nothing compared to Madame Nabet, who insisted Jools vacuum her annoying little Chihuahuas. Jools rubbed her wrist where one had clamped onto her. Neither had paid since . . . well, Jools would need to look over her largely non-existent records to be sure.

So in the last month, once she took out insurance payments, wages and all the other stuff you needed to run a company, Jools earned negative £2000. Not exactly the lucrative business she'd been hoping for. She'd thought she could deal with it, though.

Until Eugenia, her last remaining employee, burned down Mrs Pho's house. Who knew burning incense near a gas burner would cause explosions? It wasn't like there were warnings – on either the stove or the incense! Eugenia might have noticed the top-floor studio was on fire if she hadn't been bonking her boyfriend Nutto on the kitchen table. By the time Jools arrived to supervise (as per the contract with Mrs Pho), the place had burned to the ground.

Literally, it burned to the ground. Jools had assumed it just a saying, but no – Mrs Pho's beautiful, white Victorian terrace was indeed reduced to a pile of black soot.

'How could you!'

What could she say? Clearly she could because she had.

Or at least Eugina and Nutto had. In more ways than one.

'Mrs Pho, I can explain everything.'

But Jools' most important client (and landlady) wasn't in the mood to hear anything.

Not even the hunky fireman with the ever-so-subtle goatee was on her side. 'Pretty bloody hard to explain how you blew up a whole house, without trying to.'

Eugenia piped up: 'Actually, it wasn't that hard – '

Mrs Pho stomped her Manolo on the footpath. 'What do you mean, stupid girl? I pay you to clean my beautiful home, and you burn horrible stick in mother-in-law's room and blow up house!'

Then it was Jools' turn. 'How come you alive anyway? You supposed to watch cleaner. How come you not dead?'

She made it sound like Jools being alive was a bad thing. Looking at the fierce frown on the face of the cute fireman, it seemed a popular opinion.

'Well?'

Oh shit. 'I had an emergency, Mrs Pho. I've been here all the other times, I promise.' Total lie – she was in Harrods' foodhall most other times, indulging in macaroons at *Laduree,* but there was no point in upsetting the poor woman any more, was there?

Mrs Pho moved in close. Her Botoxed face shone like her brass door-knocker – before it was blown off the front door and became a projectile. She grabbed Jools by the neck.

'I would love to say you fired – and evicted. But there no business, no house, and no point!' She jabbed

Jools in the chest as she spoke. 'But I promise you,' she spat, as one of the firemen somewhat begrudgingly dragged her off Jools, 'you never work in Knightsbridge again. Not as long as I breathing.'

Soon after, the insurance company informed Jools they wouldn't cover her anymore. Shockingly unprofessional, Jools thought – what was insurance for, if not for incidents such as these? She was probably their best customer!. Then the stuffy Royal Borough called to tell her if she worked without insurance, they'd put her in jail – if the police didn't get to her first for something called criminal negligence.

Jools updated Mel on the latest bit about the council. She knew the rest of the gory details already.

'God, Jools, what are you going to do?'

'What everyone else does when they go bankrupt – go on the dole. At least I'll be able to live.'

'Oh.' Mel went quiet.

'What is it?'

'I think that little problem a few years ago might work against you.'

Shit, she'd forgotten about that. Jools had claimed for a non-existent child for three years. It hadn't been total bogus in the beginning – she had honestly thought she was pregnant for a week or two. And she'd paid it all back. Surely that must count for something?

Mel shook her head. 'Not really. They had to threaten you with jail before you paid up. Remember?'

'I was broke – a uni student. Talk about stingy!'

Mel shrugged. 'Not big on fraud, the government.'

'Unless they're the ones with their noses in the trough,' Jools spat. 'Like that guy who claimed second home allowance on a wheelie bin.'

Mel reminded her he actually was in jail as they spoke. 'May I suggest you try to drum up some more business and avoid bankruptcy? Surely you can work as a cleaner for someone else? That way you avoid the whole insurance problem?'

Jools groaned. God, she was sick of bloody working. Cleaning other people's muck for ten quid an hour wasn't exactly a dream job.

She stared at Mel enviously. Life was alright for her – sitting at a desk and lording it over people. And even though she tried to distance herself from her aristocratic family, her mother insisted on buying the Kensington crash pad, and her father was constantly sending cars round for the drive back to their Hertfordshire country estate. (Apparently when her father had said he disowned her, he meant for five minutes, on full trust fund.)

Jools' life looked even more rubbish in comparison. She lived in a studio flat near the Willesden Green bus garage. Well, 'near' was putting it nicely. She was so close to the drivers' canteen that remarkably consistent farting could be heard day and night through the flat's only opening window.

'Well, what else are you going to do? Maybe Deepak will give you a job at Handimart?' Handimart was the nearby 24-hour off-licence where Mel and Jools were infamous late-night regulars seeking emergency alcohol supplies.

Jools turned a deep shade of puce. 'Deepak caught me pinching a packet of Tampax last week.'

'Jools!'

'Oh, come on, Mel! I was desperate and there was a huge queue. I was going to pay for them right after I went to the loo.'

Mel was silent.

'I was, I just forgot.'

'Well, if not Deepak, then someone else. You'd better start looking for work, or you'll get evicted.'

'I figured that out for myself, thanks very much.' Jools was slightly indignant. 'In fact, no matter what you say, I'm going to apply for help, join the queue of the great unwashed. Isn't this what our taxes – ?'

Mel interrupted. 'Actually, isn't Inland Revenue chasing you too?'

'Whatever.' Mel was such a stickler for the law. 'All that preggers stuff was ages ago. Surely they can't hold a grudge that long?'

Chapter 2

Dear Mr Fortescue,

Thanks for your letter. Horace is a unique name. You must be a very special man. As I recall, you're extremely buff as well. Alright, well, to the issue at hand. I can assure you I am doing everything I can to bring down my overdraft. In fact, I hope to hear of a new, secure income stream in the next few days. Meanwhile, I don't suppose you would consider extending the overdraft by an extra £2000 to cover my out-of-pocket expenses in establishing this vital new addition to my business model?

Kind regards,

Julia M. Grand

APPARENTLY THE unemployment office was busy catering to those even needier than Jools, and she couldn't get an appointment for two weeks.

The nice man on the toll-free number assured her

they could pay from the moment she'd lost her job, as long as she had all the relevant paperwork and she met the criteria for Jobseeker's Allowance.

Relevant paperwork? Jools wondered if a copy of the call log to the Fire Brigade would do the trick, and if so, how could she get one. Maybe call her insurance company or even Mrs Pho? No. That might attract further expensive lawsuits and old Horace at the Commercial Bank would definitely hang tight on future advances if he discovered there was yet another negligence claim on the horizon.

She sank onto her musty little sofa and stared out at the brick wall of the bus garage. The cleaning business had imploded. There was no way to get new clients – she couldn't even advertise with the local rag since her account was 120 days overdue. How on earth could she pay for the little necessities in life, like rent, water and HobNobs? Hopefully, her dear friend Horace would continue to expand the overdraft until the dole kicked in. But right now the cash point was being most unhelpful. Jools had to make some money.

In desperation, she tried other cleaning companies, but the moment she gave her name, the response was the same.

'You're not the Julia Grand of Julia Grand Cleaning?'

'Yes, but . . .'

CLICK.

'Didn't you burn down a client's house?'

'Yes, but . . .'

CLICK.

'You give cleaners a bad name. I've lost three clients because of you.'

CLICK.

Mrs Pho had been busy. How had one small woman managed to spread the word so quickly? Clearly there was no chance of working as a cleaner in London again unless Jools changed her name and invested in that extreme makeover – which in turn required the rapidly vanishing generosity of her bank.

Hand creeping towards her second pack of HobNobs that day, she considered Mel's Handimart suggestion. If not Deepak, maybe one of the shopkeepers on the high street would consider giving her work?

It was time to make some money and keep the bank and her landlord from her slightly warped door.

Standing up, she shook the crumbs off her tracksuit. It felt a little tight under the arms.

Must have shrunk in the wash. She couldn't have put on that much weight, could she? After all, she'd been running around Knightsbridge cleaning houses until a week ago. Or, at least, her cleaners had.

Jools stared at her reflection in the bathroom mirror. Maybe she should change first? Shellsuit-needing-wash was hardly a great look when one was on the hunt for employment.

She turned to her wardrobe, a rickety contraption

with a missing leg supported by old textbooks. But when it was impossible to get a leg through one of her skirts – let alone her sizable bum – it soon became apparent nothing suitable would fit.

When had she stopped wearing normal clothes? How long had it been since she'd been to Topshop? Or even Primark? The one pair of jeans that did fit had a nasty stain right near the crotch from a ketchup incident at Sticky Finger's in Kensington two weeks ago.

Jools had been meaning to do a load of laundry, but depression and lack of coinage had scuppered that particular plan.

There were some vaguely attractive knickers and bra combos, but she could hardly mince down the high street in those, could she?

There was no choice but to wear her only clean pair of trousers: navy tracksuit bottoms with 'Living It Is Large' written in neon across the derriere, purchased as a joke from a market stall in Chinatown after a rather merry evening with Mel and Gracie, another uni chum.

Sighing, Jools tugged on a clean but furry, lime-green jumper, adding a string of faux pearls she'd bought with a dress that now wouldn't go further than her thighs. At least she was clean. That had to be a plus point.

She set off on her mission.

A few doors down the high street, a squiggly

handwritten sign in *A La Mode* boutique beckoned:

Assistant Wanted Sat and Sun.

Saturday and Sunday? Working on weekends would definitely curb her social life. Hang on, apart from Mel, she didn't have a social life, did she?

'Can I 'elp you?' The pristine girl behind the counter looked Jools up and down.

She took a deep breath and tried to look confident, motioning towards the front window and the sign. 'I've come about the job.'

'Oh.' The Carla Bruni look-alike took in Jools' trainers, tracksuit bottoms and rather tight-fitting jumper.

'Do you 'ave ze experience?'

'Well, I've recently run my own company and …'

'What was zis company?'

'Sorry?'

'What do ze company do?'

Shit. Jools was hoping she wouldn't ask that. 'Um, cleaning.'

Silence, then: 'What 'appen to your company? Did you zell it?'

Double shit. Jools was hoping she wouldn't ask that either. 'No, I had a bit of trouble.'

'Trouble? What sort of trouble?'

Shit, shit, shit. She was really hoping she wouldn't ask that.

'Well, one of my employees burned down a . . .'

Carla had heard enough. 'Well, maybe you zend in the CV and we call you for interview. Maybe.'

There was no doubt that response translated as: maybe if hell freezes over and the devil skates over to me wearing a leotard, does a triple twirl and offers me a double chocolate mocha with cream and Baileys.

Leaving the boutique, Jools longed to run back to the comfort of her HobNobs, but forced herself to wander up and down the high street.

The only other place that needed help was the Goldilocks' Theme Pub. Steeling herself to inquire, she discovered employees actually had to wear themed outfits – either the shortest skirt known to man (obviously a male interpretation of what young girls wear on a morning hunt for porridge), or a bulky bear suit. 'You'd make a great bear,' the manager said enthusiastically, eyeing the tagline on her tracksuited bottom. Jools wasn't sure if going from a chicken costume to a bear was a step up or a step down. Either way, she certainly wasn't going to find out.

Suddenly, a firm hand gripped her shoulder. Hoping for Hunk of No Fixed Abode, she turned to find her landlord, Rocco Martucci, eyeballing her, arms full of kebabs. Jools' stomach leapt at the delicious spicy smell.

'Joolsy, Joolsy,' his voice betraying the fact that a tracheotomy wasn't far off.

'I been looking for you, innit? You owe me £1,349.'

Oh-oh. She couldn't run or hide – Rocco knew exactly where to find her and besides, he had a set of keys. Not to mention that in her current state, Jools could neither run nor hide. She feigned surprise. 'Really? Didn't you get my cheque? I sent you the full amount.'

Rocco was having none of it. 'No. I want money, Joolsy. Now!'

'Well you know how the Royal Mail is, Rocco. I'm sure it'll turn up soon.' She licked her lips. 'I don't suppose you have an extra kebab?'

Grabbing her arm, Rocco began dragging Jools to the nearest cash point. 'How about you cancel the cheque and pay me now? Make things easy.'

She tried to squirm free but his grip tightened. Jools thought fast. 'Maybe the cheque was stolen and cashed? The money won't be there.'

'That's your problem.' They were in front of the cash point now. 'Money please. £500 will do – for today. I'm a reasonable guy, innit.'

Promising God she'd convert from carbohydrates to a proper religion if he commanded money out of the machine, Jools cupped her hands at the slot of the cash point and prayed.

But like the rest of London, God must have been watching a repeat of EastEnders. The stupid machine ate her card, a message told her to contact her branch immediately, and Rocco began clicking his knuckles in anticipation.

Chapter 3

Dear Miss Grand,

Thank you for your undated letter, which we received on 3rd March. Whilst I appreciate the exuberant compliments, unfortunately Commercial Bank London cannot extend further overdraft privileges to you, no matter how attractive you perceive me to be, until the balance is brought down within the agreed limit.

We look forward to receiving such sums within the next week, and urge you to contact us immediately should you experience difficulties making payment.

Yours faithfully,

Horace Fortescue
Commercial Bank London

WAITING FOR THE response to her plea, Jools glanced around Mel's roomy Kensington pad. The luxury flat stretched across the second floor of a Victorian mansion block in the rich heartland of W8. It was so far removed from Jools' smelly little flat near the bus garage she expected someone to tap her on the shoulder and ask if she was lost and lead her quickly along the posh streets to the tube.

Taking in the slick interior, the familiar pang of jealously gnawed. Why couldn't she have been born into money, instead of a home where everything was quite literally broken, stolen, or – like her father – so far past its sell-by date it was practically worthless. Everything here was so glossy; even the people seemed to shine with wealth. The pristine tree-lined streets doubled as Maserati or Porsche dealerships, with almost every car worth more than the two-bed, South London semi she'd grown up in.

Picking at the scabbing Chihuahua bite, Jools wondered how to approach the money issue with Mel. She'd shed what little pride she had left to beg Mel for money to pay Rocco. If Mel refused, there would be the kind of trouble that ended with a visit via ambulance to the local NHS pit. Rocco had agreed not to bash her face in if she paid in full, plus two weeks in advance, by the next morning. The deal expired in exactly two hours.

Mel wasn't exactly thrilled at being hit up for cash. 'I'll lend you money, but in the meantime, be proactive. Sell something, make something. Anything.'

'I tried to get a job,' Jools protested. 'Absolutely no luck. And I *did* ring up to apply for the dole.'

Mel sighed. 'That was a waste of time, I told you, remember?'

'Well, I managed an appointment, so it wasn't a total loss.'

Mel told her she needed to grow up. 'Jools, you always take the easy way out. You fell into cleaning because you didn't want to bother with a proper job, then you didn't vet your employees properly, and now you're hardly even making an effort to get a job. I mean,' she pointed at Jools' tracksuit bottoms, 'I hope you didn't go job hunting in those?'

Jools looked shifty.

'Jools!'

'But I don't have anything else.'

'You have loads of clothes.' Mel launched into high-gear ticking off. 'That's why you're broke. You wasted too much money on designer gear. £800 for Prada trousers, if I recall correctly. What about them?'

She pouted. 'Too small. Everything is too small.' All those HobNobs have taken their toll. It wasn't fair. Comfort eating shouldn't make you look worse. Where's the comfort in that?

'You need to pull yourself together. Maybe it's time to ask your dad for . . .'

Shaking her head furiously, Jools wondered how could Mel even suggest that?

The last anyone had heard, her dad was living with a 26-year-old lap dancer – the very thought put Jools off HobNobs. Well, for about five minutes, anyway.

'Look, I'm sorry. I just thought that . . . Oh, never mind. Why don't I take you out for breakfast? We can get cash for Rocco on the way. How much is it again?'

Deep down, Mel was a sweetheart and couldn't resist a charity case, even though Jools was about as close as Mel would ever get to a real down-and-out, unless you counted the bag lady who sat in front of Tesco's on Kensington High Street asking for money for cat litter.

The thought of food cheered Jools immensely. Maybe they could go to Gladstones, the posh place around the corner.

Mel made a face. 'Not wearing those tracksuit bottoms. How about McDonald's? The one up the road does a particularly good coffee.'

'Forget coffee. It's all about the hash browns,' Jools said, linking arms with her friend.

Two-and-a-half hours and a bus ride later, Jools was back on her own smelly sofa, thinking blissfully of Bacon and Egg McMuffins just consumed.

Mel's comments floated through her head. Sell something. Isn't that what she had said?

How did you sell stuff? Wait a minute – didn't people make a fortune selling stuff online?

She looked around her shabby little cubicle of a flat. Well, they said one man's rubbish was another man's treasure – though to be frank her things were more on the rubbish side of things. What did she have to lose?

A few biscuits and a cup of tea would help give her energy to sort through her stuff. But halfway through a HobNob, Jools fell asleep. She awoke with the soggy remnants stuck to her tongue, wondering what it was she'd planned to do right before phasing out.

Sell her stuff. That's right. A quick lunch of bread and Nutella and Jools went to work, ferreting through everything in her flat to find sellable items.

One pair of Adidas trainers; slightly used, slightly stinky from a run-in with doggie-do on the way to the chippy.

Four size 14 and 16 sweaters, all with at least one immovable stain located somewhere obvious.

A four-year-old iPod Shuffle that might or might not be working – she'd lost the power cord, box and every accessory that had come with it.

A toaster that had blown up when she'd tried to jam a crumpet into it.

And finally, the item she was banking on to pay this month's rent – one brand-new pair of size 10 Prada trousers, purchased as an incentive for weight loss, still gorgeous in their original black and white Prada packaging.

Picking up a massive *Online Selling for the Mentally Challenged* she'd found in the specials' bin of the local bookstore a year ago (purchased for buying cheap cleaning supplies that turned out to consist largely of water and sugar), Jools skimmed the section on 'Setting Up Your Shop'. Halfway through the chapter, it was clear making a fortune online might not be as easy as she'd hoped.

Thanks to the fire at Mrs Pho's, she was minus a computer and camera.

Great. What was she going to do now? Maybe go to an Internet café but they cost money, and right now, every penny borrowed from Mel was going straight to Rocco to preserve her life. It wasn't polite to ask Mel for more money – besides, the lucky cow had taken off to New York for a work conference.

Jools stood up and gazed out of the grimy window for inspiration. There, tempting her, was a lovely new computer, sitting in the bus station's staff canteen.

Ideal. If only she could get in there, just to get the auctions started. Then she could use just the Internet café to check emails, without having to spend too much.

Alright, there was still the camera issue to contend with, but she could be good with words – like those advertising copywriters who entice people with snazzy syntax.

The canteen was empty. It might be possible to jump out the window and sneak into the canteen, but what if someone noticed. Besides, there were no guarantees she'd fit through the window.

'Psst.'

What was that? Not Rocco! But after quickly scanning the tiny flat, she was relieved to find it free of kebab-scoffing lunatics.

'Psst!'

It was coming from outside.

Hunk of No Fixed Abode was standing in the door next to the canteen, eating a doughnut.

'Want one?'

Was he actually a bus driver? It wouldn't surprise her. Some London bus drivers *did* look like a Darwinian dream of the missing link. But Hunk of No Fixed Abode didn't seem to own a uniform. If he wasn't a driver, he definitely couldn't be management – that required at least a shower and some form of hairbrush.

He must have just snuck in there to steal food. Jools hadn't eaten for at least forty-five minutes and right now a calorie-loaded treat would hit the spot perfectly. Ignoring the little voice in her head that said being an accomplice to doughnut-pinching was just as bad as stealing, she leaned out the window.

'Yes, please,' she replied in a whisper, in case someone caught them in the illicit act.

Taking a plate from the table in the canteen, Hunk of No Fixed Abode came over to the window – which was only slightly higher than him. He must be around 6 foot 2, Jools estimated. Impressive!

A plate of fresh, deliciously-iced doughnuts was held up. They sat in a neat pile, begging to be eaten.

'Thanks,' said Jools, taking only one. It wouldn't do if Hunk of No Fixed Abode thought she had no self-control. Luckily, he couldn't see the contradictory expanding backside from out there.

'You're welcome.' He was surprisingly well spoken.

Posh, even. And those eyes! Plus, up close, he looked cleaner than from afar. The hobo outfit was definitely third or fourth-hand, but the skin underneath seemed relatively clean. His cuticles seemed well cared for too, though the hands were grubby. Interesting, thought Jools, a hobo with good personal hygiene. She couldn't wait to tell Mel. Surely hygiene in a hobo was a major plus point? And he didn't appear pissed or stoned either. The plus points were stacking up!

The plate was raised again. 'Another?'

Jools shook her head. It wasn't good to come across as greedy. As a distraction from the lure of the doughnuts, she jerked her head towards the canteen: 'I don't suppose they have a computer in there they aren't using?'

Wide-eyes stared back, unblinking.

Shit. He thinks I want him to steal one. 'No, I don't mean nicking one,' Jools spluttered. 'It's just, I need a computer to make money and if I could just pop in and use one… '

Hunk of No Fixed Abode didn't reply, just smiled and passed her the plate once more. 'Have another.'

I'll take that as a no. Unable to resist, she grabbed another high-in-every-kind-of-fat no-no and sank back onto her dirty little sofa to enjoy it – and to contemplate the hobo's bum as he wandered back towards the canteen.

How did he manage to make those manky old combats look so bloody sexy?

Chapter 4

Dear Mr Fortescue,

I'm sure an intelligent man such as yourself appreciates that in order to make money, one must spend money. Therefore, I can assure you that should you allow the cheques I have written to a number of establishments during the last week to be added to my overdraft, you can expect a speedy and swift payment in the very near future.

Fondest regards,

Julia M. Grand

TWO DAYS LATER, as Jools was preparing a delicious supper of instant noodles and white chocolate mousse (virtually free from Handimart since they were well past their sell-by dates), she heard a soft *thump* outside, right by the front door.

Fearing Rocco, she held her breath and hid in the shower until receding footsteps could be heard, then opened the squeaky laminate door to investigate.

There, sitting neatly on the step, was a dirty old laptop with a power cord taped to the base. A scrappy note attached to the screen said:

fond in scip, al yours. Bus intnet works.

Hunk of No Fixed Abode had come through for her. Jools' heart skipped a beat. He went skip hunting just for her. For her! There must be some feelings there.

Then reality set in. Feelings or not, any laptop found in the rubbish by a hobo ran the very real risk of not working. There was a reason such things were in skips in the first place. Jools grabbed the cord, plugged it in and turned it on. There was a whirring and a dainty 'ping' and the familiar PC logo sprang to life. Yes! It actually worked. Hunk of No Fixed Abode deserved a medal. Well, he probably deserved a good meal and a decent roof over his head but Jools was in no position to offer that, was she?

More miraculous still, upon clicking the Internet icon, the connection launched immediately. The bus garage must have unsecured access – not extremely wise. (Someone who lived within spitting distance of Mrs Pho's had downloaded the entire Beatles back catalogue, courtesy of Julia Grand Cleaning, and BT had hit Jools with a huge bill which, as she recalled, she had yet to pay.)

Quickly putting aside thoughts of her ever-mounting debts, Jools thought about the hot hobo and wondered how to thank him. Maybe make him a meal? But what did she have to offer but close-to-the-sell-by-date beans? Still, he was a hobo, so maybe he wouldn't mind risking salmonella for the chance to eat? Yes, when she saw him again she would ask him over for a spicy date of beans and cider. At least she didn't have to be embarrassed about her paltry circumstances, did she?

Jools was longing to shift her online sales career into high gear, but she'd arranged to meet Mel in a nearby café to hear all about her trip. She reluctantly trundled down the stairs from her flat and out onto the damp pavement. Outside, buses coughed and mumbled exhaust that made the garage look like a grim nineteenth-century mining town. Through the haze, she narrowly avoided a newly deposited pile of vomit just outside her building. Flip-flops were a little too precarious for this neighbourhood.

After her latest job rejection – from Lucky Loo 'We Want You' Cleaners of Willesden Green (who told her 'we no want you type of clean') – she'd grabbed the closest thing to hand and lobbed it out the open window into the street. Problem was, it was the left shoe of her only decent pair of flats. So now the choice was between too-small Adidas trainers (which she planned on selling anyway) or £1 Primark flip-flops.

She checked her watch. Shit, better get moving – Mel didn't appreciate being left alone around here. She flipped and flopped with determination to Mama

Blue's Café, buoyed by her gift from the hunky hobo and the possibility of making enough of a living to avoid being unceremoniously evicted and/or bashed by the evil, kebab-hoarding Rocco.

Mel was already waiting inside, hands warming around a steaming double-shot café latte, feet cosily encased in expensive Uggs that were kicked up on a chair. Jools waved and headed to the counter – no such thing as table service at Mama Blue's.

She was starving, as usual. She checked the menu for the cheapest item: a coffee and plain-toast combo for a quid.

'That's supposed to be for retirees,' scowled the barista as she took Jools' money.

'Well, as it happens I'm currently retired.' Jools held her head high. 'And put some whipped cream on it.'

'The toast or the coffee?' the barista snorted.

Jools shrugged. 'Both.'

She lifted Mel's feet off the chair and squeezed herself into it.

God, she was only 28 but she felt about a hundred. She deserved that retiree deal.

'Alright?' asked Mel, looking pointedly at her feet. 'Bit cold for flip-flops, isn't it?'

'Doing great, thanks. And I can't afford new clothes, or shoes, so don't start.' replied Jools more snappishly than intended. Hunger did that to her.

'How's the job hunt going?'

'Still looking, but, you know, I have a few ideas.'

'Your ideas are what got you into this mess. I don't suppose you've heard from social services yet?'

'Still waiting for my appointment, but I'm sure it'll go well. They say they'll back-date the payments.'

'Good luck with that.' Mel bit into her pricey-looking almond croissant. Jools couldn't take her eyes off the flaky goodness.

'Thanks. You're very supportive.'

Somehow, Mel missed the sarcasm. 'That's what I'm here for, Jools, to cheer you up.'

'I think you must be mistaking these convulsions for laughter. I'm actually suppressing the biggest anxiety attack you've ever seen.'

'You can always crash with me if things don't pick up. There are people who love you, you know.'

'Well, one person. You.' Jools took a big slurp of cream to make her life seem less pathetic.

'What about your dad? I know you hate talking about him, but if things got bad I'm sure you could stay with him couldn't you?'

Jools bit into her slice of burnt toast. It was so black that its origins as bread were hard to discern. At least the cream tasted good. 'Last resort, Mel. That hovel in Tooting is definitely the last resort.'

'Well, like I said, you're more than welcome to move in with me. Ever since Michel left . . .'

Jools interrupted the start of her routine lament with a wracking cough barely masking an underlying 'Arsehole!'

Mel frowned. 'I know you think he's no good and I agree, he was then. But not anymore.'

Jools dropped her charcoal toast. 'What? Anymore? Don't tell me . . . Have you talked to him?'

'Just once. He called, I answered, he apologised and... '

This wasn't looking good. 'You slept with him, didn't you?'

Mel was affronted. 'No! Are you insane? After he left me for a fifty-year-old stripper? What kind of sucker do you think I am?'

Quite a large one – literally and figuratively, if you could believe Mel's boasts. 'You've taken him back twice before.'

Standing up, Mel grabbed her stuff. 'Look at the time. I've got a meeting to defend some misguided youths. Poor things, they've been accused of a laptop scam or something. I'd better get going.'

Jools was immediately reminded of Hunk of No Fixed Abode and his computer. She was definitely not telling Mel about his gift now. She'd only force her to report it to the police, and Jools needed that particular piece of equipment to survive, at least until the dole kicked in.

Mel gave her a quick hug. 'I'll call you tomorrow, alright? Hang in there.'

'Have fun at your important job. In the meantime, I'll enjoy the walk back to my rat-infested flat whilst my kneecaps are still intact.'

But Mel just smiled and raced off.

Jools watched her tiny frame walking briskly towards her car. Was Mel hiding something from her? Whatever it was, it better not involve that cretin Michel Matthews. Jools clenched her jaw thinking about what a true arsehole he was – the kind who changed names from Michael to Michel and put on a fake (and frankly, terrible) French accent to seem more exotic. The guy was about as exotic as her burnt toast.

Mel, being Mel, had fallen for his bullshit. But there were things Jools knew about him that made her blood boil. If Mel decided to take him back yet again, Jools wasn't sure she'd be able to hold her tongue – or stop herself from attempting to suffocate him with one of her rapidly disintegrating flip-flops.

It was relatively easy to get started as a seller online. Seller! Much better job title than cleaner. Jools was surprised at how efficiently her rubbish-esque laptop managed all its functions – it was faster than her old business computer, and it seemed to have loads of memory. Funny that someone should throw out a gem like this.

There were no photos to upload, but as decided she could make do without – how hard could it be to write a few pithy enticements instead? Considering the state of the merchandise on offer, keeping the offers mysterious might entice more interest.

In a few moments she managed to list the items.

Near new Adidas trainers, size 4. Slight brown stain to canvas. Only adds to the trendy grunge effect.

Pristine iPod. Hot pink. All you need is the charger and battery and you're ready to go!

Prada trousers. White. Size 10. Still with tags. Paid £800. Massive bargain. Don't miss out.

Toaster. Slightly temperamental. Might work for patient handyman. All offers accepted.

Finally, she keyed in her credit card details to pay the fees, crossing her fingers the card would be accepted with the unrealistic hope of a two-headed cripple at Lourdes.

Buoyed by the possibility of a sales career that could be carried out in close proximity to the telly and HobNobs – and the fact that her card hadn't been immediately rejected online – Jools set off for the supermarket in case the miracle of available funds could be repeated at Sainsbury's.

When she returned to her flat an hour or so later, the little red light on her answering machine was flashing wildly. The phone bill was about five months overdue. It was a wonder they hadn't cut her off yet.

'Joolsy, baby! Alright? It's your old dad! Listen, I need to talk to you. Somethin' important.'

Jools rolled her eyes. In the background she could make out a woman's shrill voice yelling: 'Just ask her now! Ask her!'

'Huh? Alright, uh, honey, listen. Suze and I – hey have you met Suze? Right little looker!'

'Hieeee Charlie's daughter!'

Christ, she sounded about 17.

Jools hoped she was at least 17.

'Suze and I are going to Ibiza. Remember how I went there last year with, uh, thingy, the 26-year-old? Amazing pins.'

'CHARLIE! I knew you still thought about her!'

Charlie Grand continued unabated: 'Well, anyways, we had such a good time I want to show Suze how great it is. But the thing is, well, remember how I loaned you money for school all those years ago? Well, I know you paid it back but maybe I could get a loan from you this time around . . . You know, 'cause I'm your dear old dad and you love me and . . .'

BEEP.

Thankfully, the answering machine had decided enough was enough.

Jools staggered to the window, wrestled it open and leaned out, taking deep breaths of stale, petrol-scented air. She'd thought maybe her dad had grown up a bit since the fiasco with the 26-year-old, but no. He was onto a new vacuous bimbo.

The thought of him dating anyone at his age was obscene. That he was dating women even younger than her was enough to put her off HobNobs.

Well, nearly enough.

When her mum died five years ago, Jools' hopes of her parents ever getting back together were finally laid to rest. She'd assumed her father would follow the usual route of acceptance, sink into a fading armchair somewhere, and live out his life watching *Countdown* with the odd pint down the pub for fun.

But her dad had other ideas, the only path he had committed to was growing old as disgracefully as possible. Jools shook her head. He could at least find someone his own age. Or at least within twenty years of his age.

In an attempt to forget the message, she settled down to watch the *A Place in the Sun* marathon, but the lobster-red holidaymakers only reminded her of Charlie Grand. The nerve of the miserable bastard. To ask for money when he knows I'm dirt poor. If she continued to ponder the mysteries of her dad, her head might explode, so she decided to check her online shop. Maybe the sight of all that soon-to-be-available cash would perk up her afternoon?

A host of messages were waiting in the inbox. Brilliant. Her sales patter must be doing the trick. Eagerly, she clicked onto the first one.

Question from GinaBuys09: Used trainers? How do I know your feet aren't covered in fungus?

Evil troll. If you don't want them, just move on.

Question from NickySize36. Hi, I'm interested in your sweaters. I am a size 36 and I wonder if they might fit?

What was wrong with these people? She wasn't a size 36. Well not yet, anyway.

Question from Techdude899: Hey lady. if u want to do a online scam try something less dum than selling a shitty old ipod without the cords. U must have nicked it. u can't even buy that shit new anymore so whats n it fur us?

WERE R NOT IDIOTS.

Clearly. Jools didn't bother replying. What was the point? Christ. She scrolled down. The only item that anyone had bid on was the new Prada trousers. They were already up to £200! If the auction kept going at this rate, those trousers alone would cover her rent and maybe her telephone bill.

Jools went to the kitchen to find some alcohol to celebrate. Ah, Latvia's finest. Opening the bottle of red wine and taking a large swig, it crossed her mind it might have been a good idea to sell the wine along with the trousers, but the cork was already pierced, so never mind. Grabbing a glass and the 10p custard tarts from the clearance section of the supermarket, she sat down to watch a group of feral foodies slag each other off in *Come Dine with Me*.

Two glasses later, Jools heard a knock on the door. Who the hell would visit at this hour? Maybe Hunk of No Fixed Abode looking for a bed for the night? I'll give him more than a bed, Jools sniggered through her alcoholic haze.

She arranged her features into a sexy, come-hither gaze and swung open the door to find her worst nightmare. Rocco 'Pay the Rent or Die' Martucci was leaning against the chipped frame, eating a kebab.

'Rent, Joolsy, rent. You only gave me two weeks. I need a month, in advance.' Some red sauce dripped down onto his chin. Jools watched it trickle, repulsed. Even in her current pathetic state she wouldn't go there. Well, not immediately. Maybe if he bought her dinner and . . . Stop! She told herself to pay attention, she was in mortal danger! There wasn't any money to give Rocco until the auction ended on Thursday.

'Really lovely to see you, Rocco. You look like you've been working out.' In fact, he looked like something out of a mattress factory reject shop, but whatever.

'Yeah? I never work out.'

Quelle surprise. 'Hey, can I offer you a glass of wine?'

'Got beer? Wine don't go great with my kebab.'

'Sorry, just wine. Come on, try some, it's great. From Latvia.' Jools went into the kitchen to get him a glass.

Rocco poured it down his throat and a second later said: 'Where the fuck is the rent, innit?'

'Oh, the, ah, the rent? Oh, uh. Yeah. I have it, just not in cash right now.'

Rocco cracked his knuckles, not an easy feat considering he was still holding half a kebab. 'That's bullshit, Jools. Then how do you have it?'

Jools shook her head. 'It's not bullshit. See those white trousers over there?' She pointed at the Pradas thrown over a solitary dining chair. 'Those are worth three weeks' rent alone. Trust me. When my online auction ends tomorrow, it will provide plenty of cash by Monday at the latest. I guarantee it.'

Rocco grabbed her chin, kebab grease sliding down onto the only unstained top she had left. 'You'd better, because if Monday comes and there's no money, there will be trouble. I guarantee *that*.'

The next morning Jools woke with a splitting headache. She vaguely remembered drinking wine and distracting Rocco from violent acts by showing him the trousers. God, she felt rough. Promising never to drink again, she dragged herself out of bed to get some water. On the kitchen counter was a pile of white material, decorated with a large, surreal-looking red patch. What the – ? She squinted, making out the squat silhouette of the Latvian plonk lying right beside the white heap.

'Shit!' Jools snatched the white pile off the counter, catching sight of the telltale gold button fly. The Prada trousers! Her legs gave out and she sank to the grimy kitchen floor.

With a brain that pounded with the bass of a malfunctioning speaker, she shakily picked up the phone. Maybe Mel could help, suggest something to get wine out of white trousers without washing them. Maybe – oh God, Jools was going to be sick.

After emptying her stomach of Latvian wine and HobNobs, she dialled Mel. Perhaps it was okay to let the auction ride, then blame the Royal Mail when the trousers 'mysteriously' never arrived? No, that wouldn't work. miSell, the online auction store, said you had to get proof of postage or you were liable. Shit. Shit. Shit. Mel would know what to do. And if not, at least Jools could stay with her when Rocco broke both legs and threw her carcass out onto the grubby Willesden Green pavement.

A male voice answered the phone, groggy.

Jools recognised that voice. None other than that pretentious twat Michel Matthews.

'You!' she spat. What else could you say to the deviant who had crushed her bestfriend's heart by running off with a rusty whore from Bada Bing. And not just any rusty whore. Jools couldn't tell Mel the truth about that, could she? It would kill her.

'It's been too long, Joolsy! You should come over for dinner tonight, to celebrate!' He tried to give the word 'celebrate' a French twist but it sounded Indian, which made him an insult to Indians as well as the French. Tosser.

'Celebrate what?' Jools felt her stomach twist again in revulsion at the thought of seeing him again.

She had already seen far too much of him.

'Mel did not tell you? I'm moving back in! We are *tres, tres* excited!'

Feeling *tres, tres* sick (again), Jools hung up without replying. So much for the option of crashing with Mel. There was no way. Not if that bastard was there too, especially after – yuck, it didn't bear thinking about.

She logged back onto the auction. The Prada trousers were now at £500.

Why was life so insanely unfair? Idly, she clicked about the site. Exercise bike for 10 quid. Rip-off! Antique Hush Puppies without a heel about to go for 4 quid. Honestly. The trash people sell. Then it struck her. If people were willing to pay that much for last season's Prada, how much would they cough up for a whole person?

What if she sold herself?

Not in the prostitute sense, of course, but weren't there thousands of illegal immigrants running around London looking for a way to stay? Surely one of them would be willing to part with some cash to marry a fully-fledged English girl like herself? What was it called, a marriage of convenience? There might be enough to pay off Horace Fortescue and the very insistent Commercial Bank.

At least she should be able to give Rocco enough to ward off eviction through the rest of winter and some of spring.

However, hand poised over the 'Start Selling' key, Jools came to her senses. What if some nutter decided to bid? There were plenty of weirdos out there; the papers were full of them. She didn't fancy finding herself bound and gagged in the dungeon of some rancid place in New Cross, or even worse, Slough.

Seeking solace in her HobNobs, Jools went back to the telly and tried to forget about her money woes for a few hours.

Or at least until the HobNobs ran out.

Chapter 5

Dear Miss Grand,

Following our letter of 14 days ago, we write to remind you of your obligations pursuant to the contract you signed with our bank last year.

As you know, we have been extremely lenient with regards to the extra expenditure on your account, but as you are now £5872.11 over your agreed overdraft we ask you to contact our offices with a plan for payment as soon as possible.

In the meantime, you will have noticed your account and credit cards have been frozen and no further withdrawals will be possible.

Yours sincerely,

Horace Fortescue
Commercial Bank London

JOOLS WAS DREAMING of the Hunk of No Fixed Abode. In her dream, he had a fixed abode – several, actually – and he rode to her door on a white Vespa, offering unlimited accommodation in a white Georgian terrace in Chelsea. Even better (well, almost), she fit perfectly into the pristine white Prada trousers, which bore no signs of stain.

Ring, ring, went Hunk of Many Fixed Abodes on her doorbell. Ring, ring.

RING RING.

She sat up. Shit, that wasn't a dream, and it wasn't her doorbell. It was the telephone. The answering machine clicked on, and a voice like gravel rapped her ears with unintelligible syllables. All she heard was 'RENT! RENT! RENT!' Even in a partial state of unconsciousness it didn't take much to realise who it was. Rocco. The creep. What did he want now? Hadn't they decided it was due on Monday? Today was only . . . Monday. Shit. Tucking her head safely under the pillow, she decided to stay in bed until a brilliant idea came to mind.

Another hangover, the second in a row, wasn't helpful in trying to formulate plans to prevent her eviction. Well, it was punishment for agreeing to go to Mel and Michel's last night. That particular episode was excruciating on so many levels, not the least because of Jools' massive, national-deficit-sized resentment towards fake-Frenchie for scuppering Plan B to keep her from the ranks of the street scourge. If not for that manipulative arsehole, she'd happily be packing her humble possessions right now, telling Rocco he could stuff his vermin-infested hole.

But whenever Jools looked at Michel's face, all she could picture was the rather saggy backside of an all-too-familiar woman. What had he been thinking? As for the woman – it was disgusting in the extreme!

Mel was a successful lawyer, and exactly twenty-two years younger to boot. The greater injustice, though, was on Mel's part, for forgiving him. Again.

Jools' reflections were cut short by the second phone call of the morning. Popular girl, Jools thought, expecting Rocco's threats to resume momentarily. The machine picked up again, which was good because it'd offer a friendlier greeting than she could muster.

'Jools here. Tell me your troubles and I'll call you once I fix mine! Cheers!'

'Horace Fortescue, from Commercial Bank London Limited. Calling for a Miss Julia Grand. We need to speak to you regarding your loan and overdraft repayments. Please call me back on the following number as a matter of great urgency.'

Jools deleted the message before the machine saved it. Like that was going to happen! When she finally got her moment in the sun at the dole office – in approximately two hours – all her newfound money would be going on rent and food. That bank would have to wait until she was employed again. Banks had plenty of money anyway, didn't they? Why hassle temporarily insolvent but entirely innocent people?

The nearest social security office was conveniently

located just a few doors from the bus station. Jools pulled on her tracksuit bottoms, added what seemed to have become her 'going out top' – the furry green jumper – and set off for a date with destiny (or at least a meeting that ended with the presentation of a cheque large enough to appease Rocco).

The waiting room was like a leper colony – what *was* that weird weeping sore disease the old guy by the loos was sporting? Hopefully abject poverty wasn't catching. She didn't plan to be on the dole for long, so just enough money to survive a month or two would be perfect. After all, she wasn't greedy.

Taking a number from the slick, automated machine, she found herself sitting next to a mentally-deranged woman who said she liked Jools' jumper. 'I have one just like it,' crooned the hag, smiling through a set of teeth with more gaps than Jools' CV.

'Julia Grand.' A prim woman with hair in a bun (a bun!), wearing a tight fawn cardigan with matching acid-wash skirt (like that was *ever* in fashion outside Texas), led her into a tiny grey cubicle. 'Miss Grand, we won't keep you long.'

Excellent. Hopefully they had the cash in an envelope, ready to go. In two hours, she'd be living it up in Sainsbury's, buying proper food. And more HobNobs.

Jools sat down on an itchy grey chair and smiled.

The woman plopped down opposite and fumbled with some papers.

Looking for that envelope, I expect, thought Jools.

'As you know, this department sued you for fraud a few years ago.'

Oh-oh. Not exactly a promising start. Jools squirmed and the chair edge bit into her soft thighs.

'And at that time, you were informed that the prosecution would stop at the plea stage, on the condition that you would repay all the sums defrauded.'

'But I did. Every penny.'

'Yes, but you also agreed to have no further recourse to public funding for twenty years.'

Jools stared at her in horror. It was just as Mel had said. 'But how will I survive? I'm going to be homeless if I don't pay my rent. Can I at least get a council flat?'

'I'm afraid that comes under the umbrella of obtaining public funding.'

What the hell did that mean? 'Is that a no?'

'Yes, Miss Grand. That's a no.'

'But what am I going to do? Live on the street?'

'There are charitable organisations that can help you. I've made a list for you to take away.'

And with that, Jools was bundled out of the grey cubicle and back out into the waiting room, a single sheet of useless paper in hand.

'I think I've got those trackies too,' squawked the deranged woman as Jools lurched to the door.

'Terrific,' Jools snarled. 'I'm so glad for you.'

And the old bag would probably get financial aid,

no problem. Probably offer her a *Porsche* instead of a bus pass. Life was so unfair.

Back home, Jools consumed the last remaining packets of HobNobs and washed them down with past-sell-by beer in an effort to try to cheer up. But nothing could mask the fact that all options for survival had been neutered. No Mel – and no dole. What the hell could she do now?

Logging on to miSell, the bittersweet results of the Prada auction taunted her: they had sold for £600. That would have been enough to shut Rocco up for ages, had she not been such a clumsy lush. Looking at the now-familiar website, the idea of a few days ago resurfaced. Maybe she *should* try to sell herself – in the nicest possible way. An auction for a quickie marriage to some poor sod who had his own, entirely above-the-navel reasons for wanting a wife – fast.

This could be a golden opportunity for both her and the highest bidder too – she was almost a catch, right? Previously unmarried. Young-ish. Sure, desperation wasn't necessarily attractive, but they said men liked damsels in distress, didn't they?

Down to practicalities. Going down the asylum-seeking route probably wasn't advisable – offering marriage for money and residency in a public forum might bring Immigration to her door faster than she could say 'highest bidder.'

Pretending her motives were purely for love rather

than money might attract nutjobs with dungeons.

Maybe taking a fun angle would do the trick – call it an 'experiment with fate'. Yes, that seemed the best option. Make out she was sick of dating the wrong men, so was playing with fate to find a perfect match.

Obviously, there would be no sex involved. She would make that very clear. Okay, maybe she would make it clear that the choice would be hers. Once the money was in bank, the deal would be a marriage for at least three months. If someone wanted more, they'd need to get approval before bidding. And they'd need to provide a photo.

What about a photo of Jools? She might be a slight disappointment to the buyer in her current state, but without it, she might be breaching some sort of trade misdescriptions' Act for failing to give an accurate rundown of 'the goods'. The auction Ts&Cs could say 'no refunds available' – but if the bids rocketed (one could dream!), emotions and expectations would be running high and the winner might complain.

Jools told herself she could handle it. It was better than being homeless. Taking a deep breath, she considered the 'Listing Your Item' section of the handbook.

Right, which category to list in. 'Dolls & Bears'? 'Other Real Estate'? No. The only category that seemed appropriate was 'Everything Else', which wasn't exactly complimentary but as least it was generic. Why restrict the clientele? She clicked and a secondary list appeared with 'Adult Only' at the top.

How depressing. I've sunk so low, Jools sighed, I'll probably get bought by Charlie Grand. She shuddered at the thought.

In the end, Jools settled on 'Other' in the 'Everything Else' category. Even if no one found her there, at least she could hold her head high in the knowledge that the 'Adults Only' label did not apply.

Right. Now to fill in the form. Descriptive title: Girl to Marry. Excellent Condition. Jools relaxed a little, encouraged by how straightforward the whole thing seemed to be.

Next. Insert photograph. Hmm. No so easy. Perhaps Mel could take a photo with her fancy phone and Bluetooth it to Jools' laptop? But looking down at her hips – difficult to miss with all that HobNob padding – it might not be a good thing to send prospective buyers running before they'd had time to fully contemplate the offer. What about posting a photo of beautiful, refined Mel? Her gorgeous mug would go for at least £20,000. But no; imagine the fallout once the buyer saw Jools' lumpy bod after fantasizing about Mel. Anyway, her friend would throttle her for even thinking of it.

The best idea was to upload a photo from five years ago. It was her phone screensaver, the one from a boozy vacation to Spain. In it, a brown, fit and relatively slim blonde girl with a beer in each hand laughs nonchalantly at the camera. A far cry from who she was now – well, except for the beers.

Now, describe the item for sale. Hmm. Should she be vague, or extremely vague?

Girl. 28. Never married.

Or maybe just leave it open?

Ask any and all questions before bidding. No refunds.

The first option could limit the number of bidders and keep the price low. The second might attract an unholy number of creeps and psychos. But the less specific she was, the more buyers might fantasize – and the higher the bids would go. It was a huge risk not to agree on stipulations beforehand, but so was becoming homeless and completely devoid of HobNobs.

At the last minute – thoughts of mad men with whips and chains running through her head – she added:

Young woman till death do us part, or at least a season, to the highest bidder. No sex. Perverts need not bid.

Leaving the starting bid price and auction length at the default setting to stop any red-flags being raised, Jools had the uneasy feeling that maybe this sort of auction wasn't exactly legal. Maybe she should ask Mel before embarking on the adventure — but Mel would only try to talk her out of it, and Jools didn't want to listen to a lecture right now. Anyway, it could be argued, both to Mel and miSell, that the auction had a noble purpose.

Yeah, as a scientific experiment, to examine human nature or something.

Having convinced herself of the legitimacy of her actions, Jools moved on.

Form of payment: PayPal. Definitely PayPal. The faster I get the money, Jools thought, the better. Finally, the money-making masterpiece was reviewed. Rubbing her hands together, she clicked 'List'.

For the next three days, Jools stayed close to her laptop, monitoring her auction. At first, very little happened. On the second day, there was a flood of emails, asking for details, informing of her status as a whore, a sinner, crazy, hot, courageous, desperate (all fair enough, Jools thought) – every manner of insult and compliment.

The good news was that the total was climbing. By the end of the third day, the bid was up to £1000. Even if it didn't go any higher, she'd at least buy some time. And if she were lucky, she might even fall in love – or at least find a new, flush roommate. Scrolling through the inbox, there were a few sincere messages. Two bidders wanted to meet before they continued to take part.

Not a bad idea, actually. It would be nice to see who was bidding, but she didn't want to put them off. After all, once the auction ended and the highest bidder paid up, whether they liked the merchandise or not wasn't her problem. But now that the auction was underway and there was a large amount of money involved, Jools was curious to see who these people were. It might be best to make sure they weren't totally insane (although some allowance should be made for marginal insanity, given the situation). Maybe there would be a bit of free grub in it too? Her stomach rumbled at the thought.

She quickly emailed the two bidders and arranged back-to-back meetings at Mama Blue's the next day.

'On you!' she added cheekily at the end of each email, just in case they were planning on leaving their wallets in their cars.

Not being completely barking, Jools thought an objective opinion on her prospective husbands might be in order. And who better to ask than her best friend? Sure, Mel had taken up (again) with the biggest loser ever, but Jools trusted her judgment on anything non-Michel related.

Her best friend's reaction was not altogether unexpected. 'Are you completely out of your mind? Do you realise what kind of psychos are running around out there, drooling onto their keyboards all night long, just waiting for some naïve idiot like you to step right into their trap? Jesus, Jools. Use your brain. People go to court to protect themselves from crazies, and here you are teasing them into your own flat. Christ!'

That did it. Jools couldn't sit by and be insulted when Mel was shacked up with the human form of excrement. 'Like you're any sort of example of purity and good decision-making! You and your so-called boyfriend – or should I say, *boyfiend*.'

They both sat and stared angrily at each other. Mel caved first. 'I'm sorry, Jools, I just care about you, and this, well, venture of yours isn't safe. You can still move in with me, you know.'

'I can't. Not while Michel is in residence. Anyway, I think my new online career is going to be a great source of income for me.'

Jools looked at her watch. 'Oh shit, you have to go.'

Mel got up to leave, but Jools grabbed her arm. 'Wait. No. Stay here and watch so I can say 'I told you so'. Niles Crisp should be here any second. I bet he's gorgeous! He certainly sounds yummy.' Jools felt her tummy leap at the thought of crisps.

'That's his name? I can tell he's a weirdo without even clapping eyes on him. Come on, let's leave while we still can,' Mel hissed. 'Right now!'

'No, shh. Someone's coming in. Quick. Sit over there!'

Mel rolled her eyes and moved to a table in the corner behind the door.

A short, skinny bloke in a long black leather trench coat walked over to Jools. He flashed a grin. One of his teeth was black.

Shit. Jools shot a look at Mel. She had the sinking feeling that she might need fairly prompt saving, but

Mel was adding sugar to her coffee and didn't see.

Niles Crisp sat down and leaned in. 'Hi, babe. You're everything your photo hinted at and more, eh?' He peeked under the table. 'I like your tracksuit bottoms, darling. I love sporty birds.' His breath smelled like old cheese and sweaty socks. Jools recoiled.

'What's the matter, baby? You scared? I'm harmless. I like it fast, hard and often. I can tell you do, too. I spend my days selling, selling, selling. I spend my nights teaching naughty young things like you how to behave.'

A thin thread of spittle hung from the corner of his mouth.

Jools' heart bumped in her chest. 'My listing made it clear there's no sex involved. This isn't exactly what I had in mind . . . I just need to pay the rent.' She tried to keep her voice steady.

'Ooh, baby, let me assure you, we'll get your rent paid. You just have to work hard – if you know what I mean.' He licked his lips.

'No. I mean, yes. I know what you mean. But no, that's not going to work, alright? I've got to go.' Jools stood up, grabbed her coat and looked hard at Mel who was already halfway to the door.

Niles Crisp wasn't the type to take rejection well. 'You little bitch, where do you think you're going? You can't run from me!'

Jools and Mel broke into a sprint and ran three blocks before Mel pulled Jools into an alley and screamed that she was certifiably insane. 'I should get a doctor and have you sectioned. I'm going to take you back to your flat, you're going to pack your shit and move in with me. Don't you dare say no.'

Jools could barely breathe. That was the fastest she'd moved all year. 'Thanks, Mel, but I keep telling you, I can't live with the boyfiend. I respect you enough to let you make your own decisions. You need to treat me the same!'

'Fine. Call me when you're being tortured by a psycho whilst tied to his bed. I'll save you, if I can.'

Jools smiled. 'Is it wrong that the thought of that isn't entirely unpleasant?'

But Mel just shook her head and stalked off, disappearing into the nearest Tube station. Jools ducked into the loos at the Tube and fixed herself up for Bidder Number Two. Maybe she shouldn't go through with it. But, she reasoned, the last one was so bad that surely it couldn't get much worse. Anyway, this next bloke sounded honest and professional: Would be delighted to make your acquaintance with a view to discussing our possible business arrangement. What a gentleman. In fact, he might be extremely refined – and maybe even handsome. With a username like 'HotRod38' he sounded promising in one aspect, anyway.

She made her way back to Mama Blue's. There was no mistaking who was Bidder Number Two, HotRod38. Sporting a navy polo and dark glasses that obscured his eyes, she saw that his jaw was square, his nose straight and his hair shiny and groomed. As she approached, he didn't stand up or even look at her, just slipped into the chair opposite and launched into a polite speech that had clearly been rehearsed.

'It is nice to meet you. Let me explain my situation, entirely in confidence, of course. I am a politician about to be preselected as MP for the safe seat of Kensington and Chelsea. I'm gay, but I have told my party I'm about to be married. I must find a wife or any chance of becoming an MP is ruined. I would require a prenuptial agreement, as well as a legal contract from you stating that you will never disclose the circumstances surrounding our marriage as long as we both shall live. The marriage should last long enough to be plausible. I would not expect you to be faithful, just discreet. Think about it. I will be bidding on your auction up until the end. Thank you and have a lovely evening.' With that, HotRod38 walked out of the café and into a waiting car.

Jools took a deep breath and watched as his car edged along the busy high street, then disappeared around the corner. 'HotRod38, I like the look of you,' she said aloud, relieved there was at least one normal bidder out there. Detached, wealthy, and with a strong ulterior motive, he was a perfect candidate for marriage.

She wondered if he lived somewhere nice.

Chapter 6

Dear Ombudsman for Social Services,

I am writing to complain of my appalling treatment at the hands of the Willesden Green Dole Office.

As a person who has paid most of her taxes on time (well, when I had the money), I cannot believe that this country, a supposed democracy, would allow me to starve to death on the street over one small indiscretion when I was young. Despite my pleadings, I have been left to my fate. Please see what you can do immediately.

Yours starvingly,

Julia M. Grand

NILES CRISP WASN'T finished with that bitch who'd put herself up for auction online, not by a long shot. Such opportunities didn't come around often, and he was willing to invest a significant amount of time to get a cute (albeit fat) young wife. Niles had tried conventional relationships, but they bored him. He was meant for something wild, unorthodox, and just plain hot. So the day after meeting Jools, he arrived back home from his job at the call centre and buckled down to hatch a plan to possess her.

Despite the fact that she didn't seem to fancy him (that could just be a matter of time, couldn't it?), it was shocking to find she had retracted his bids. What nerve! After all, he was the customer, and wasn't the customer always right? She didn't deserve to slither away that easily, and he was more than willing to teach her all about customer service.

Staring at the shagpile carpet that graced his mean little kitchen, Niles finally concocted the perfect plan for ensnaring his future wife.

First, a polite email, acknowledging that their chemistry did seem off and he had no bad feelings about his cancelled bid. However, he wrote, it had been nice to meet her and if she felt like it, perhaps they could be friends. Of course, she wouldn't respond – she'd already shown she had no customer service skills to speak of – but it would divert any suspicions that might arise when he made his next move.

Which was to become someone else.

Niles Crisp began to create a new miSell user account. Buyer name: Brad Brown. A small smile twisted his lips. Perfect. Innocent and wholesome. Maybe even make him American. Yes. Throw her off any scent of Niles, and make it impossible to meet him, given his location several thousand miles away.

Image upload: Hmm, where to get a convincing picture? Niles Googled manically. Stockphotosmales had a nice one of a tall, lean catalogue model, posing at a lakefront chalet in boat shoes, shirtless, with flat-fronted chinos. A sales assistant had once told him that girls love a man in flat-fronted chinos.

Wait. Perhaps the model was too good-looking? Someone with that poncy floppy hair – the sort of bloke who obviously looked in the mirror a lot – would hardly be shopping online for a wife. Who'd be dumb enough to believe such a thing? Niles sniggered. Probably the kind of girl who auctioned herself online. Besides, once she got a look at that photo, it'd be game over.

Brad, Wisconsinesque hunk, would seal the deal.

Once his new ID and bid were entered, Niles immediately found Jools' auction, and clicked on 'Send Question to Buyer'.

I am absolutely taken by your beauty in this photo. Even more, I find your courage and confidence to put yourself out in the world in such a way totally irresistible. Though I can't meet you immediately, because I live in Wisconsin, USA, I would love to speak with you on the telephone. I need to find a wife so I can stay in England permanently to look for work in the finance industry. If you're not interested in a possible relationship, I would completely understand, and would settle for the possibility of staying in a country I know I would grow to love like my own. Please write if you are interested.

Quashing his growing nausea at writing such drivel, Niles started a 'To Do' list:

1. Get American phone number – or maybe just a silent UK number that can't be easily traced?

2. Practice American accent.

3. Start preparing basement.

Excited, Niles allowed himself an hour or so of defacing that day's paper before he went to bed. He was a happy man. No more dull evenings surfing the web from his mid-terrace in Slough, searching fruitlessly for naughty women to teach a lesson. He had a purpose. He had a goal. And when he reached that goal, he would have a wife.

Jools sat at her computer, satisfied with the power granted to her index finger via the mouse. One click and Niles was gone. At least, he had the good sense to understand she couldn't stand the sight of him. Well, he did mention something about being friends, but hopefully he was just being polite. Her skin was still crawling with thoughts of his twitching, pock-marked face peering under the café table to perve at her tracksuit bottoms.

Luckily, there seemed to be no hard feelings at the deletion of his bid.

Pity she couldn't delete kebab-squaffing Rocco with one finger – and that twat Michel Matthews too, come to think of it.

Tempting fate by leaning back on the back legs of

an ancient dining chair, Jools smugly acknowledged she was now worth £5000. At least. That was a major improvement on the negative £25,000-odd figure that sad little dweeb of a man from the bank insisted she was worth. Horace Whateverhisnamewas.

Flicking idly through her auction statistics, she saw that some wealthy bloke – a Brad Brown from Wisconsin – had helped up the bid to £5000. A more sensible person (Mel, for example) might have asked why someone would try to bid from the States, with no guarantee of clearing Immigration, but she was willing to believe anything at that point, so God bless America. And with a name like Brad . . . well, if a Brad was good enough for Angelina, a Brad was good enough for Jools.

Okay, it was highly likely this Brad was bored, intoxicated or addicted to online fraud, but Jools was unperturbed because there were now two serious bidders again.

Plus, her favourite, HotRod38, was still winning.

Suddenly the inbox pinged, indicating a new message. Wow. Must be telepathy or something. A message from Brad himself.

Jools read it quickly, then looked at the photograph he'd sent. Well, okay, not exactly Brad Pitt, but nearly as gorgeous, and, from what she could work out, heterosexual too. No sign of man bags or makeup.

Feeling carefree, she emailed her mobile number, instructing him to call anytime after 11 am London time. Then, deciding it might be worth getting into shape for a prospective video-cam affair with Brad, she flip-flopped out of the flat for a bus ride then brisk-ish walk in Kensington Gardens, where there was a lot less doggie business than in any park near her.

At last things seemed to be picking up.

As she waited for the number 52 – along with a rancid old man who kept shouting 'piss' and a young mother who mumbled 'off' each time he did – she felt a dim fear that the bids might be a hoax, or a result of peoples' alcohol-induced mistakes, or that if Brad won, Immigration would interrogate her using disposable gloves and lie-detectors and expose her highly illegal plot. In any scenario she wouldn't see a penny – unless the judge was understanding enough to let her keep some money to aid rehabilitation after being released from prison.

The bus arrived as Jools considered another option – Ross was actually a Russian pimp and she would be kidnapped and sold as a sex slave in Thailand, or horror of horrors, Blackpool.

Calm down, she told herself sternly. Precautions have been taken. Sort of.

Rodney Wetherspone (although she preferred to think of him as HotRod) checked out – he even had a grainy mugshot on the Rising Right website.

As for the American, well, he was so far away that he really wasn't worth worrying about, was he? If she liked the sound of his voice, maybe, just maybe, he might have a chance. If not, one click and he was history.

The sun suddenly made an unexpected appearance, which was slightly eery in a British winter, but Jools was pleased that even the London weather was cooperating today. Finally things were moving in the right direction.

Spying a familiar cross-street, Jools got off the bus one stop before the park, deciding that a short walk to Mel's flat was a vast improvement on an exhausting trek through the Royal Park.

It was only when she had spent 15 minutes loitering at the front of the building, buzzing at two second intervals, that she remembered Mel worked until at least 5 pm and it was only mid-afternoon. It wasn't a good idea to hang about – being in Kensington in a rather smelly tracksuit was risky if one wanted to avoid persecution for bad fashion – so Jools gave up on the whole thing and headed for home, where a nice new packet of HobNobs was waiting.

A half hour later, the bus pulled into the garage and the doors swung open. The only upside of living near the toxic bus station was the proximity of the bus stop to her flat – about five metres.

Walking the few steps home, she spotted Hunk of No Fixed Abode heading towards the canteen again. God, had he no shame, carrying on like he owned the place? Although a few of the drivers threw him strange looks, no one actually questioned his presence.

Lucky bugger. If Jools tried that they would probably mistake her for a woolly mammoth and shoot her in the bum with a tranquilliser dart.

Jools watched as he rounded the canteen door. As hobos went, he looked reasonably well-kept. In fact, you could clean him up and put him to work in a bank or law firm without too much effort.

Rats. Hunk had caught her staring. What to do? Hide? A wee bit difficult given her girth. Instead, Jools went bright red and waved. Remembering his laptop gift she tried to sign drinking and eating to invite him for dinner.

Thankfully (because she had no food and drink except tea and Hobnobs), he shook his head and pointed at the canteen, then headed inside. In spite of her relief, she was a tad insulted. Was he, a hobo, to good for her, an almost hobo? No. Maybe the bus drivers had offered him supper tonight? God, her love life was officially as dead as roadkill if she couldn't even attract a hobo with an offer of food and drink.

Before she had a chance to begin scoffing her HobNobs, she saw the answering machine flashing. Must be from Rocco. She deleted it without listening.

'What can he do, throw me onto the street?' she muttered, wrestling with the tightly-packed biscuits. 'Tenants have rights too.' She'd no idea what those rights might be, but Rocco didn't scare her. Well not much. Not when she was in here with the door locked and a chair propped up against the door knob and he wasn't outside jangling keys and kebabs. Plus, there were better prospects than this dingy old flat on the horizon, such as HotRod and a nice abode fit for a politician. And, of course, the gorgeous Brad from America.

The phone rang again. Jools answered tentatively, hoping for Mel. If it was Rocco she'd pretend to be from an overseas call centre and hang up.

'Joolsy, alright?'

Great. The sponging father. 'Oh, um, everything's fine. Are you having a nice time in Ibiza with, uh, what's her name?'

'The name's Tash – er, sorry, uh, Suze. You'll have to meet 'er, a right sweetheart. Great boobies on her. Listen, have you found a job yet?'

Jools felt nauseated, which went with the territory when in conversation with her dad. How could she even consider moving in with him? Jeez. Living on the street was infinitely better than having to slap away his constant hand out all day long.

'No Dad, there are no jobs out there. I've looked.'

There was a pause. 'How about a new boyfriend? I tell you, it sure is great to have a partner in crime, eh, Suze? What a sweetheart, she's still passed out from last night. It was a wild one, alright.' Another pause as he reminisced about his gross and possibly illegal activities with the much-too-young Suze.

'Listen,' he said, 'You should look on miSell if you're lonely. Must be a new thing in online dating.

I found this sweet girl, sorta looks like you when you was a skinny little teen. Real cute, a bit old for me, but only going for a few thousand pounds. You couldn't lend me a few thou to bid, could you?'

It was all Jools could do to stop from losing her lunch then and there. 'Christ, Dad, you're sick and I'm still broke. I've got to go.'

'Come on. You know I'm kidding, only kidding. Well about the girl, not the money, I do actually need the money. But the girl wouldn't hurt, eh . . .'

Jools hung up. If he whined about it later, she could pretend they were cut off, which was bound to happen any moment now. Charlie Grand bidding on her was making her re-evaluate her whole miSell career.

Speaking of which . . . she sat down to check the current auction value when the phone rang again.

She hadn't been so popular since forgetting to wear a skirt to school after a cider binge in Year 10.

'Hello?'

'Yes, hi. May I speak with Jools?'

The American! Jools threw a hand over her mouth to keep from squealing out loud.

'Ahem. Yes. Speaking?'

'Oh, hi there, Jools, this is Brad, I believe you read my message on miSell? I wanted to call and touch base with you, let you know that I am real, and not one of those weirdos who tend to lurk around online.'

'Oh, I didn't think that for a minute,' said Jools as seductively as possible.

'See, I was browsing online for women's life preservers, looking for one for my mother who is coming out on my, ah, yacht for the weekend, and accidentally deleted the word 'preserver' and your profile was the only result that showed up. Naturally, I had to click and . . . Anyway, I'm so sorry to ramble on like this. I hope I'm not interrupting anything?'

So far so good, thought Jools. He sounded just as gorgeous as he looked. 'Oh no, no. I was just, I was just getting some Hob . . . er, fish. For dinner.'

'Oh, well, be careful you don't overcook it! There's nothing like a perfectly moist trout fillet with a touch of lemon and dill. But I suppose you folks prefer the battered and fried variety?'

'Right, that's what you all think of us over there, isn't it . . . ' Jools laughed awkwardly. Was dill food? 'No, I'm actually just going to broil a nice fresh Scottish salmon with butter, pepper, and you said it, lemon.'

'Ah, my second favourite fish!'

Jools was charmed by his ability to take anything she said and make it sound like the most interesting thing he'd ever heard, particularly as Mel once said she could bore for Britain when she was nervous.

Blushing deeply, even though they were thousands of miles apart, they chatted for another twenty minutes – about what, she had no idea – she just loved listening to his accent.

'Well, the way your price keeps going up, I'd better not spend all my cash on international phone calls.'

Because it was going so well, and Jools didn't fancy any grim incidents involving cardiac arrests and ambulances at Heathrow should Brad eventually make it to the UK, she decided to come clean about the rather out-of-date photo.

'One last thing, Brad. Would you like me to send a photo of myself, besides the one that's on miSell? I have, um, changed a little.'

'Don't be silly! I'm not a superficial guy. A bit of weight, a darker hair colour, who cares? You're still you; the same person.'

Busy thinking what an outstanding chap he was to appreciate a girl's inner beauty, Jools failed to note how he somehow knew she was darker and heavier.

Hanging up, she forgot all about her HobNobs and longed to call Mel but she suspected her friend was camped out in Boujis at South Kensington with Michel, who in turn was no doubt ogling women old enough to be his great-grandmother the minute Mel turned to take a sip of champers.

If Mel was busy ruining her life, who was Jools to interrupt her, even if she had the best news ever!

Rodney Wetherspone was greatly relieved the miSell girl wasn't the old slapper he'd imagined – just a normal, if slightly overweight, woman. Smart but not too smart, pretty but not memorable and generally a forgettable wife – the ideal consort for a gay politician trying to look straight.

What he wasn't happy about was the price. His yearly 'Fun and Entertainment' allowance didn't include a wife – and besides, he had been saving for a brand new Aston Martin.

What other desperate fool had racked the price up to £5000, with days still remaining in the auction? Surely not his arch-enemy and other candidate for preselection, Roland Harris? What were the odds of both of them being gay? Okay, quite high, given who graced the bars and clubs of London's homosexual community, but still.

Maybe he should just give up on the whole thing. He asked himself just how badly he wanted that preselection, and the answer, as always, was more than anything. He needed to show his unsympathetic and slightly bonkers parents he could do something worthwhile with his life.

The phone rang and he answered without enthusiasm. After hanging up, he felt even worse. His hands were shaking and a headache was building at the back of his skull. Some woman from the Party had requested the presence of himself and his fiancée at a boring Family Values symposium to promote his view that stronger families equal stronger countries. If he won the preselection in Kensington and Chelsea.

Bleeding hell. He needed a wife – fast. Logging back onto miSell, he upped the bid to the amount equalling the down-payment on his coveted Aston Martin: £20,000.

The car was preferred, of course, but the wife was much more of a necessity.

Jools headed to a nearby soup kitchen for breakfast, mouth watering at the thought of a scrumptious full English dripping in grease. But when she turned up at 10 am, the grumpy volunteers were just cleaning up and wouldn't even give her the last charred bits of bacon she could see still clinging to the grill. Worse, they told her they had other jobs to go to and if she wanted charity, she needed to get off her lazy backside and turn up before nine.

Shamed, Jools trudged home, looking forward to taking a hot shower and climbing into bed to watch TV. Nearing her block, she saw a mountain of dingy, wet junk on the pavement at the bottom of the stairs leading up to her building. God, people were pigs. London was really going to the dogs.

Then she saw a note, wet and barely legible, pinned to some familiar white trousers stained with wine.

`You was warned, Jools. Now you know I men busness. I took laptop and telli as payment for the rent. And here is the bill for the money it cost to cleeen your shithole flat.`

Rocco! The bastard.

Chapter 7

Dear Julia Grand,

On the 31 March you made the following purchases in our store: two bottles of Pretende Beaujolais, five half-pint bottles of cider, one case of Heineken and 48 packets of crisps (mixed flavours). We agreed to let you pay by cheque because you are a long-standing customer and you told us your wallet had been stolen, along with your cheque guarantee card.

We now find that your bank refuses to authorise the £59.20 you spent, and we ask that you make restitution immediately, to avoid further action.

Yours sincerely,

John Haines
Johns Liquor Limited
Willesden Green

JOOLS SAT ON her sofa. Somehow Rocco had managed to shove it through the flat's narrow bathroom window. It had landed upright in a hedge, and was serving as a very effective sponge for the rain. Already wet from head to toe and not knowing what else to do, she'd climbed up onto it to wait for a brilliant idea to eventuate. A few people passed by and politely looked away. Jools didn't blame them. She must be a sorry sight on her grubby, soaking throne, and her predicament must be fairly obvious to the general public – especially after last night's news broadcast about homelessness being on the rise.

The rain had now subsided to a light mist, and Jools tried to remain optimistic. Life was a wild and crazy adventure! Who needed material goods? But she couldn't deny her longing for a warm shower, cosy bed and a sofa that didn't double as an absorbent. Earlier that morning, Jools couldn't imagine pining for her nasty little flat. But now it seemed like the Promised Land. She even missed the farting bus drivers.

She plastered a big fake smile on her face – hadn't someone said smiling made you feel better? – and lifted her head only to find Hunk of No Fixed Abode staring at her from across the street.

Great, thought Jools. What's he going to think of her now? Sure, he was homeless too, but if you evened the playing field and she was minus a roof over her head, she wasn't exactly a hobo's young dream. There must be loads of hot, newly homeless girls with bendy bodies and eager lips who were looking for a clean, handsome vagrant like him.

'Hey, they get you, too?'

Jools wasn't sure how to respond. He was right! They got her. Rocco. That cow from social services. The bank. Mrs Pho. Michel Matthews. Yeah, they'd definitely got her, and got her good.

'Look, you can't live in a hedge, not in this weather. Come to my place. It isn't much, but I'm happy to share.'

Jools' heart jumped. Living with the Hunk of No Fixed Abode? Now that would be a treat. Maybe it would be just like in her dreams – the Chelsea terrace, the white Vespa. Then she reminded herself that his accommodation couldn't be much better than the hedge. And she really didn't know anything about him. He could be a complete psycho, like that Niles Crisp. 'I don't know. I need some time to think.'

He picked up a handful of her stuff and started walking away. 'What's to think about? I offer you a rent-free home and you have to think about it? I'll tell you something – if you stay out here all night you'll freeze, be murdered or worse. Come on. I promise, I'm harmless.'

Yeah, that's just what Niles Crisp said, Jools thought. 'There's something worse than being murdered?' she asked to buy some time.

He grinned. Perfect white teeth. So the hobo flossed. Interesting.

'Believe me, there are lots of things worse than being dead. Now are you coming or not?'

What choice did she have? It was past noon and the wet sofa was freezing. It was either go with the hobo, or get on a bus to Mel's where she'd have to live in the same space as the cretinous Michel. Jools knew who was dirtier, and it wasn't the man who probably hadn't bathed in two years.

Jools jumped down off the sofa. 'Alright. Let's go. Are you going to help me with this or not? It's half yours now, anyway.'

He held out his hand. 'Skuttle. Pleased to officially meet you.'

'Oh, uh, Jools.' She took his hand and he pumped it up and down. His grip was strong but his hand was soft.

Skuttle lifted the sofa up onto his right shoulder and told her to load the rest of the stuff onto it. When all but some rubbish she didn't want (like letters from debt collectors) was on board, they carried the little sofa towards the back of the bus garage. Jools admired his biceps. For a hobo who probably didn't eat much, he was certainly strong.

They squeezed through a small alley – barely wide enough to accommodate Jools. With one hand Skuttle pushed away a flattened refrigerator box, revealing a small door that looked like the entrance to a black hole.

'Is this it?' Jools was worried all over again. Living

in a dark hole was about as low as you could go. Well, unless you were begging for kitty litter in front of a Tesco.

Skuttle smiled. 'No, this is the way into it. Let's push the sofa down in front of us.'

They manoeuvred the soggy rectangle into the square hole and with a slow tilt downward it disappeared into blackness.

Skuttle stood aside. 'Okay, now you go.'

'Me?'

'No, not you. I was talking to Harvey.'

'Harvey? Who's Harvey?'

'My mate, Harvey. He's standing right beside you.'

Jools looked around but there was no one there. Christ, the Hunk of No Fixed Abode was a nutter. She was ready to politely excuse herself and find her own doorway to sleep in when she saw the cheeky grin forming on Skuttle's face.

'Brilliant! Gotcha!'

Jools punched him on the arm. 'Nice one. Real funny. You know, you don't have to pretend to be crazy to be homeless.'

'I agree. Being drunk, poor and smelling like rotten potatoes does the trick perfectly well.' Skuttle looked up. 'Get in the hole, it's starting to sleet.'

'Right.' Jools entered head first.

'Other way round!' Skuttle called, just as she started to free-fall into the humid, dirt-smelling space.

*

Niles Crisp was more than a little annoyed with the bidder who kept raising him by thousands of pounds. The bloke must be loaded – or really desperate. Problem was, Niles was running out of savings. If the bidding war continued he might have to take out a second mortgage on his dumpy semi-detached in Slough. He didn't mind doing that, as long as he got his wife. He told himself that if the amount went to £22,000, he'd pay a visit to the bank.

There were other details to worry about too, like how to keep Jools in his possession after winning her. It was one thing to convince her online that he was Brad Brown, but it was another to trick her in person. No way could Niles pull off a transformation of that magnitude. This would have to be an unconventional relationship – that's for sure. Maintaining this marriage might have to involve force.

And given that Niles had a penchant for force, he didn't mind that aspect of this little game. Not at all.

The next night, Mel searched online for Jools' auction. She hadn't heard from her friend in awhile and she was worried an Internet psycho had got to her. As the only item in her category, Jools certainly wasn't hard to find.

'Bloody hell!' £22,000 and four days left? That was more than Mel earned in a year! What kind of person bids that high? From what Mel had seen at the café last week, only insane lunatics and perverts.

Picking up the phone she dialled Jools.

'I'm sorry, the number you are calling has been disconnected,' was the only response she could get.

'Oh Jools,' Mel whispered to herself. 'I hope you're okay.' She'd go over to Jools' flat later to check on her. Right now, she and Michel had an anniversary dinner to commemorate the old days, before their love had run amok – or to be accurate, before he'd run amok with an old bag and his todger.

The dinner had been Michel's idea, and Mel was touched. Jools couldn't believe that Michel had changed, but their renewed relationship was living proof – he hadn't so much as looked at another woman since they'd rekindled their love.

Mel put on the old but still elegant red dress she'd worn on their first date, and the strapless gold heels she'd bought in Harvey Nicks a few years ago but had never had the chance to wear. It was getting dark out, but she decided to walk to the restaurant. It wasn't far, and besides, the rain had finally stopped. She and Michel had planned to meet at the restaurant, as if they were just meeting for the first time all over again. God, he was so romantic, she thought.

By the time she got to the west corner of Kensington Gardens, there were blisters down the sides of both toes. Stopping at a bus shelter, she sat and rubbed her feet. Dim street lighting cast narrow pools of yellow on the pavement, but the enclosed space in which she sat was shrouded in black.

Just as Mel decided she better get moving, two figures moved towards her.

She slipped her shoes back on, stood and turned towards the street with the intention of hailing a cab for the rest of the journey. But before she could, footsteps came up behind her and a female voice whispered: 'Not a woman, leave her alone.'

Mel turned, her heart racing and face hot with fear. A heavyset woman in an oversized coat and a misshapen figure with a beard were standing right behind her.

'I can't do this. It's wrong. We can't take people's money!'

Mel should have sprinted away but she was transfixed by something familiar about the woman. Mel stared hard at her until the woman turned her face up and the light from the streetlamp illuminated it.

'Jools?' Mel shrieked. The woman's mouth dropped open and she sunk to the ground The man jumped the fence and ran off into the park.

Mel pulled her up and onto the bench. 'Good God! What are you doing out here in the dark, and why are you wearing that hideous mac?'

'I, I, I'm . . .' Jools trailed off and looked at the ground.

'No! Don't tell me . . . don't tell me you were about to mug me?'

'Of course not.' Jools was indignant. 'I was just

going to ask for money. I'm homeless.' Mel rolled her eyes. 'That's what homeless people do.'

'You're not bloody homeless, you fool.' Mel pulled her off the bench. 'You live with me now. You're coming home with me, and you're going to live in my flat until you get back on your feet. Listen, I'm on my way to dinner with Michel. I'll just go explain things to him. Then we'll get a cab home. Tomorrow, we can go get your things, wherever the hell you put them.'

Jools didn't say a word as Mel flagged a cab. She never should have agreed to wander in the park at night with Skuttle. He'd insisted there was lots of good food – and other expensive stuff – just lying around. When they'd seen Mel, he'd suggested Jools ask for some booze money. Initially refusing, the thought of a nice Cab Sav to go with their rubbish-bin dinner was so alluring she'd finally agreed.

Where the hell had Skuttle run off to? Some friend he'd turned out to be. It really was dog eat squirrel on the street, wasn't it?

The thought of eating made her stomach rumble.

Night-time for future MP Rodney Wetherspone meant one thing: clubbing. He loved to dance and he loved the anonymity of club-land. Either people who followed politics didn't go to clubs, or people just left that all behind when they were out. Or maybe he just looked so different in his tight, silver-spandex leggings and snakeskin boots that no one recognised him as Rodney Wetherspone. In any case, he could slough off his professional image and just be himself. He had to be careful, though, because he was liable to forget all about politics and do things that would not impress the party or his parents – especially if they read about it in the morning papers.

For instance, tonight, over by the water fountain in the shape of a huge penis, was his ideal man. Even more tempting, the guy was staring him down like a piece of meat. But should he risk it? An isolated flirtation was one thing, but he'd hooked up with this guy – Mike, he'd said his name was – a few times over the past few weeks, and his internal alarm was sounding. Rodney longed to go the distance with a male friend, but the risks were too great. Maybe once he had a wife, the press wouldn't be so interested in him. Eligible single men from aristocratic families over a certain age attracted rather too much attention.

So he dragged himself away from the club – and Mike's overly suggestive eyes – and went home to engage in the increasingly important sideline of upping the bid on his prospective new wife.

When Jools and Mel reached the restaurant, Michel was already inside swigging wine from an expensive bottle of something rare on the table.

'Look, Jools. Do you mind waiting outside for a bit? This is kind of an important night and I should just go inside for one little drink.'

Jools shrugged, which Mel interpreted as 'no problem, go and live it up drinking your fine Merlot while I wait out here in the cold,' and she disappeared into the warmth of Chez Françoise.

Jools turned on her heel and walked north towards the bus station. It was the height of rudeness to expect her to sit and wait for them to finish their fancy dinner. Besides, seeing Michel's smug mug reminded her there was no way she could live with that useless idiot. Someday Mel would have to be told exactly why Michel was such a tosser, but even in her current state of annoyance, Jools knew that it would kill her friend to discover the truth. Right now, it was easier to stay away and say nothing.

Besides, Jools was surprised that the thought of spending another night with Skuttle in his basement hole wasn't exactly awful. After almost drying out her sofa with a nearly new hairdryer he'd apparently found in rubbish behind 'Hairs That', he'd provided some sheets and a pillow (which also seemed brand new – another miraculous find!). She'd slept comfortably in the main living area, and even though it was damp and chilly despite the small heater Skuttle had hooked up, and rats could be heard skittering around inside the walls all night, she was so happy to be rid of Rocco (not to mention the money-grubbing bank) that she'd slept solidly for ten hours.

When she slid back down the chute to the basement squat, all was quiet. There was no sign of Skuttle. Not that surprising, considering the desertion at the park. She'd lie low too if she were him.

But he'd obviously come and gone, for on top of the pile of scrappy items that had once hung in her wardrobe was another laptop. Like the first, it was dirty but remarkably modern. It even had a sticker on it saying 'Wi-Fi'.

Jools tapped the keyboard, and the screen came to life with the message: TO JEWELS FRUM SKUTAL.

She logged on and the MSN home page appeared instantly. The power and speed of the wireless connection amazed Jools, even – especially – since she was living deep in a basement. Quickly logging on to miSell, she was delighted to discover the bids were all the way up to £30,000.

Absolutely bloody brilliant! What a great couple of days. Her new home was dry and safe-ish, plus thanks to the auction's success, a decent home was on the horizon. And there would be enough so that Skuttle could move too.

I knew things would work out, Jools thought as her eyelids dropped. Falling into a deep sleep at the small kitchen table Skuttle had rescued from the tip (she could have sworn she had seen it in Harrods; her hobo friend certainly had a good eye), Jools only woke when she heard someone coming down the chute.

She opened one eye to find Skuttle looking at the screen of the laptop intently.

Shit. She'd forgotten to log off.

Chapter 8

To whom it may concern at the Willesden Green Post Office,

I am writing to complain about my mail delivery service. Despite my best endeavours to stop you (please tell the postman I apologise for threatening him with a day-old baguette), you continue to redirect my mail to the basement of the bus garage. Whilst it is true that I am currently living at the garage, I have never instructed, for my mail to be redirected here. I am quite happy for my mail to continue to be sent to my previous address, and hope I will receive no further unauthorised redirects.

Yours,

Julia M. Grand

RODNEY BLAMED HIS parents for the conflict between his political career and his true desires. Everyone outshone him, no matter how hard he tried.

He'd graduated with a first from Cambridge, but that particular feat was about as exciting as an M25 traffic jam to a family like his. His father was a retired High Court Judge, his mother a former model and muse of Yves Saint Laurent. His cousin Harry finished Cambridge, then built the UK's biggest Internet provider, marrying a bright but mouthy girl from a horrendous soap opera. His nephew Ronald managed to win a coveted scholarship to Oxford, despite his dyspraxia and Ecstasy addiction, while his aunt wrote a book that fascinated half the world's population, including a fair few Booker Prize judges. And what had Rodney done? Nothing, he thought glumly. At least nothing that would impress his family.

He was branded the family underachiever. His mother loved to tell the story of how the doctor had left him in a drawer an hour after birth and mistakenly set a heavy, jumbo-sized box of wooden tongue depressors on top of him – certain proof that poor Rodney's brain wasn't all it should be. It didn't matter that Rodney's ideal image of his future involved dancing on tables in seedy little Soho clubs, dressed in stilettos, black fishnets and a red patent leather halter dress. He had to achieve something that would make his family sit up and take notice – something that didn't involve stilettos. Becoming prime minister might just do it.

Of course, for that he needed to be a minister – and for that, he needed a wife. Now, thanks to Jools and miSell, he might be finally moving closer to his dream.

Not only that, the marriage would also appease his parents. They'd been on at him for years, saying how embarrassing it was that their 38-year-old son was still a bachelor; that it was a sure sign of loose morals and a lack of substance.

God, loose morals was an understatement. Imagine if they knew the truth! Unlikely, now, as Rodney calculated that if he won the auction on Friday, Jools would be sitting in his parents' overly-opulent Eaton Square living room by Saturday evening, celebrating their engagement. He had even hinted as much in that morning's weekly interrogatory phone call with his mother.

Moving to his state-of-the-art, home-office ensemble, Rodney voice-activated his computer and checked the progress of the auction.

'That's an extremely simplistic view of the complex man I love!'

Jools felt ill. She hated when Mel used her lawyer voice to defend stupid Michel, he wasn't worth an ounce of her intelligence. How could Mel be so blind? 'Mel, I can honestly say that I'm better off homeless and selling my soul on miSell than you are sticking with that loser.'

'You're selling more than your soul, Jools. And how you can compare the mess you've made of your life with my relationship with Michel is beyond me.'

They were standing outside the bus garage,

screaming at each other. When Mel had tracked Jools' down in the middle of the night, calling pitifully outside the garage until Skuttle told Jools to go and chase away the waiting cats, she'd assumed it was to apologise for abandoning her for her twat of a boyfriend.

But Mel had other things on her mind. She'd been near hysterical with anxiety because Michel had disappeared. She'd woken up and he was gone. So she'd started driving around, fearing the worst, and ended up near the bus garage. Even though Jools was trying to comfort her, secretly she was glad the pinhead had finally made a wrong move.

But a few minutes later, Michel had rung Mel's mobile, wondering where the hell she was. He'd just returned from a 'drive' and was craving a good bacon butty. He needed her to make him one.

Jools told Mel that 'I just felt like driving around' was no excuse – particularly as Michel didn't even have a car. Jools couldn't fathom tolerating a man so pathetic he couldn't even be bothered thinking of a valid excuse after pissing off to traipse around with strippers. But when it came to Michel, Mel had her blinkers securely fastened.

Maybe she should finally spill the truth about Michel, Jools thought. But looking into her friend's eyes, Jools saw the relief in her eyes. God, Mel really did love him. How could she break her heart?

Instead, she hit her up for a tenner (well, she was

a hobo now) and told her it was time they got some sleep.

Niles had finally formulated a plausible plan for his future wife. As soon as he won the auction, he (as Brad) would tell her to meet him at Heathrow, just outside whichever terminal housed flights from Wisconsin (where the hell was that, anyway?). Once he got her to his hire car (a van with blackened windows would do the trick nicely), he'd tell her they were going to a romantic location for a meal. Then he'd smuggle her to his house in Slough and lock her in the basement until she agreed to be his wife – forever.

The plan meant he had to get busy enhancing the windowless room under his kitchen so that she would be cooperative and eventually warm to her circumstances. Then she could live upstairs, cook his meals, clean his mess, and behave just like a real wife.

Going downstairs he investigated what needed to be done to make the cellar a pleasant home. The scratching claws of rats scurrying into the walls greeted his ears. The floor had a large puddle in the middle, surrounding the drain. He walked through the thick sludge water and kicked at the pile in the middle. A spray of pellets the size of raisins skidded to the opposite wall.

'Rat shit,' Niles muttered. He was going to have to give this place a good scrubbing. He'd need to unclog the drain, replace the broken window, paint the cement and get some furniture. A bed and a chair, at least – and maybe a TV, if she was a good girl. His lips lifted in a smirk. He'd have to hook up some plumbing for a bathroom too, since she wasn't going to be leaving the room much. He'd better get working right away. There wasn't much time until the auction ended.

Niles went back upstairs to gather supplies. He stopped by the breakfast nook, where he'd stuffed his computer, and checked the auction. To his dismay, the bid had been bumped way beyond his means!

£75,000?

Who had £75,000 to throw around?

Niles wished he could find out who HotRod38 was. He would pay him a visit with a truncheon and force him to retreat. However, that wasn't an option. He had tried to get miSell to release personal details before and was given short shift.

£75,000. That was over twice as much as his last bid. Even with his re-mortgage he couldn't afford to better that. Or could he?

Niles gathered his credit cards. He had four, with varying limits. He tallied the remaining balances and discovered he had just enough to make one final bid and buy the supplies he needed. There would be a small amount left after that to stock the pantry with food to prepare for Jools' arrival, although losing a few pounds wouldn't do her any harm.

He placed a bid of £76,000. If the other arsehole

outbid him again, the quest for a wife would be over for Niles and the wholesome American Brad.

Maybe he could convince Jools to drop the other bidder? Maybe win her heart with a phone call? If Brad turned on the charm, she might be willing to go outside of miSell and pull the bid. He could offer her a small tempter – say £20,000 – and then carry out his original plan.

Finding the old email with her phone number, Niles made the call, but a robotic voice said that the number had been disconnected. Niles broke into a cold sweat. Where was she? Had HotRod38 lured her away? He called once more, only to get the same message. Finally, he sent her an email as Brad, trying to sound cool and asking where she'd gone off to, and was she alright?

Now the ball was in her court, and Niles didn't like it. But he'd be the one in control soon enough.

Rodney now regretted mentioning the 'special someone' to his mother.

She'd been calling him twice a day, changing the dates they were available for dinner. If he didn't give her final confirmation soon, she would start thinking it was all a lie to impress her (which, to be fair, it was). If he didn't win this auction . . . God, it didn't bear thinking about. To shut his mother up, he told her that he and his new fiancée would come to dinner as agreed Saturday evening. That was a day and a half after the auction ended; hopefully plenty of time to makeover Jools and present her as eligible marriage material, with a little help from an old flame.

Once the auction was over with, he could work out how to combine married life with his newest attachment – Mike from the club.

Rodney had raised his bid to heights that would surely drown the competition: £75,000. All hope for the Aston was gone, but who was he kidding – his career rode on the auction, and considering the very tasty lump sum he would inherit from his parents (if they continued to think he was mentally stable and heterosexual, that was), money wasn't an issue.

A day before the auction ended, Mel found Jools near the bus stop around the back of the high street, rooting through the skip behind Bounty Bakery. Skuttle had taught her well – you could find entire loaves of bread early morning when the bakery replaced the old loaves with fresh ones.

'Jools! Jesus! Are you insane? You'd rather eat out of skips than live with Michel?'

Well, frankly, yes. Jools was surprised her new life was not totally horrible. She was beginning to function almost normally, short of having to forfeit a daily hot shower. It was possible to keep fairly clean by bathing under the powerful hose used to wash the buses, which did the job but was far from relaxing.

She felt like an elephant being hosed down before

the circus. She imagined she looked a lot like one too.

When she wasn't looking for food, Jools was window shopping, in preparation for when she actually had money. With the bids way up past the £75,000 mark, it wouldn't be long before her life changed dramatically.

Until then, Jools felt life wasn't half bad. She was a little lonely during the day, given Skuttle's mysterious daytime life. Always up early in the morning, despite having stayed up late with her, laughing and talking and occasionally going upstairs to spook the nightshift. She was certain there was more to him than he let on, but he seemed to respect her privacy and so she respected his, too.

He'd obviously seen her auction, but he never once mentioned it to her. She still found him very attractive but as the days wore on and he made no move in the 'more-than-friends' direction, Jools had to concede he clearly didn't feel 'that way' about her.

'Look, I've got to go, but will you at least come for dinner and a shower?' Jools looked up. She had forgotten Mel was there.

'Okay, maybe tomorrow.' Jools blew Mel a kiss.

'Try to stay out of jail unti then,' quipped her friend.

Hilarious. Bread for the day secured, Jools returned to her squat and her makeshift desk, an old refrigerator box with one side cut off for her legs to rest under the tabletop.

She logged onto miSell to see what numbers the bidding war had reached.

£76,000!

There were still only two bidders (Rodney and Brad) battling each other, up-bidding back and forth. Go boys, she thought gleefully.

Then she noticed a message in her inbox – Brad, wondering why he couldn't reach her by telephone. He said he missed the sound of her lovely voice, and the charming lilt of her English vowels. Jools giggled, and looked around, embarrassed, hoping Skuttle hadn't returned to find her laughing to herself.

Writing to Brad, she thanked him for the kind words, and told him not to worry, she had recently moved and would call him as soon as the phone was hooked up (but that it would be a couple of days due to an unexpected and violent storm that had destroyed all of the telephone lines in her neighbourhood).

She couldn't very well tell him she'd been evicted and was living with a homeless bloke in a basement squat, could she?

Jools still couldn't believe her good luck. She was definitely going to share her money with Skuttle; he'd been so kind and generous to her.

Turning to back the computer she saw there was a new message. Perhaps Brad again?

Her heart beat faster, but when she clicked on the message the subject line almost put her into cardiac arrest.

Administrative Message: Auction Terminated.

With shaking hands, Jools opened the message.

Important message to Jools700

We regret to inform you that due to a conflict with miSell's legal policy, your auction has been terminated. miSell does not support the sale of human life. miSell hopes that you will continue to use its services only for the sale of items such as inanimate objects and plants. You will not be charged for your listing. Thank you for your understanding.

Jools sat, frozen into place. All she could do was stare at the screen. She didn't even hear Skuttle slide down the chute and walk into the room behind her until he started singing *Girls on Film*. She turned and as soon as he saw the expression on her face, he stopped.

'What happened?'

Jools motioned towards the computer screen and burst into tears. 'What am I going to do now?'

Skuttle quickly read the message. 'Don't worry. We'll get on fine, you and I.'

Jools stared at him. Christ, he looked good – her very own hobo in grubby, third-hand, business suit. She took the back of his head (how did he get his hair so soft without proper conditioner and hot water?) and clamped her mouth on his.

But Skuttle's lips stayed deathly still under her

frantic ones. Slowly, he pushed her away. 'Jools, I don't think you're thinking straight.'

Shit. Double shit. Jools' chest heaved and sobs escaped like snorts – she'd never been a lady-like crier; just one more thing to add to her loser list. 'I know you know what I've been doing. You must think I'm such a freak. You've been so nice to me. I'm sorry I was keeping a secret from you but I was going to share the money with you, honest.'

Skuttle put a hand on her shaking back. 'Jools, we've all done things we're not proud of; not told the whole truth. It's no big deal.' He handed her a silk hankie with a Hermes logo in the corner. 'Now why don't we go and get lunch at that charity kitchen in the West End. The one with the Yorkshire puds you love?'

'No thanks. I'm not hungry. I just want to lie here on my sofa for a while.' Jools turned her face away. She couldn't stand for him to even look at her.

Skuttle looked at her for a moment then stood up. 'Alright. I'll let you nap. But you should remember that nothing is what it seems. You might be in the middle of a fairytale and not even know it.'

Of all the hobos, she had to get stuck with a philosophizing one. She was so not in the mood for cryptic messages. If this was a fairytale, then Jools was one of the ugly sisters. The shoe was never going to fit her size 7 hoofers.

So this is how people fail, she thought as she listened to Scuttle leave the squat and silence descended. They lose their jobs, lose their homes, lose their friends – then lose their minds from the stress of it all. She was either about to go insane, or she already had. If trying to sell yourself on miSell and thinking it would all be fine wasn't insanity, it must be the closest thing to it.

Maybe she could contact Brad and work something out with him. It would seem strange, though, now that the formal aspect of miSell was gone, to actually have him hand her money and then go home with him.

The whole thing was starting to make her nauseous. But she needed to face the facts: the only way out of this mess was to put herself at the mercy of a stranger and become a kept woman.

There was nowhere else to turn.

Chapter 9

Dear Miss Julia M. Grand,

It is Royal Mail's job to deliver the post; if we have knowledge of a correct address, we cannot simply overlook it because the recipient asks us to.

May I suggest that if you no longer wish to receive post, you contact those trying to send it to you and ask them to cease. In the meantime, we will continue to deliver to the chute at the back of the bus garage.

Yours sincerely,

Edward Blatherwith
Director, Customer Services

'JOOLS, HAVE YOU completely forgotten that just a few months ago you had a job, a home and a firm grip on reality? What the hell has happened to you?' The pixie-face was set in a deep grimace.

'I thought you'd be happy that my miSell days are over, Mel. I thought you might respect me again.'

'I can't tell you how happy I am that you're no longer indulging your miSell fantasy. But even that wasn't by choice! If they hadn't booted you off you'd still be doing it. No, the real problem is this homelessness thing you're doing now. It's not funny anymore. Hell, it never was funny, for that matter.'

'It's not a joke, Mel! I really *am* homeless!'

Mel called over the bitchy guy behind the counter at Mama Blue's and asked for two more takeaway coffees. 'I've told you a thousand times to come live with me and Michel. How on earth could Michel possibly be worse company than that wino you're living with? God, next thing you know, you're going to be sleeping with him.' Mel paused and squinted. 'You aren't sleeping with him, are you?'

Jools certainly wasn't going to tell Mel that Skuttle had rejected her. The bitchy guy returned with the coffees, and they walked outside and started towards the bus garage. 'You know, Mel, you don't have to be such a snob. Skuttle is a good man and I'm sure there's far more to him than we know.'

'Obviously. Broken home, mental institution, stint in prison. Take your pick. And what's with that name – Skuttle?' Mel made a face.

'He might look like a hobo, but he knows what he's doing and he's been nicer to me than anyone. He brings me food, he warns me about the really dodgy street people, he's emotionally supportive. And he's funny! When was the last time Michel did anything nice for you? Skuttle is a better candidate for marriage than anyone on miSell – including your own live-in *boyfiend.*'

They had made it to the chute and were standing in Jools' living room.

'Yeah, Skuttle the alco sounds like a great catch.'

'What are you talking about? He never drinks!'

Mel pointed to the corner, where a large mound of crushed beer cans leaned against the wall. 'Then what are those? Your bedding? An art project?'

'Oh. That. Well, you know I have so much time on my hands, and, well, it can be a little cold at night down here and beer is warming. And filling.'

'So you're the alco? Jesus, Jools, this isn't good. Come on, why won't you live with me? It would be fun. We can stay up late drinking, but because we're having a good time, not because we're miserable and homeless.'

'I will move in with you.'

Mel's face lit up. 'You will? Great!'

'But not until Michel is gone.'

The smile disappeared. Mel plonked herself down on Jools' sofa. Thankfully, it had finally dried out and no longer made the strange squishing noise.

'Will you just tell me what you've got against him? I know about the other woman, remember? That's why I left him in the first place.'

Jools was tired of trying to hold it all together. 'Fine, I'll tell you.'

Mel rolled her eyes. 'Let me guess, you saw him bonking a coat-check girl.'

'No, not that.'

'Who then? A waitress? A shop assistant? His dentist?'

The voice inside her head screamed for Jools to stop while she still could. But somehow her mouth and the words flew out.

'Your mother.'

Mel's own mouth dropped open. Then she shook her head, as if trying to dislodge the putrid image. 'You're making that up. Just because he made fun of your jiggly arse you've decided to break us up. Using my mother is stooping to a new low, even for you.'

'It's true,' Jools said, already wishing she hadn't said anything.

'Really, and you know this how?'

'Because, well . . . I saw them.'

Even though she'd tried to block the memory many times, her mind flashed back to the vision of Michel with Mel's mum.

Jools had Mel's keys for emergencies, and one day she'd run out of bleach while working at a nearby flat. She decided to run across to Mel's to grab some. Mel wasn't home so she'd let herself in.

And there, on the kitchen table of all places, was pinhead Michel. And underneath him – Jools had to bite back a yelp – was Harriet Smythe-Brooks. Ergh. She was old enough to feature in the Old Testament. Her legs in the air, his pimply naked body on top of hers, grinding away. If there was ever something to propel a person straight into therapy, that was it. Jools had crept out unseen, *sans* bleach.

And until today, she'd told no one.

But Mel was having none of it. 'You're delusional, you know. Really, Jools.'

'Me? Well, you're delusional for not believing me, your best friend. I've never lied to you, Mel.'

They stared at each other. A whole minute passed. Then Mel gathered her things and headed for the chute. 'All I've ever done is try to help you, and this is the thanks I get.'

'Mel, I promise you, I'm telling the truth.' It was going to be tough to get anyone to verify her story, given that Harriet Smythe-Brooks and Michel were hardly going to offer themselves up.

She never should have told Mel. She was an idiot. A stupid, homeless idiot.

'Bye, Jools. I do hope your life gets better, even if you don't deserve it.'

Jools felt so bad after Mel left that she needed to talk to someone. But who?

Although it was unthinkable just a short while ago, she rang her father from the phone Skuttle had hooked up – line and call costs courtesy of the bus garage. Maybe she could go to Ibiza for a while? If she could raise enough for the airfare, a nice spell in the sun might be just what she needed.

The phone rang ten times and just as Jools was about to hang up, he answered.

'Who the hell is this? I told you lot to leave me alone.' A tad aggressive, but maybe that was the way Spaniards answered the phone.

'Hi, Dad. How's Spain?'

'Joolsy! You're a voice for sore ears! Listen, I need your help, alright sweetheart? I need you to testify for me. I'm being charged with trying to get it on with a thirteen-year-old. Well Christ, I thought she was nineteen! Now I want to come back home to avoid jail, but the Old Bill over 'ere says I ain't going nowhere. To be honest, I don't really want to leave – the women here are amazing. Thought maybe you should get on a train or a plane and get down here and help me out of this mess. I can't leave my pretty little Suze here alone! She's a little angry about the, you know, the teenager. I told her, I said . . .'

So much for relying on support from dear old Dad. She should have known better. Jools put down the phone, grabbed a bottle of cider that Skuttle had appropriated from the bins outside a house party around the corner, and prayed that if she actually fell asleep that night, she wouldn't wake up.

Or worse, that if she did, she wouldn't dream of her father molesting girls young enough to be *her* daughter at nightclubs.

*

Rodney was optimistic as he sat down at the computer to check the state of the auction.

The Party insisted he was a shoe in for the preselection and given he was in a safe Tory seat, in less than a month Rodney Wetherspone would become odds on for the role of MP for Kensington and Chelsea. His chest puffed up with pride as he imagined his parents' faces.

Luckily, there was plenty of cash sloshing around his bank account, and no other reason why this wouldn't work out. Even if that other bidder raised him to £100,000, he was liquid enough to handle it. Rodney took a deep breath, typed in his username and password, and logged onto miSell.

He had one message in his inbox.

A MESSAGE FROM MiSELL

Dear HotRod38,

The Auction 'Girl for Marriage' has been cancelled owing to a miSell's policy violation. We apologise for any inconvenience, and advise that all bids have been retracted and are no longer legally binding.

Rodney read the words over and over again until his vision blurred. Cancelled? Against policy? He stood and paced the room angrily. All this time and effort invested into preparing for his marriage, his career as an MP, and now some idiotic policy was going to ruin it.

He tried to stay calm. Jools must be in the same position as him. This wasn't over yet. They could do the deal face-to-face – all he had to do was track her down in person and make her an offer she couldn't refuse. Rodney didn't know much about women, but he was fairly certain they liked money, they liked to feel pretty, and they liked security. He would come up with a package that was irresistible.

He gathered his coat and car keys and departed on a city-wide search for Jools. He would start in the neighbourhood of that nasty little caf and radiate outwards in concentric circles until he found her.

Thus keeping his MP dream alive.

After his initial shock, Niles decided the auction's termination was not, in fact, a bad thing. It actually put him at an advantage because Jools and Brad had a personal relationship – maybe he could get her to agree on an outside arrangement?

Better still, his competition had been helpfully scuppered by miSell, giving him plenty of time to get his basement ready and to woo his future bride further. Even better yet, there was no doubt he could get her for less cash now. Maybe Jools wouldn't even ask for money. He might be able to seduce her with the prospect of a fine cottage by a secluded lake in

Wisconsin – before introducing her to the less-than-stellar reality of Slough.

Drafting his response, he finally had the perfect combination of words. Brad would implore her not to let the trivial laws of the Internet keep them apart. He'd suggest a meeting in London in two weeks. Plenty of time to get the house ready.

Jools moped about the basement squat, feeling restless. She picked up the phone to call Mel, then put it down again. Mel might be living a lie, but Jools' truth wasn't exactly worth boasting about. Okay, Skuttle was entertaining and mysterious, but he wasn't interested in her, so pining after him was pointless and pathetic. And living down a chute at a bus garage wasn't adult behaviour either, was it?

Maybe some hunting and gathering would lift her spirits.

Scooting out of the basement and up the chute, she launched herself into surprisingly bright sunshine.

The skip behind the bread shop around the corner was loaded with goodies that morning and Jools took her time seeking out a nice loaf. Digging about, she came across an olive ciabatta, a rare find. Sniffing it and poking her finger inside to make sure it was only from yesterday, she then took a big bite out of the top.

Accidentally inhaling some of the flour that was

heavily sprinkled on the surface, she started coughing uncontrollably.

God, she needed some water. She was just about to drink from a kerb-side tap when she turned and found herself face-to-face with a tall man in dark shades and a well-tailored grey suit.

'Ah!' Jools shrieked in surprise, inhaling even more flour and coughing harder.

Rodney Wetherspone took a couple of steps backwards, holding up his arms in surrender.

'It's me, Rodney, remember? From the miSell auction? Terribly sorry to startle you.'

Jools swallowed a couple of times. 'It's, um, okay. How did you find me?'

'Well, the café we met in is two doors down from here.' Rodney took in Jools' appearance. 'I'm sorry, but may I ask, what on earth are you doing? Had I known you were so hungry, I'd have asked you to accompany me to dinner.'

'That's um, nice of you.' Jools was horrified. What a sight she must look. 'You're probably relieved that miSell didn't let you spend all that money on me!'

Taking her arm, Rodney led her towards the street. 'On the contrary, my dear, I am truly delighted to have found you.'

'Really?'

Maybe she had got it all wrong. Maybe Rodney, not Niles, was the nutjob.

Rodney turned to face her. 'Would you be prepared

to go through with the original deal, for the top bid of £76,000?'

For once rendered speechless, Jools opened and shut her mouth like a fish heading for a plughole.

'The plan would be to marry, and then live separate lives. Of course, I would fund a reasonable lifestyle, including food and accommodation.'

Jools was still doing a good impression of a breathless marine creature.

'Tell me, do you like Percys?'

The most expensive department store in London? Silly question. She found her voice. 'I, ah, I guess. Who doesn't?'

'Let's see.' Rodney glanced at his watch. 'Why don't we take you there and have your hair and nails and er, bits and pieces done. Maybe a few new clothes? Then you can come home with me – the guest room of course – and tomorrow morning the instant the bank opens I'll deposit the lump sum in your chequing account. What do you say?'

Jools opened her mouth to scream 'YES!' but all she managed was another feeble cough. So, she nodded vigorously.

'Well, gather your things, and let's get going. Do you have to give notice at your flat?'

Jools couldn't quite work up the courage to tell him she was a homeless squatter. 'Why don't you wait in your car and I will be just, ah, just a second.'

Back in the basement she looked around. As usual,

Skuttle was absent, which was probably a good thing. Jools might cry if she had to say goodbye to him right now. There wasn't much of her current life she needed or wanted, but there was the rock shaped like a poodle that Skuttle had given her on the one-week anniversary of her homelessness.

She went to unplug the laptop, then had second thoughts. What would Skuttle use if he wanted to do a little online surfing? Hobos had needs, too. Besides, she could use it to leave a note for him. She opened the word processor and began typing, not noticing the tears streaking down her flour-covered cheeks.

Dearest Skuttle,

A friend has offered to let me stay with him. He wants me to leave right now, so we can't say a proper goodbye. I really appreciate all you have done for me and I promise I will drop by soon and give you a special gift to say a proper thanks for your kindness.

Loads and loads of love, Jools

PS: Sorry for trying to snog you.
PPS: But I don't regret it.

With a final look at the tidy, cosy little basement squat, Jools wiped her cheeks and climbed up the chute towards Rodney and her new life as a wealthy politician's wife.

Halfway up, she encountered a familiar boot. She let herself drop back into the dark little room. Skuttle dropped down after her.

'Jools?' He eyed her bags.

Feeling more than a little guilty for running out on him, Jools tried to explain. 'This bloke offered me a home. And money. A chance to start again. Please understand. I'm not cut out for homelessness. I'm not exactly a natural, am I?'

'Who is? Listen, Jools, there's something I should tell you –'

But a loud, insistent car horn interrupted him. Rodney. God, the last thing Jools needed was for him to drive away without her.

'I really must go, but I will be back soon, I promise. I left you a note, over there… '

And Jools gathered up her things, gave Skuttle a chaste kiss on the cheek, clocked the fact that he smelled wonderful (where had he found that incredible aftershave?) and raced up to meet her destiny.

Chapter 10

Dear Miss Julia M. Grand,

As representatives of Commercial Bank London Ltd, we have been asked to bring proceedings against you for the amount of £25,681, plus interest and costs.

As you have not contacted the bank, despite numerous letters and phone calls from Mr Horace Fortescue at the Business Lending Division, it can only be assumed that you have no intention of paying this amount voluntarily. If you wish to formulate some sort of payment plan, however, please contact me as soon as possible to discuss this option. If we don't hear from you within seven days, we will lodge a claim in court for recovery.

Sofia Andersson
Associate
Little, Barry and Morton Solicitors

ON THE WAY TO Percys, Jools couldn't shake the image of Skuttle's sad eyes from her mind. Rodney was rambling on about his job, the upcoming election and the expectations people would have of her now that she was to be his wife, but she was still in that basement squat, thinking about Skuttle and those blue-grey eyes. Rodney glanced over and realised she was a hundred miles away.

Jools,' his voice bordering on sharp, 'have you heard a single word I've said?' Jools returned to the present, turned to her new fiancé and nodded.

'Of course,' she told him. 'Dinner at eight and I get to meet your parents.'

Rodney rolled his eyes and let out an exasperated sigh. The caring man by the bread bin seemed to have vanished – along with that olive loaf, come to think of it. At the thought of food, Jools' stomach began to rumble, but the look on Rodney's face told her there would be no eating until she'd been transformed from lump to stick.

Or as close to stick as she could get, anyway.

'That was the first part, but you missed the rest.' His voice was calm, but when Jools looked his way she saw his teeth were clenched and a muscle was jumping in his jaw.

'Listen, you're going to have to shape up and get serious if this is to work. I'm not just handing over £76,000 so that you can ruin things for me. There is a lot of press interest in me and my family, so we have to watch out. You're entering a whole new world now, Jools, and in this world there is a code of conduct. We'll have to concoct some sort of love story and you'll have to be able to retell it on demand to anyone who will listen, including the press.'

The press? Shit. Jools didn't particularly like the idea of being in the public eye – at least, not without going on a major starvation detox. Her stomach rumbled again – this time with nerves. Surely it would be extremely difficult to sell any new life story to the people who had known her since she was young.

Like Mel.

What on earth would Mel say if the press questioned her? She was so angry at Jools she might tell the truth. Then Rodney would demand his money back, and she would be homeless once again. Only this time, Skuttle might not take her in. Why would he? She'd pretty much deserted him.

'What if someone finds out about us?'

'People will believe what you tell them to, Jools.' Rodney was back-combing his hair with one hand, and trying to negotiate a corner with the other. 'That's the first rule of politics. And the second rule of politics is to pay off whoever refuses to believe you.'

Interesting. Jools had assumed the first rule of politics was to flip a non-existent second home. This bloke was even dodgier than her, and that was saying something. Then again, he didn't know about the debts, the fire, or her letch of a father.

Maybe now was the best time to let Rodney in on her chequered past. Even though she was terrified it might be the end of their arrangement, she'd always (okay, sometimes) thought honesty was the best policy – not that it had served her well with Mel. But she didn't want to be the centre of any potential scandals down the line – and judging by Rodney's desperation to marry her, she sensed he didn't want to be, either.

'There are some things I should tell you about me,' she said, trying not to look at him.

'Let me guess, you've got a few credit card debts?'

'Well, more than a few but that's not . . . '

'Look, as long as you're not committing bigamy by marrying me, I don't really care what you've done in the past. People forget.'

Mrs Pho was extremely unlikely to forget, thought Jools, and she tried again. 'But you see, I had this business and . . . '

'You went broke. So what? That puts you in the same league as half the self-employed in this city. It's just good tax practice to go bankrupt occasionally.'

'Well, some people weren't exactly happy with the way things turned out.'

'Relax, will you. People are greedy and can be easily appeased. It's simple: I need a wife, you fit the bill, so just don't act up and we'll be fine.'

As hungry as she was, Jools smiled. For the first time in a very long while, she felt things might be actually alright.

'Now,' Rodney said as they pulled up to Percys with a screech, 'the only thing you need to concern yourself with is getting rid of that toxic body odour, and that moustache.'

Her hand sprang to her top lip. God, living with Skuttle she had forgotten all about the rudiments of feminine hygiene. No wonder he hadn't wanted to kiss her. Who would? Upper lip bum fluff was hardly going to entice a man, even a homeless one.

Rodney reached over Jools and opened her door for her. 'Go on, they're waiting for you. I've got an account, so buy whatever the personal shopper tells you and toss what you're wearing in the bin. Just give them my name and tell them you're the woman I rang them about.'

Jools crept out of the car, clutching her bag of meagre belongings to her chest. Standing there on Oxford Street she felt like a garden gnome in a sea of Vogue models.

'Jools!' Rodney pointed to the bag in her hand. 'You won't need any of that. Tell them in there to burn the lot, will you. I can't have a stinking pile of festering hobo clothing in my house.' Obediently, Jools took her sad bag of dirty possessions and headed inside.

The beauty salon was on the fourth floor. It took Jools a while to find it – no one seemed to want to give her directions. Alright, so she was a bit smelly and her hair was tangled around her face like a bird's nest – she certainly didn't look the sort who'd frequent

Percys – but you'd think people would at least point her in the right direction instead of sniffing rudely and asking each other where security was.

As Jools approached, the salon receptionist's eyes bulged. She dropped the phone and her mouth sagged open, then twisted with disgust. When she could finally speak, she told Jools that if she took one step closer, she'd call security.

'Rodney Wetherspone sent me. He said he'd called.'

Christ, she didn't look that bad. Jools wanted to deck the prissy bitch but somehow managed to restrain herself. She was supposed to be a lady now, and for £76,000, she could definitely begin behaving like one.

'Rodney Wetherspone sent you?'

'Yes.' Jools stared her down. Gleefully she noticed the receptionist's left eye twitching.

'You are Julia? His, his, fiancée?'

'I believe that's the term used when one is to marry, yes.' God, this was exhausting. Strange how your body got used to hanging about doing nothing but eating. Which reminded her, she could do with a nice muffin or two and a latte. They should be complementary in a place like this.

But the snooty cow was still unconvinced.

'Oh, well, then, you won't mind me calling Mr Wetherspone to confirm that you are who you say you are?'

'Go right ahead,' Jools told her. 'I don't suppose I could get something to eat while I wait?'

Asking for food seemed to confirm the suspicions bouncing around the salon bimbo's tiny mind.

'Why don't you spare yourself the humiliation of being revealed as nothing more than a derelict street person with absolutely no right setting foot in an establishment like Percys, hmm? If you walk away right now, no harm will come to you. I might even give you a free sample or two for use in the bath – that is, if you can find a bath to use.' She laughed at her pathetic joke.

Suddenly, a muscular bald black man with flawless skin and glowing white teeth appeared alongside them. His periwinkle blue muscle tee hugged his body and the fabric of his white linen pants strained over his legs. A belt around his narrow waist held all manner of beauty implements, which looked to Jools like a set of medieval torture devices.

Maybe she should run before they got near her with those things, she thought, eyeing a particularly evil-looking pair of pliers. But Rodney hadn't given her his mobile number. She would have to hang about on the street and wait for him, and she guessed that seeing her loitering in front of Percys in the same state he'd left her wouldn't exactly thrill him.

'Ivory,' he barked at the receptionist. She turned away from her nail file and, seeing him, shrunk to the size of a dried plum in her seat.

'This woman is Mrs Rodney Wetherspone-to-be. How could you speak to her like a common hobo?'

'How was I supposed to know?' Ivory asked, on the verge of tears. 'She looks like she just crawled out of a bog!'

'Enough,' he commanded. Ivory snapped her mouth closed and scurried away.

'Julia, yes?' the man asked, stepping forward.

'Jools. Um, yes.' Jools was tired of all this now and hungrier than ever. If they didn't give her something to eat soon, she was going to start gnawing the bamboo sticks in the corner.

'I'm Debonaire, head stylist and make-up artist to the stars. I am also a very good, er, friend of Mr Wetherspone.'

Debonaire extended a hand for Jools to shake.

She reached out but shrank back the minute she caught sight of her own gnarled fingernails, overgrown cuticles and dry, scaly skin. But Debonaire didn't seem to mind. He grabbed her hand and kissed the top of it. Jools smiled. Finally, a little respect.

'Rodney has spoken very highly of you,' Debonaire said, 'and since Rodney is one of our most valued clients, you are more than welcome here at Percys.'

Debonaire led Jools to a small changing room where she was given a soft, fluffy white bathrobe and a pair of black sandals with tiny massaging bubbles on the insoles – it was as though she was standing on a bed of marshmallows. Bliss.

In the limited days she'd been homeless, she'd almost forgotten this sort of thing was possible.

A small Asian woman appeared at the changing room door and made a disgusted face when Jools stepped out.

'Stinky, stinky!'

She led Jools to a shower room and pushed her inside. Normally Jools would be offended, but right now she was so excited by the prospect of a real shower, with piping hot water, that she didn't give a second thought to being called stinky – frankly, it was the truth.

She turned on the water full force and let it run until she nearly burned herself. Her muscles loosened and she felt her whole body relax. An assortment of expensive lotions, shampoos and face washes were stationed on a small shelf in front of her. She tried every single one of them, particularly enjoying a jasmine-scented body scrub. It smelled great even if it did take off an extra layer of skin along with the dirt that had accumulated on her body over the last couple of weeks.

The Asian woman appeared again and handed Jools a giant bath towel. Jools didn't have time to even dry off before the tiny lady was buffing, clipping and polishing the nails on every single toe and finger. Then she led Jools to a chair in a small room. Three other women entered, all staring at her like she was some kind of puzzle they needed to decode.

'No idea what to do with those brows,' one said.

'Brows?' another laughed. 'What about the upper lip? You're going to need a tanker of wax just to get started.'

'The poor girl's ends are more split than me and my ex-husband,' the third woman cackled as she examined Jools' hair.

Lucky they were beauticians not comedians, thought Jools, as she rolled her eyes.

'Pretty eyes, though.'

'Yes, very pretty, eyes.'

They all looked down.

'Too bad about the feet.'

'Ew, yes. Even with the pedicure. Maybe some more polish?'

'Maybe some socks?'

'And sandals? Seems like her style.'

They all laughed.

'Hello!' Jools waved a hand in front of them when she couldn't listen any longer. 'I'm right here!'

'We know.'

'We know.'

'We're not stupid.'

'Or blind. We can see you there.'

'Couldn't really miss you, could we?'

They all sniggered.

The big one, the leader, Jools reckoned, leaned over and grabbed Jools' face in her hands. 'You have to understand, darling, we're like doctors. But instead of making you feel better, we make you look better and in order to make you look better, we have to first diagnose what's making you look bad, which, in your case, is everything. Don't take it personally. We're on your side, after all.'

Jools' chair was whisked around suddenly so that she was facing the opposite direction. Then, before she knew it, the chair-back dropped and the seat pushed out so that she was flat on her back, staring up at the ceiling. Someone put a steaming towel on her face and pressed down. What was this? Were they trying to kill her? She opened her mouth to scream but the towel came off, and Jools found herself looking up through a round, lighted magnifying glass at the big woman's huge, distorted face.

'Dear Lord, look at the pores. Moon craters, they are.'

'Let me see, Maude,' the littlest one said, pushing her way over to the magnifier.

'Oooh,' she cooed, 'I've never seen them like that. Cool.'

'Lola, you're a little sicko,' Maude told her, backing away. Suddenly, and without warning, Lola was going at Jools' face, squeezing and popping and smashing her pores. It was excruciating and Jools screamed.

'Now, now,' Lola said, 'don't be such a drama queen. It'll only hurt for a minute and then we'll get you some steam.'

Lola continued her torture until Jools could stand it

no more and announced she might faint. The woman took mercy on her and brought over a small steamer. Then came a soothing cucumber and aloe rub, then a citrus peel followed by an apricot exfoliate. All that fruit reminded Jools she was starving.

'I don't suppose you have any food?'

They looked at each other in bemusement. 'Food? In here? No one's ever asked for food.'

'We don't have food here, do we?' asked Lola.

'Only in the foodhall,' said Maude.

So no food then. Well, they must be nearly finished in any case, and then Jools could investigate that foodhall.

Before Jools' stomach could even think to rumble, Maude returned with the hot wax and tweezers. Every single hair on Jools' face was systematically ripped off or plucked out without one word – kind or otherwise – from Maude, who went about her business like an assembly line worker.

The third woman (called Tangerine, no doubt in honour of the colour of her fake tan) descended on Jools. She dragged her off to a sink to work on her hair and scalp: scratching, massaging, washing, conditioning and finally towelling dry. Then she pushed Jools towards a chair and mirror. She could barely make out the fast blur of Tangerine's hands as the woman snipped and clipped.

The whole process took the better part of three hours and when Jools finally made her way back out to reception, she was completely spent. The Terrible Trio had kept her well away from the mirrors, and she was too exhausted to even care what she looked like now. All she wanted was food and sleep. She sank onto a plush sofa and closed her eyes.

'No napping, darling,' Debonaire told her as her eyes began to droop. 'I need you awake and alert.'

'No, please, what are you going to do to me now? Give me a nose job?' Jools asked.

'You have a perfect nose, lovely. No, I'm going to do your makeup. I'm going to give you an overall look that you'll be able to recreate. With a little practice, of course.'

'But I'm terrible with makeup,' she told him. Working as a cleaner hadn't really called for Jools to excel at foundation and lipstick. She hadn't even excelled at cleaning!

'Well, you're going to have to get good, baby, because Debonaire can't be there for you every time some pap jumps out of the bushes and snaps a picture.'

Oh God, Jools thought. This is my life now. Paparazzi and TV appearances and photo ops. For a moment, she thought she'd made a terrible mistake. Maybe she should have stayed in the basement squat with Skuttle.

'Don't be scared,' Debonaire told her. 'We'll find a way to make it all work.' Jools smiled. She felt the same warm, safe sensation sitting in Debonaire's chair that she had in Rodney's Benz. And with Skuttle.

When Debonaire finished working on her face, Jools pleaded with him to let her have a look. But Debonaire told her there was one final thing she had to do before the grand reveal. He led her to the changing room, where she found a garment bag hanging from one of the wall hooks.

'We took the liberty of choosing for you. Rodney told us the sort of thing you prefer.'

She unzipped the bag. Inside was a very classic – but very boring — Chanel suit and a string of pearls. She'd been hoping for more Posh Spice and less royal garden party. Never mind, maybe she could get the skirt taken up? Jools put on the suit and the pearls and exited the dressing room to where Debonaire was standing with the Terrible Trio. They all gasped when they saw her.

'What?' she asked. 'It's horrible, isn't it? I look like somebody's grandmother.'

'Tangy, give her your shoes,' Debonair commanded.

'But… what? Why?'

'You're about the same size. Come on, Tangy, you've only got fifty pairs exactly like those.'

'But these are my favourite Prada strappy sandals," she whined. Debonaire didn't need to say more; he just gave her a look. Tangy walked over to Jools and handed her the shoes.

'Take care of them,' she said, her eyes filling with tears. 'They're my babies.'

Jools put the shoes on. 'Now can I see myself?'

Debonaire led her to a mirror and Jools lifted her eyes.

Bloody hell! Was that her? She looked like another person: someone beautiful and confident. Someone who looked as though they belonged in Knightsbridge, living next to Mrs Pho, not working for her. Her new blonde hair glowed, lighting up her eyes. For the first time Jools could remember, it hung straight and glossy around her face, arranged into a neat, fashionable bob. The suit fit her figure perfectly, the chic tailoring stripping her of twenty extra pounds. Tangy's prized Prada sandals made her legs look slim and shapely.

'Dear God,' she breathed as she took in the new woman before her. She finally realised just how much her life was about to change.

'Wonderful. Just wonderful,' another male voice announced. Jools turned to find Rodney standing in the doorway, a smile stretched clear across his face. 'You look simply marvellous. Debs, I can't thank you enough for making my, er, one true love, look even more, um, beautiful than she already did.'

Debonaire folded his arms across his broad chest and rolled his eyes at Rodney. 'Well, it's the least I could do for you and your one true love, isn't it?'

'Shall we?' Rodney held his hand out to Jools, ignoring his friend's sarcasm. Her perfectly polished nails glistened in the salon lights as she placed her hand in his.

*

When the Benz pulled up in front of a large building in Eaton Square, Rodney turned to Jools and told her not to worry about his parents. 'Really, they're quite harmless.'

'I'm not worried,' she said truthfully. 'I spent the afternoon being tortured. Could it really be any worse than that?' Rodney smiled. 'I'm feeling pretty good right now. In fact,' Jools continued, 'I don't remember the last time I felt quite so good about things.'

'Excellent,' Rodney said, still smiling. 'Let's hope it stays that way.'

'I can't wait to see your parents' flat.' Jools stepped out of the car and looked up. 'It's a brilliant building. How many flats are there here?'

'Flats?' Rodney asked, looking perplexed.

God, they didn't make the people smart in this part of town, did they? Jools took a breath to stay patient. 'Yes, how many flats in the building?'

Rodney laughed. 'There are no flats here. My parents own the whole place.'

Oh God, Rodney's parents must be Saudi-oil rich to be living here by themselves. Jools was nervous now. With all that money to protect, surely they were going to be a little suspicious of her sudden appearance in their only son's life?

But Rodney grabbed Jools and led her through the wrought-iron gate that stood before the massive house.

There was no time to escape.

Chapter 11

Dear lawyers at Little, Barry and Morton,

I refer to your rather narky letter of last week.

The reason I haven't responded to the bank's calls is because I was momentarily homeless. In fact, come to think of it, if the bank had agreed to loan me more money to tide me over, as I'd asked, I would not have become homeless. Do you think I might have a claim against the bank? Surely that would wipe out the debt I owe them? Maybe you could take the case on a 'no-win no-fee' basis. Of course, I'd need to see your schedule of fees, because I saw on telly once that some law firms take far too much of any court-awarded funds, and I wouldn't want to be ripped off, would I?

Yours sincerely,
Julia M. Grand

PS: I swear on the Bible that everything above is true – just to speed things up.

THE FRONT HALL of the Wetherspone mansion was four times the size of Jools' old flat and probably ten times the size of Skuttle's squat. A white-haired man wearing an impossibly wrinkle-free tuxedo appeared. In fact, his entire demeanour was wrinkle-free: there was not a single hair out of place on the man.

Jools stepped forward, arm outstretched. 'Mr Wetherspone, pleased to meet you.'

The man made a small noise and Rodney pulled her back. 'That's the butler. Good evening, Clement.'

A butler. Wearing that outfit? In the 21st century?

'Good evening, sir,' Clement responded, averting his eyes from Rodney.

'Clement, I'd like you to meet my fiancée. Jools, this is Clement. He's been with us since I was a boy.'

'Hiya,' Jools said, holding out her hand again. Clement nodded slightly and Rodney cleared his throat, throwing her a glance that clearly said you never shake hands with the help.

'It is my great honour to meet you, Miss,' Clement responded gravely. Jools couldn't stop a laugh from escaping before correcting herself and curtsying awkwardly. Rodney rolled his eyes.

'You only curtsy to the Queen, Jools,' he whispered through clenched jaw. 'Now give the man your coat so we can proceed, will you?'

With the coats safely deposited into Clement's capable hands, Rodney led Jools into a sitting room so huge that the ceiling seemed four storeys high.

He took a seat on a small chaise and patted the space beside him.

'Are you sure?' she asked. She'd lost a little weight during her period of homelessness, but even Kate Moss might threaten the stability of that chair. 'Seriously, it doesn't look like it's for sitting.'

'Of course, it's for sitting,' he told her. 'We are in the sitting room, after all.'

'Everything looks so perfect,' she said, admiring the glimmering set of Fabergé eggs proudly displayed on the huge marble mantel, each one in pristine condition without a single speck of dust. The other chairs and settees scattered about the room looked just as immaculate. It didn't seem as though anyone had ever set a single foot onto the exquisite Oriental rug spread out underneath it all.

'Mother is very particular about maintaining an appearance of cleanliness, tranquillity and grace. That is why she has such a large staff. But she still expects people to use the furniture.' Just then, as if on cue, Rodney's mother appeared in the doorway.

'He's quite right, darling,' she said, taking a step into the room, her white Maltese nestled like a baby in her arms. 'What would be the point of having all this furniture if no one ever got a chance to enjoy it?'

Rodney stood as his mother made her grand entrance. She was a tiny woman with dark hair pulled into a tight bun at the top of her head. Her skin was ivory and her eyes were rimmed perfectly with jet-black liner. Ruby red lips contrasted dramatically with her cream-coloured trouser suit. For such a tiny woman her presence practically filled the room.

'Mother,' Rodney said, planting a soft kiss on her cheek. 'This is Julia.'

'Well, of course it is, Rodney. Who else would it be? Charmed, my dear.' Rodney's mother extended a tiny, manicured hand in Jools' direction.

Jools froze. She wasn't sure if she was supposed to shake Rodney's mum's hand or kiss the massive emerald ring on her middle finger. She opted for yet another uncomfortable curtsy, almost toppling over onto the rug. She even went so far as to drop her eyes to the floor.

'I'm very pleased to meet you, Mrs Wetherspone.' Her voice sounded high-pitched and reedy.

She heard Rodney groan. 'It's Lady Wetherspone, Jools.'

His mother shot him a foul look.

'Judging from that greeting one would think she's meeting with the Queen. No need for such formalities, dear. You may call me Lady Margaret or even Mother, since I am soon to be that very thing to you.'

Jools straightened up. Rodney's mother wasn't all that bad; a definite improvement on the cow in the beauty salon, that was for sure.

'Aren't you pretty?' Lady Margaret said, admiring Jools' perfect hair and makeup. 'She's every bit as charming as you described, Rodney.'

'And you said you didn't believe me.' Rodney sounded more petulant child than loving son.

'I believe it even less now that I've seen her in the flesh. Tell me, Julia, what on earth is a smashing girl like you doing with my ridiculous son?'

Jools wasn't sure how to answer. She had no idea how much Lady Margaret knew about their arrangement. She didn't even know if Rodney's family was aware that he was gay.

'Actually, I find your son quite smashing himself,' Jools said, looking at Rodney, who suddenly perked up at her support.

'Is that so?' Lady Margaret was clearly not believing a word of it. The Maltese suddenly came to life, barking and struggling to get out of her mistress's arms. 'Hush now, Ping Pong!' Lady Margaret ordered and immediately the dog went back to sleep. Margaret Wetherspone was obviously used to being obeyed. 'She's an old bitch, Ping Pong, but I love her dearly. Rodney will tell you that I love her more than I love him but that's not true. It's a different kind of love. Ping Pong is so loyal and Rodney is just… well, my son. I do see quite a bit more of Ping Pong, however.'

'I'm sorry but I've been a trifle preoccupied these days,' Rodney began. 'What with the preselection coming up–'

Margaret cut him off. 'Oh, please, Rodney, I don't care to hear how busy your life is. It's so dull.' She turned to Jools. 'Has he told you of his silly plan to become an MP? They don't call it the House of Commons for nothing, do they?' She stroked Ping Pong's head. 'Shall we go to the dining room? Langston should be down any moment. He had a very trying polo match this morning and he's been resting ever since.'

Margaret placed Ping Pong on the chaise and extended her hand to Jools, who took it, allowing her tiny hostess to lead her out of the sitting room. She glanced back at Rodney and flashed a 'Dear God, help me look' at him but he was staring at his feet.

Rodney's father was already seated when they entered the dining room. A short, stout man with a few tufts of white hair atop his otherwise balding head, he wore spectacles and tight-fitting, grass-stained polo attire. Even Jools was slightly shocked to find him dressed so casually for dinner.

He was one of those men who appeared to subsist on copious amounts of cheese and lager. His belly was round and solid as though hiding a keg under his shirt and his cheeks remained perpetually flushed throughout the meal. He reminded Jools of a gruff, pissed Santa Claus.

Like Lady Margaret, Langston seemed quite taken with Jools – more than he was with his son, anyway. 'My son is, of course, a great disappointment,' he told her. 'I had hoped he would go into the law. Instead he's wasting his time with blasted politics.'

'Langston was a High Court Judge,' Lady Margaret told Jools, patting her husband's hand, 'and despite the fact that he managed to secure Rodney a position in a chambers of note, Rodney insisted on doing his own thing.' She made it sound x-rated.

'How interesting,' Jools said, trying to follow the conversation even though she had no idea what they were talking about.

'And law is the only profession, I tell you, the only profession worth bloody anything in this modern world. Politics,' Langston continued, 'bollocks! Who in their right mind takes politicians seriously?'

He prodded manically at one of the colony of garlic snails that sat before him, swimming in a shallow bowl of butter. At least Jools thought they were snails. The small apparatus in his hand was proving an inadequate tool as he attempted to wrest the small, rubbery creature from within its once-mobile home.

'What is it that you do . . . uh . . . Jools? Is that what Clement said her name was?' Langston bellowed at his son.

'My heavens, Langston, of course her name is not Jools. It's Julia. I've told you twice already.'

'I can't be expected to keep track of things like names,' he huffed.

'Don't pay any attention to him, Julia dear,' Lady Margaret advised. 'But do tell us what it is that you do to stay busy.'

She nibbled daintily on one of her snails. Langston had abandoned his tool and was stuffing as many as possible into his mouth at one time. A small trail of greasy garlic-butter ran down his lip and into the crevice of his chin.

Jools opened her mouth to speak, hoping that her mind would work faster than her lips and that whatever she thought to say would not make her sound like a complete fool. Thankfully, Rodney responded before she had a chance.

'Julia does most of her work online,' he said.

'What does that mean?' Lady Margaret asked.

'Internet sales,' Rodney responded.

'Jesus, man!' Langdon slammed his fist on the table. The few remaining snails in his colony bounced out onto the table. 'Would you let the girl speak for herself? You're not her bloody keeper!'

'Temper, darling,' Lady Margaret said to her husband, patting his hand again. 'You know what the doctor said about your blood pressure.'

'It's that damned boy!' Langston took a large swig from his glass of red wine. '*He'll* send me to an early grave, not the blood pressure.'

'I'm at leisure, actually,' Jools said, finally working up the nerve to take part in the conversation. 'I'm lucky. I sold some of my, um, assets and made a quite a bit, so I've been able to focus on myself lately.'

'Ah!' Lady Margaret clapped her hands together. 'An independent woman! How lovely.'

'Bah!' Langston stuffed more snails into his mouth. 'Where's the next course? These snails are far too much work.'

Margaret rang a small gold bell by her plate. As if by magic, two tuxedo-clad waiters appeared.

'Well, Rodney, I can't believe I'm going to say this, but it looks like you've finally gone and done something right.' Margaret nodded towards Jools.

'Rubbish!' shouted Langston. 'He'll have to work harder than that if he's to start getting any compliments from me. So he's found himself a decent girl to marry. Any half-wit with a fancy car can do that.'

Lady Margaret smiled, obviously humoured by her husband's insults.

Jools didn't understand why they were so down on Rodney. By all accounts, he was a success: the kind of man any parents should be proud of. Even if he *was* gay, that was nothing to be ashamed of, was it?

'So have you given any thought to the wedding?' Lady Margaret asked.

'Not really, Mother, but . . .' Rodney began.

'I wasn't speaking to you, Rodney. The wedding has nothing to do with you. It is the bride's affair entirely.'

'Sorry.' Rodney fiddled nervously with the cloth napkin in his lap.

'I'm not sure yet,' Jools said.

She needed to talk to Rodney before she said anything more to his mother.

'Rodney tells us that you're motherless. Is that true?'

'Yes, I'm afraid. My mother is no longer with us.'

'Ah! Well, you leave everything to me. I'll make all the arrangements.'

'Brilliant.' Jools shot a nervous look at Rodney.

'We'll have it at the Dorchester on Park Lane. And I don't see any need for a guest list greater than three hundred, do you, Langston, darling?'

'Leave me out of it,' Langston grumbled.

'Three hundred people?' Jools was shocked. 'Isn't that a lot?'

'Not if you want all our respective family and friends in attendance,' Lady Margaret responded.

Jools had to stop a snort from escaping. All of her family! That was a laugh. Jools could fit all of her family members and close friends into a small walk-in closet these days. She hardly needed to rent out the Dorchester for a ceremony that was all business, no pleasure. Then again, it might be nice to have a fairytale wedding at a beautiful venue.

Athough a man batting for the 'other side' didn't exactly meet fairytale criteria.

'I'm afraid I don't have much family,' Jools admitted. 'It's just my dad and he's… out of the country at the moment. He won't be able to come.'

'Nonsense!' Margaret commanded. 'Give me his contact information and I'll handle everything.'

Jools nodded although she couldn't even begin to imagine that particular conversation. But she couldn't very well tell them her father was wanted in Europe for having it on with teenagers. She gave Lady Margaret her father's address in Ibiza, praying to God he was banged up in jail and wouldn't be able to respond.

An hour or so later, they were back in the car.

'I think that went well,' said Jools.

Rodney was gunning the car west, the driver having disappeared into his parents' house. 'Yeah, they liked you.'

They sat in silence for a while, then Rodney pulled up in front of a small terrace not far from Harrods.

'I've got, er, work to finish up. Do you mind going in and making yourself at home?'

'Sure.'

Once she was out of the car – house keys and alarm code in hand – Rodney roared off. Suddenly, Jools had little desire to investigate her new home. She almost wished she was spending the night back with Skuttle, or at least Mel.

Mel. Yes, she could take a stroll over to Mel's place. She didn't want to gloat, exactly, but she did want to let Mel know that her plan had worked out after all. Of course, Mel hated her guts right now, but she might be so shocked at her appearance she'd forget all about the *boyfiend* and her mother. Or she might not recognise Jools and let her in by mistake. Whatever it took, Jools needed to talk to her.

She arrived at Mel's building just as someone was leaving. Scurrying through the open door, she made her way to Mel's flat.

Testing the handle, she found it unlocked.

'Mel?' Jools pushed the door open and walked into the dimly lit foyer. She waited a moment before calling Mel's name again. There was no answer so Jools decided to leave a note telling Mel that she'd stopped by and could now be reached at Rodney's swank little SW7 terrace.

Jools heard a noise coming from the bedroom. She couldn't place it at first. There was something animalistic about it but at the same time mechanical. A grunt and a clank, a buzz and then someone screaming – Christ, was that a man or a woman? She walked hesitantly towards the noise, wondering if Mel had been stricken by some horrible stomach flu.

'Mel? It's Jools. Are you all right?' Jools was about three feet from the bedroom when the door swung open. Michel appeared, red-faced and wearing only a giant smile and nothing else.

'Gross.' Jools slapped a hand over her eyes.

'Jools! How'd you get in here?' he asked, jockeying to block her view of the bedroom. Unfortunately all that jiggling attracted her eyes to his nether-regions.

'The door was unlocked. Is Mel here?' she asked, quickly moving her eyes to his face again — not that it was much better. She tried to look behind him into the bedroom.

Michel shook his head. 'Nope. Just me. Just me here in the apartment all by my lonesome.' He stretched to block her view again. 'I'll tell her you stopped by.'

Right then, Mel's voice called out from the foyer. 'Babe?'

Mel came down the hallway towards them. Her mouth dropped open as she took in the sight before her. Why was Jools there – wearing Chanel and Prada, to boot? And why was Michel naked and panting?

'Um, hello,' Mel started, her eyes moving from Michel to Jools and back to Michel.

'Hiya, darling. Jools popped by for a chat – I was just doing some, er, push-ups. Why don't you two go out for a late feed, on me?'

Jools glared at him. She was sure there was someone in that bedroom, but the last thing she wanted was to upset Mel all over again.

'Sounds great.' Jools linked her arm with Mel's. 'I've got so much to tell you.'

Not sure what else to say, Mel allowed herself to be led away.

Soon after, Jools and Mel were seated at their favourite cosy booth in a fabulous but cramped Polish eatery in a tiny Kensington backstreet.

'So, given that I have no choice but to forgive you for saying those unforgivable things about mummy, will you explain how you came to look like this?' Mel popped half a cheese and spinach pierogi into her mouth.

'What do you mean?' Jools responded. There was a bowl of thick hot borscht in front of her but she wasn't interested in eating. Not after the meal she'd had to endure with Rodney's parents. 'Don't I always look like this?' She thought it better not to mention Michel again – ever, if she could manage it.

'Yeah, right. So let's have it. Who did you mug?'

'No one,' Jools said, trying to hold back a smile. 'And don't worry about dinner. This time it's on me. Well, maybe not this time, but after tomorrow, definitely.'

'What have you done?' Mel was almost afraid to hear the answer.

Jools explained everything. She told Mel how Rodney had appeared at her squat and taken her to Percys; about the Wetherspone house and Rodney's parents; and lastly, that all of her financial worries were over. Finally finished, she waited for Mel's response.

Mel ate another pierogi, chewing thoughtfully before speaking. 'I suppose it's better than dumpster diving and living with a hobo. But I still can't condone you selling yourself like a geisha.'

'Geishas are very well taken care of, Mel. Besides, the joy of this arrangement is that Rodney is totally and utterly into men. I'm completely safe from any unwanted advances.'

Mel's eyes narrowed. 'You're not attracted to him, are you? First a hobo, now a homosexual. You really have great taste, my friend.'

'Do you mean that?' Jools asked.

'What? That your taste sucks?'

'That I'm your friend?'

Mel shrugged. 'You're on probation.'

Jools grinned. 'That will do.'

While Jools enjoyed dinner with Mel, Niles was staring at his computer screen, anger growing with each passing second. Why hadn't that little bitch responded to any of his emails? It was a monstrous affront to his dignity and there was no way that she was going slip through his fingers without a fight.

Niles had an idea. He dressed in black and scurried out of his flat. He knew where Jools lived, or at least he knew where she'd been living when they'd first met. If he could find her, he'd just need to gag and smuggle her back to Slough. All his careful planning need not go to waste.

After an hour on the M4 he arrived at her flat and buzzed. No answer. He walked around to the other side of the building, found what looked to be her kitchen window – in fact, the only window – and heaved a large chunk of concrete towards it. But his aim was poor and he missed. The concrete chunk ricocheted off the brick façade and came crashing back down towards the pavement, narrowly missing Niles and landing, instead, on the head of a tatty hobo who was making his way down the street.

'Ah!' Skuttle cried out when the concrete chunk hit him. 'The sky's falling!' He fell to his knees and covered his head with his hands.

'The sky isn't falling, you idiot wino!' Niles barked. 'Get up.' Skuttle carefully removed his hands from his head and, sensing no immediate threat, stood up and dusted himself off.

'You look like a regular on these streets,' Niles said.

Skuttle eyed him suspiciously. 'Maybe I is and maybe I ain't.'

'I'm looking for a girl. She lives here. Jools. Plump. Blonde. Pretty. Do you know her?'

'Who's asking?'

'Cut the crap!' Niles shouted, offended that a wino dared to question him. 'You tell me where she is and you tell me now.'

'I don't know nothin' about no Jools,' Skuttle said, sneering at Niles as he moved towards his chute.

Alright, then. Niles thought. If Jools wanted to play hard to get, that was fine. But he would get her eventually. And when he did, he won't ever let her go again.

Which reminded him, he needed to get to Homebase for some rope and masking tape.

Chapter 12

Dear Miss Julia M. Grand,

We refer to your application for Jobseeker's Allowance. Unfortunately, as was made clear to you during legal proceedings three years ago, committing benefit fraud renders you unsuitable as a candidate for government assistance. However, we have attached a list of shelters and groups that provide free meals in various locations throughout London, should you require them.

Shakeriana Pemena
Ombudsman for Social Services

STUPID, SANDAL-WEARING dole people. Jools tossed the letter aside. Never mind. It wasn't as if she needed them anymore. Serves her right for giving Skuttle her new address.

'Are you listening, Jools? You'll come?'

Rodney and Jools were sitting down to breakfast and he was rabbiting on about some neighbourhood meet-and-greets he had to do. She took a giant bite of her toast, spread thickly with juicy strawberry jam, and considered his request.

'It's my duty now, I guess.' She tried not to speak with her mouth full but failed miserably. Bits of gooey toast fell onto the glass table.

'You have free will, Jools. I certainly can't force you to come.' He sipped his tea and flipped through the pages of *The Times.*

But after everything he'd done for her, she really couldn't say no. He'd paid her all the money as promised, and when she'd returned to Knightsbridge after dinner with Mel, a stunningly furnished bedroom, in various tones of white, was waiting. The balcony overlooking the small garden made her feel like Juliet. Unfortunately, given Rodney's sexual orientation, that's as far as that analogy went.

She couldn't believe how lucky she'd been to find Rodney – or rather, how lucky she'd been that Rodney had found her grazing by the bins that day. Not only did she have someone to take care of her now, but she didn't have to share a bathroom with him, fend off his unwanted sexual advances, or deal with his loud snoring and cold feet at night. Rodney was the best boyfriend she had ever had. Well, apart from a brief fling with a fast-food manager from Birmingham, it was the only relationship she'd ever had.

Occasionally she let herself fantasize about Brad and possibly enticing him to London for a little fun and games – a man to satisfy her physical needs without losing the man who was taking care of her material ones. Then life really would be ideal.

She had no idea what Rodney did to satisfy his own physical needs. Some nights he would disappear around ten and she wouldn't see or hear from him until the following afternoon when he called from the office to check up on her.

That morning, though, they were enjoying a small domestic moment, dining on tea and toast, the newspaper spread out on the table before them, engaging in the kind of customary conversation that one would expect from a couple in their situation. Would she accompany him on a campaign meet-and-greet around Knightsbridge this week? Would she play the happy, supportive political partner? Would she smile and shake hands and tell his constituents what a wonderful man he was?

'Sure, I'll do it,' Jools said. 'I suppose that means I'll have to wear that awful suit again, though.'

'That awful suit,' Rodney snapped, 'is classic couture.'

Jools had to remind herself she was living with a man who actually knew the names of top designers. To Rodney, Chanel meant a history of couture. To her it was a perfume you sprayed under your arms for free at Boots.

Jools emerged from the shower the next day to find a large white gift box, wrapped with a bright red bow, on her bed. A grin lifted her lips – she couldn't remember the last time she'd had a present (well, one that was new, anyway). Skuttle had been generous but his presents looked like they'd fallen off the back of a lorry, which they probably had.

Pushing Skuttle and the memory of his sad face to the back of her mind, she tore at the silky bow and lifted the lid. Inside, wrapped in delicate gold tissue, was a stunning new suit – Armani, this time. She gasped as she stroked the rich fabric. It was gorgeous. Pulling it on, she was chuffed to see that it fit her perfectly. It was a bit annoying, though, that Rodney had correctly managed to estimate her size.

Size 14 was hardly a compliment.

Gliding down the stairs in her sleek suit, she found Rodney was waiting at the bottom, dressed to the nines in his own impeccable steel-grey Hugo Boss ensemble. He held a pair of perfect black Jimmy Choo stilettos in his well-manicured hands.

'I figured you should have at least two pairs of heels in your collection,' he said. Anyway, he hadn't been able to resist buying them. He eyed them covetously as he handed them over.

Jools squeaked and clapped her hands together, then chided herself for becoming so materialistic so quickly. Come on, who was she kidding. She'd always been materialistic, she'd just never possessed the financial means to satisfy her clothes cravings sufficiently. Now, she had a man who was not only keen to buy her all the things she wanted, but was also fully capable of selecting them himself. Having a gay husband was definitely the way to go, Jools mused as she climbed into the Benz. This time the driver Louis was present, and Jools waved to him happily as she launched herself into the backseat.

Louis winked and Jools blushed. She was certainly enjoying the attention the makeover was causing.

'You might want to pull your skirt down,' said her fiancé dryly.

En route to their first destination, Rodney briefed Jools on what he expected. 'You are there to support me; to make me look good. You must make it obvious that you adore me, but don't fawn. Hold my hand and gaze at me as though I am your one true love. But do not, by any means, speak on my behalf.' Jools nodded as she admired a manicured toe through the peep-toe of the Jimmy Choos.

'If anyone asks how we met, tell them that I caught your eye in a café, and had an espresso and chocolate biscotti sent to your table. You were intrigued by me but not immediately smitten. It wasn't until I came over and we started discussing our favourite book that you realised I was the man you would someday marry.'

Rodney was speaking at lightening speed and Jools almost wanted to take notes so she would be certain to get everything right if anyone asked.

'So what's our favourite book?' she asked.

'We both adore Tolstoy.'

'Don't know that one.' Sounded boring, though. Give her *Heat* or *OK!* any day.

Sighing, Rodney replied: 'He's an author. You know, *Anna Karenina*?'

It still wasn't ringing any bells.

'No one's going to ask you for a book report, Jools!' There was more than a hint of annoyance in his voice.

Jools wasn't stupid – she'd gone to uni, after all, but she was by no means an intellectual. Did she mind that Rodney might look down on her? No. What did it matter, really? This was a business deal. All she had to do was act like a loving wife. And for all that money, she could surely do that.

The car dropped them off at the end of a long street and together, arm in arm, Rodney and Jools started to knock on doors, shake hands, allay fears and fill the hearts of the good people of Knightsbridge with hope for a brighter future. Or at least more tax breaks.

All was going very well. Jools was a natural actress and therefore, she decided, the perfect candidate for a politician's wife. She even managed to remember the entire story of their first meeting and so delighted an elderly woman with her dramatic retelling of the event that Rodney thought for a moment she might actually believe it had really happened.

When asked if Rodney was a good man, she

answered sincerely without gushing. When asked if her political views were similar to Rodney's, she was self-deprecating enough to yield the spotlight, but smart enough to seem involved. It finally dawned on Rodney that Jools was so good with the hoi polloi because she was one of them. She had all the characteristics that Rodney was lacking – an earthy, simple spirit – and without even trying, she was winning over his constituents-to-be.

Then they got to a small house in Petersham Place.

Rodney rang the buzzer and the front door swung open to reveal Mrs Pho – like a scene from one of those American horror flicks. And keeping with the theme, she took one look at Jools, did a double take and started to scream.

'Not you! How dare you touch my doorstep after what you do? You have no shame?'

'Let's go, let's go now, please!' Jools begged Rodney, yanking on his jacket sleeve and tugging him away.

He held his hand out. 'Wait a second, Jools. What's going on?'

'I tell you what going on,' Mrs Pho shouted. 'I living here, in this dirty, rented little craphole because this girl she burn down my beautiful house.'

Oh shit. Jools edged backwards, trying to drag Rodney along with her.

'Is that true, Jools?' Rodney shrugged her off.

'Sort of.' Jools gnawed her fingernails. A hunk of

sour-tasting polish slid off into her mouth and she tried to spit it out. 'I'll explain everything back in the car.'

But heading to the car was not on Rodney's agenda. He made a beeline for Mrs Pho and extended his hand. 'My dear woman, let me introduce myself.'

Jools had never seen him smile so brightly. Someone had done a good job on those teeth.

Mrs Pho, blinded by his charm and good looks, held out her hand, whilst her beady eyes darted between him and Jools.

'My name is Rodney Wetherspone and I want to be your MP.'

'I am Clare Pho,' she told him, 'and if you with that evil woman I never vote for you. Ever! Your career – your reputation – be ruined. Just like my beautiful house.' She added a small wail for effect.

Rodney thought for a moment.

'Mrs Pho, it sounds like you might be having some problems with your builders?'

Mrs Pho nodded vigorously. 'Problems, yes but not with builders. The council. They won't let me rebuild to five storeys. They say my top floor illegal. How can that be? Mother-in-law live there for ten years. Are they saying she illegal too?'

'Is she?' asked Jools innocently.

Mrs Pho and Rodney stared at her as if she had a bomb strapped to her waist.

'Why don't you wait for me in the car, *Julia*?'

Shit. He had never called her that. He must be pissed. Jools trudged off and leaned on the car, only a few feet away.

'Mrs Pho, can I call you Clare? What if I said I can help get your five storeys back?'

Her round Botoxed features relaxed as much as they could. 'You call me Mrs Pho. If you get me back into my house like it was, I not pass word around you are with that nasty witchy girl.'

Uncalled for, thought Jools.

'I think I can help, Clare,' Rodney said, flashing the smile again. 'But you need to promise not to cause any problems for my fiancée.' He nodded towards Jools.

'You joking! You marry that? Since when?'

'Since we both recognised our shared affection for the great novels of Harry Tolstoy!' Jools shouted from the hood of the car. She strode back over and took Rodney's arm with a bit more force than she intended.

Mrs Pho sneered at Jools and sucked her teeth. 'I sure.' She turned to Rodney. 'Tell you what, Wetherspone. You get me out this rat trap quick and I no tell press you engaged to known arsonist. You decide.'

Chapter 13

Dear Julia Grand, Arsonist,

We no friend, I despise you, but I please to accept invitation to your wedding, got today. But as you burn down my house no wedding gift for you!

C. Pho

A WEEK HAD now passed since Niles' last attempt to contact Jools by email. To him, it felt like years. Now, standing in his shower, ice-cold water raining down on his skinny, naked body, he tried to cool the emotional firestorm building within his frantic mind.

After his run-in with Skuttle, Niles had returned to Jools' flat in hopes of staking her out. She had to turn up at some point – if she still lived there. So he waited, hidden in a nearby tree, for nearly seven hours before deciding to give up. He took a quick tour of the neighbourhood to see if he could find Skuttle – he didn't believe that wino when he said he didn't know her – but he was out of luck there, too. Was everyone disappearing on him? Sometimes Niles would wake up in the middle of the night, cold sweat coating his body. Had Jools ever existed, or was she some fantasy he'd cooked up in his overheated brain?

Of course she existed, he chided himself. He had the emails and pictures to prove it. He had records of phone calls. He wasn't that far gone. At least not yet.

Niles managed to get Rocco's contact information from one of the other building tenants by telling them he was in the market for a new apartment. When he called Rocco to enquire about Jools, the dodgy landlord turned out to be just as cagey as Skuttle.

'Who da fuck is asking? You some sort of perv?' Rocco had shouted after Niles asked if he had any information on Jools' whereabouts.

Niles had completely frozen. 'I'm an old friend,' was the best that he could come up with.

'Well listen, old friend,' Rocco said, mockingly, 'I don't give out personal information about my tenants unless they're dead or wanted by the cops. But since Jools ain't a tenant anymore, seeing as how I booted her fat butt out, I can tell you this: she don't know how to pay her rent.'

Rocco slammed the receiver down. Frustrated he couldn't seem to get any useful information, Niles did the same, managing to catch his index finger in the process.

'Owwwwwwww.'

This wasn't supposed to happen. No woman was supposed to have this much control over him. Ever. Niles had fully expected Jools to be tied up in his basement by now. The harder she made it, the more he felt she deserved it. No woman had ever made Niles feel so powerless. He would make Jools pay for what she was putting him through – if only he could find her.

Deciding he wouldn't sleep a single wink until Jools was safely stashed away in Slough, he dried thoroughly, patted himself down with liberal amounts of talcum powder, splashed some cheap cologne on his face and changed into his favourite tracksuit. Brewing a pot of very strong coffee, he sat down at the kitchen table to do some serious thinking.

Where could she be?

He spread the newspaper out on the table before him. Mindlessly flipping the pages, he peered at the giant black-and-white images plastered beside each article. A boy on a farm had raised a five hundred pound pig; a woman in Yorkshire had given birth to identical quintuplets, all as ugly as she was; a teacher at a local boys' school was being accused of exposing herself to one of the students during Morning Prayer. Niles was disgusted. The world was full of pathetic people scrambling to get what they could before they died.

Then, there it was. On the front page of the local news section, a sign from God. The newest political golden boy, the probable new MP of Kensington and Chelsea, standing in front of a row of terraces with a giant smile on his smug face. Wearing an impeccable suit, shiny shoes and hair so perfect it seemed moulded from plastic, Rodney Wetherspone looked ecstatic.

And why shouldn't he be, thought Niles, with that pretty young piece next to him?

He looked closer.

Wait a second . . . wasn't that . . . ?

Yes, it was! His Jools!

The sight of her standing there, all dolled up in a posh suit, arm in arm with Rodney Wetherspone, was enough to make him want to tear his hair out.

Instead, he slowly sipped his coffee, cut the photo out of the paper, and started making a new plan.

Back in her perfect white bedroom, Jools swore to herself that she would do everything possible to protect Rodney's public image.

The incident with Mrs Pho had been a very close call, and further humiliating experiences had to be carefully avoided. Which meant if she and Rodney had any chance of pulling off their scam, it was necessary to sever all ties with the biggest personal embarrassment of all: her dad.

She placed the call.

'Hiya!' Jools' dad answered the phone cheerily.

Jools had been expecting him to sound just a bit more penitent and downtrodden, considering that he was wanted by the authorities in at least one country.

'Dad, it's me.'

'Joolsy! My little girl. All grown up and getting married! How do you like that?'

Brilliant. He'd received the invitation. Margaret Wetherspone was certainly efficient.

'It's great news, Dad,' Jools said, trying to find the right way to break the bad news to her father. Not only was he no longer invited to the wedding but he could pretty much never set foot in her life ever again. Not that he'd been there much to begin with.

'So, Dad, there's something we need to discuss,' Jools said anxiously.

'Don't worry, hon, I'll make sure to buy a proper suit for the ceremony. That Wetherspone bird said she'd handle everything. Joolsy, you done real good landing that bloke. His mother sounds like a right posh bit – loaded, too. The Dorchester. Fancy that!'

'Yes, Dad, Rodney and his family are very well off.'

'And he's in politics, eh? That's my girl. I knew you'd land on your feet. Just like your dad.'

'Right,' Jools said.

'I'll tell you, it sure was nice of the Wetherspones to fly me and the old lady back home. I don't know how I would have done it otherwise. And I'll be damned if I'm not going to be there on my little girl's special day.'

Charlie Grand sounded legitimately happy for her

and in the thirty seconds they'd been on the phone, he hadn't once asked her for money. A small patch of warmth began to coat her heart. As embarrassing as he was, and as much as she sometimes loathed him (and wondered if she was, in fact, his at all), Jools was touched by the sentiments and couldn't bring herself to cut him from her life.

Well, not at that particular moment, anyway.

'So what else is happening?' he asked, finally giving her the opportunity to speak.

'Oh, you know, not much. Just busy with the planning.'

'Well luvvie, I'd like to chat but I was just popping out for a cocktail.'

'What time is it there?'

'Cocktail time. Always cocktail time here, Joolsy. Cheers, talk soon.' And with that, he was gone.

Jools sat in silence for a moment. What on earth was she going to do?

When nothing came to mind she went to the kitchen to review the contents of the huge, state-of-the-art, stainless-steel fridge.

Sitting on the beach in Ibiza, his skin the colour of an over-ripe blood orange, Jools' father turned his daughter's wedding invitation over and over in his hands.

'That's quite the return address,' he mused, staring at the crisp, Smythson stationery.

Jools had really hit it big. He wasn't sure exactly how she had managed to charm this rich, handsome, successful man into falling for her. Sure, Jools was cute, but she wasn't the kind of bird he himself would go for — probably a good thing, seeing as how they were related.

They had never been particularly close but he was her father, after all. He raised her, paid for her clothes and food, put a roof over her head when she was growing up. It figured that she owed him. Wasn't it the child's job to care for the parents in their old age? Not that he was old, mind you. He was younger at heart than most men half his age. He could still get the girls, too. They loved him. Sometimes he thought he was too good with the ladies. It was his charm that had got him into his current mess.

I need to get out of here, he thought to himself. Get out of Ibiza and back to old Blighty – and live with Jools and the Wetherspones in their mansion. It made perfect sense, and it was the least Jools could do.

'Right, sorted,' he said aloud, rising from his beach chair, folding the invitation into thirds and stuffing it into his back pocket. 'I'll get out of here, back to the UK, and live with Jools and her posh new family.'

Chapter 14

Dear Miss Julia Grand,

Thank you for opening a new Black account with Imperial and Colonial Banking Group, and for your recent deposit of £76,000. Your new debit card is enclosed. We are also writing to inform you of our great interest-bearing term deposits, with high rates of interest a business woman such as yourself will appreciate. Please don't hesitate to contact us with any queries.

Rutherford Smith
New Business Manager

'I KNOW IT seems steep,' the salesman said, 'but look at it this way: time is money, right? How much time do you waste waiting for your applications to open, your files to download, your documents to print? You won't have to wait on anything with this baby. This one is cheetah-fast.' He stroked the laptop.

He did have a point, Jools thought. After weeks spent using that grubby thing Skuttle had rigged up for her, and years using her own sluggish late nineties-era model, an upgrade was definitely in order.

Besides there was still plenty of money to pay back the bank – and she might not have to, if those lawyers could come up with something shonky to get her out of it.

'I'll take it,' she told the 20-something standing behind the counter. He was a good salesman – and he was cute, which didn't hurt. But even he couldn't compete with her new computer. The most expensive Mac on the market, it was gorgeous. Super light-weight, the stainless steel casing giving it an almost space-age appearance.

This computer is a fresh start, she thought, handing over her seductive-looking black debit card. The salesman quickly rang up her purchase, along with the extra software, crystal-encrusted mouse and digital camera he'd convinced her were 'must haves.'

It was a heady feeling, being able to purchase so much, and Jools had no intention of stopping now. She headed over to Harrods, aiming straight for the handbags on the ground floor. Looking around at all the glorious specimens on offer – totes, clutches, shoulder bags – she decided she'd better set herself a limit: no more than £1000 (on handbags, anyway).

But a Vivienne Westwood Ebury Ostrich Tote for £700 caught her eye, then a Pauric Sweeney Eel Skin

Hobo Bag in turquoise for £975 called out (given her recent past, how could she refuse it?), then a brief but tantalising glimpse of the Nancy Gonzalez Crocodile Fold-Over Clutch in red for £1100 teased her . . . God, there was going to be trouble.

Ostrich, eel and crocodile: a dream safari and scuba-diving expedition. But no nasty desert dust or unflattering wetsuits required: Harrods had conveniently converted all the wild and exotic creatures into luxury fashion accessories so that she could enjoy them in every-day comfort. Buying three handbags was far cheaper than going on safari anyway, and though the shopping day was far from done, she could surely keep herself from splurging too much when she started looking at clothes.

But by the end of the afternoon, Jools had spent nearly £20,000 on a variety of items she didn't need, including £500 on matching silk bra and knickers that no one would ever get to see.

Only the realisation that she hadn't eaten all day made her stop. Imagine, food had taken a back-seat to shopping! In fact, she'd managed to lose quite a bit of weight recently. Being homeless tended to do that. Even if she did have a home now, with all this shop-ercise she'd be down to a size 12 in no time.

A few times, as the black card worked its magic, she wondered if she was going overboard, but there just didn't seem any reason to stop. It felt so good to be able to spend.

A tiny prong of guilt nudged when she caught sight of the price of the 500ml bottle of Crème de la Mer moisturiser for £900, but the girl behind the counter, whose skin was so perfectly luminescent it had a hypnotic effect on poor Jools, persuaded her to purchase another £200 worth of cleansers and anti-aging creams.

Jools sat down to grab a quick bite at *Pizza et Pasta Inc.* After all that exercise, she could afford to indulge in a few calories. Waiting for her lunch to arrive, she removed her flashy new piece of electronic love from her bag and placed it on the table, making sure to wipe down the table with a cloth napkin beforehand. She popped the lid open and the computer came to life with a soothing, harmonic hum. Jools was ecstatic when an icon at the bottom right corner of the screen flashed, indicating the computer's wireless card had picked up a signal.

She clicked the browser icon on the task bar and quickly navigated to her inbox to see if there were any new messages. Yes! Her heart fluttered as she opened an email from Brad.

Brilliant. The American hunk is still interested, she thought with relief. Maybe her plan to have a bit on the side would work out, after all.

Brad's email was short and sweet. Suddenly spending hundreds of pounds on brand new knickers didn't seem so silly.

Sad to have missed out on the greatest purchase

of my life, Brad wrote, but maybe I can still buy you dinner?

Jools clapped her hands and thought for a second about what to write back. She had to be careful. She was committed to Rodney, committed to being his wife (at least on paper), and it wouldn't do to go running around London (or America for that matter) with another man. Now that she was a public figure, she had to be very crafty about maintaining the secrets of her personal life.

She knew Rodney wouldn't care about her sleeping with other men. But he'd be more than a little annoyed if her actions tainted his public persona. It was all about keeping up appearances and now, staring down the barrel of a £20,000 shopping bill, Jools wasn't about to jeopardise her set-up. Plus, Rodney seemed a semi-decent bloke, and she didn't want to mess up his political career any more than she wanted to mess up her chances of remaining liquid.

Jools hit the reply button. Dinner's a definite option, she wrote. The auction may be over but my affection remains. Let's see what happens.

It was a perfect response, she thought: breezy and flirtatious, but sexy and mature. She hit 'Send' just as a huge Supremo pizza and a large salad arrived on a shining metal tray. Jools closed the computer and stored it safely back in its soft leather sleeve.

The waiter placed the gigantic circular dish in the centre of the table. 'Hope you don't mind me bringing the pizza out before your friend arrives. We weren't sure if you wanted to wait.'

'I'm not waiting for anyone,' Jools said, shoving her napkin on her lap. What was with these people? She licked her lips and contemplated which slice to grab first.

The waiter looked over his order pad curiously. 'Sorry, madam, I have here that you ordered a large.' He started to lift the giant tray off the table. 'If there's been a mistake, I can – '

'Stop!' Jools grabbed the tray and bit into a slice, wondering what on earth the problem was. The waiter stared, then shrugged and walked away.

Polishing off the pizza and salad, Jools made her way to the Blue Bar at the Kensington Royal Hotel for a quick drink with Mel. Hampered by all her purchases, she was 20 minutes late. Mel gave a huff of annoyance when Jools entered, laden down with shopping bags and sporting a pair of obnoxiously large Jackie O-style sunglasses.

'Sorry, darling.' Jools deposited her bags on the floor and plopped down in the booth opposite Mel. 'It's been one hell of a trying day.' She leaned over and air-kissed Mel, who was completely taken aback by her friend's continued transformation.

'Looks like it's been an expensive day,' Mel said, sipping her martini.

'Oh, not that bad, really. Just a few necessities. What are we drinking?' Jools called the waiter over and ordered herself a martini as well, but told him to make hers chocolate.

'Well, isn't this fun?' she said to Mel. 'Girls' night out. Just like the old days, except now we can sip chocolate martinis at the Blue Bar instead of drinking watery coffee at Mama Blue's.'

'Got your wedding invite,' Mel said, getting down to business. 'Gorgeous stationery. Must have cost a bloody fortune.'

'Probably. I didn't have much to do with it. Rodney's mum is handling all of that.'

'How nice for you.' Mel rolled her eyes.

'Actually, it is. It is nice to be surrounded by people who truly care about my happiness for once.'

'Rodney's mum wouldn't care an ounce about your happiness if she knew what was really going on,' Mel said, refusing to hide her disgust.

'And what's going on, Mel?' Jools asked. 'I've met a wonderful man who needs me just as much as I need him and we're getting married.'

'Bollocks.'

'If you can't be supportive, you don't have to come, you know.' Jools regretted her words the instant they fell from her lips.

'Is that what you want?' Mel looked hurt.

'Of course not.' Jools grabbed Mel's hands and squeezed. There was no point in starting another argument, not now.

'Of course I want you at my wedding. But not if

you're going to be sitting in the corner, sneering at me the entire day.'

'I won't sneer. Promise. I can't assure you I'll be smiling the whole time but I won't sneer.'

'Deal,' Jools said.

'And Michel will be there too, so at least I'll have a shoulder to cry on if things get too insane.'

'Oh, really, Mel. Do you have to bring him?'

'The invite said I could bring a guest. Who else am I going to bring? He's my boyfriend.'

'Right.' Jools sipped her drink. Obviously Mel was choosing to live in denial for the foreseeable future. 'Everything alright with you two?'

'Superb. Seriously, never better.'

Jools almost believed her for a second. Maybe, despite bonking Mel's mum, Michel wasn't the evil user she thought he was.

And maybe her dad would develop a conscience?

No way. Some things never changed.

Niles decided if he had any hope of wooing Jools, he'd have to convince her that Rodney was not who he claimed to be. He'd been online for hours, searching every possible source of information. He had a full biography of the man now, but the only relatively juicy bit of information he had managed to drag up wasn't even about Rodney, it was about Lady Margaret. Apparently, she'd been spotted dozing off during a performance of Hamlet at the National Theatre last spring and the photo of her, drooling onto her lapel, had made the society pages of every tabloid in London. So not only was it a boring news story, but everyone already knew all about it.

Niles was enraged that Rodney was so perfect. He looked perfect and he spoke perfectly – he was always smiling and shaking hands, holding babies like he actually enjoyed it. He had a top-notch education, never had any run-ins with the law, was an intelligent and charismatic speaker and had risen in the political ranks quickly and with the support of his peers. He was everything Niles wasn't; he'd been given every opportunity that Niles hadn't; and now he possessed the one thing Niles wanted more than anything in the world.

Niles wasn't the brightest but he was street-wise. He knew how low men could go if the stars were aligned in the proper formation, and he knew no one could be as perfect as Rodney seemed to be. There had to be something he was hiding; some ancient skeleton in the closet. Everyone had them — Rodney Wetherspone was just exceedingly good at keeping his quiet.

Niles would keep digging until he discovered Rodney's dirty little secret and when he did, he would use his newfound knowledge to lure Jools away from her betrothed and into his newly-outfitted basement prison in Slough.

*

Jools wasn't happy to hear from her dad again so soon.

'Listen, Joolsy. I need some money and I don't want to hear that you don't have it because I know you got plenty now, ain't you?'

'What gave you that idea?' Jools responded, applying a dab of her £1000 face cream to the tip of her nose. Weary after a long day on her feet, she'd just stepped out of a very hot bath and was wrapped in several fluffy towels.

'I know the Wetherspones are loaded,' he said.

'So they're loaded. Doesn't mean I'm loaded.' She examined her nose. For £1000, the cream didn't seem to be making much difference. Surely a few delicious donuts from the gourmet place in Knightsbridge weren't causing those blackheads?

'Alright, then I need you to go to the Wetherspones and ask them for a loaner of a few thousand Euro.'

'For what?' Jools asked, already convinced that his answer would give her heartburn.

'A passport.'

God, had he lost his mind along with his passport? 'But Dad, you already have a passport.'

'No, I don't. Not at the moment.'

'Where is it?'

'In a safe place, don't worry.'

'Dad! You tell me where your passport is or I won't ask the Wetherspones for anything.'

'It's sort of been confiscated by the Spanish

government, pending my hearing about that 13-year-old. But it's all just a formality. And I really want to come home for your wedding, sweet 'art.'

'Let me get this straight,' Jools said. 'You want me to ask the Wetherspones for three thousand Euro to pay for a fake passport because your real one has been confiscated by the Spanish government pending a hearing to determine whether or not you're guilty of statutory rape.' She took a breath. 'Do I have that just about right?'

There was a brief pause. 'Yeah, that's about right.'

What an interesting (and welcome) turn of events, Jools thought. She'd been looking for a way to tell her father she didn't want him at the wedding. Now, it had fallen into her lap. Those finicky gods up there had finally decided to smile on her.

'I can't do it, Dad.' She tried to sound apologetic. 'I can't ask the Wetherspones to do something illegal. It could jeopardise Rodney's political career.'

'No, you're right. You couldn't. You're their future daughter-in-law, ain't you?'

Jools was stunned. Could her father actually be talking sense?

It quickly became apparent the answer was no.

'No, you can't ask them,' he said, 'but I can.'

Jools' jaw dropped.

Her father had finally lost his mind.

'I'll call Lady Margaret myself and explain the whole situation. She's sure to understand that I only want to be by my baby girl's side on her wedding day.'

Yeah, she'll understand alright, Jools thought frantically – especially the bit about the confiscated passport. She'll understand me right out of Knightsbridge and back down that chute to my squat.

No way could she let her father ruin things now. As his excited wheezing came at her down the phone, Jools decided she hated him now more than ever. Of course, she couldn't allow Charlie Grand to call Lady Margaret – and suspected he damn well knew it.

'No, Dad. Leave it,' she told him. 'I'll talk to them. But I'm not making any promises.'

'Who's the best daughter in the world?'

Jools promptly hung up, letting loose a string of expletives that would do a builders' convention proud.

There was nothing else for it. She'd have to tell Rodney. It was a no-win situation: give her father money and he'd be at her wedding. Don't give him money and there was the very definite possibility that *she* wouldn't be at her wedding.

Towel-drying her hair, Jools threw on a new silk lounge suit (the sales assistant in Harrods told her she looked like a 1940s' filmstar in it) and padded down the hallway towards Rodney's room. She tried not to bother him this late at night but she knew she had to talk to him about her father at some point, and now was as good a time as any.

She couldn't keep this from him any longer, not with her dad making threats about calling Lady Margaret.

She was about to knock on Rodney's door when a funny noise stopped her. She strained to listen, pressing closer. A low hum was coming through the door, and some other sound she couldn't identify. Should she knock? Just go in? The little voice in her head – the one that usually failed to speak until after she'd done something stupid – told her to back off.

Just as she moved away, she heard a strangled yell. Good Lord, what was he doing in there? She wasn't sure she wanted to know. Maybe the voice was right. She turned and headed back down the hall to her own bedroom.

Jools pulled back the sheets and climbed into bed. She lay there for a long time, staring up at the ceiling, thinking about the mess her father had made of things. She would have to figure this out on her own. The Wetherspones simply could not know about his dalliance with that 13-year-old.

Jools would find a way to keep him away from the wedding, even if it meant telling every lie known to Michel Matthews.

That should give her plenty to work with, she thought as she drifted off to sleep.

Chapter 15

Dear Miss Grand,

Thank you for choosing Carlisle's of Sloane Square for your wedding gift registry. We have a few queries regarding the initial list you emailed to us.

Firstly, we were somewhat surprised to see that you listed several pairs of shoes from our Shoe Department, all in size 7. Shoes are not items prospective brides usually choose to list, nor, we imagine, gifts the groom's family in particular would be incentivised to purchase. Additionally, there are many other personal items such as body lotions and perfumes which we suggest might be replaced with a nice Le Creuset frying pan set or perhaps some high thread-count sheets.

Furthermore, we notice you requested La Perla underwear in size 12, including white lace crotchless G-strings. Unfortunately we don't stock that particular style in a crotchless G-string, but in any event, we would advise against listing such items as they may offend some of your more elderly guests.

If you would care to review your listings and respond as soon as possible, we would be most grateful.

Jacinta Millani
Wedding Registry Division
Carlisle's of Sloane Square

THE NEXT MORNING, Jools was working overtime to squeeze herself into a pair of designer skinny jeans for an appointment with the picky bitches at Carlisle's, who seemed to think her wedding gift list was too unorthodox for guests of the Wetherspones. As she strained and tugged, it dawned on her that becoming Mrs Rodney Wetherspone might just be more work than it was worth.

What the hell was wrong with these jeans? Rodney had bought them, and he was usually spot-on when it came to sizing. Looking at the expanding universe that was her backside in the full length Venetian-style mirror on the back of her door, Jools had to concede that any sizing issue probably wasn't his fault. In fact, come to think of it, they'd fit last week when she'd tried them on. Somehow she had managed to gain about eight pounds in five days! Was that even scientifically possible? Alright, she may have indulged in one too many Doughy doughnuts on her way to her now-daily interludes at Harrods, but still, that much weight in such a short time? Maybe she had an allergy or an underactive thyroid or something?

Jools had never been skinny, but she'd definitely hit her heaviest weight ever – even including her lengthy love affair with HobNobs when her cleaning business had crashed and burned (literally). She blamed the doughnuts, for sure, but also credited the insane amount of stress she was under these days. Stress, she had read, released cortisol, and excess cortisol led to belly bulge. Her belly seemed to be competing with her bum in the battle of the bulge. She remained small(ish) on top and she never carried weight on her face, so thankfully she could hide the extra pounds if she wore the right clothes (Prada had a line of tents, didn't they? Or muumuus?).

Of course Jools didn't go looking for doughnuts, but every time she found herself near Harrods – which was quite often because a) she was bored sitting at home all day and b) she had loads of money to spend – the friendly bloke behind the Doughy counter offered her freebies. Apparently, he recognised her from a photo in one of the numerous tabloids that had decided to make Jools a Z-list celeb.

That was another reason she was getting tired of Rodney's lifestyle. She hated being followed by the paps almost as much as she hated the now twice-weekly grooming sessions with the Terrible Trio at Percys.

Before meeting Rodney, she'd never once had her bikini line waxed. She really didn't understand why it had to be a one of the prerequisites for marrying him, anyway. It wasn't as though he was ever going to see her bikini area, let alone touch it. Although, she supposed, they would probably take a honeymoon, even if it was just for show. God, she hadn't given much thought to that until this moment.

Jools stared at her muffin-top, wondering how on earth she would ever sausage herself into a bathing suit. She'd just have to talk Rodney out of any sort of water-themed holiday. They could go skiing or to the country but under no circumstances would she set foot on a beach unless it was in one of those countries where you had to swim in a burqa.

Life with Rodney was not exactly turning out as Jools had hoped. He didn't seem the least bit interested in developing any kind of real relationship with his new fiancée. Jools wasn't delusional; she didn't expect Rodney to switch teams and fall hopelessly in love with her. She wasn't trying for a conversion. But she had hoped they could at least be friends.

Just after moving in, she'd indulged in various daydreams and fantasies that involved shopping together, dining together, watching scary movies together, talking about the boys they both liked . . . the sort of *Sex and the City* friendship Carrie Bradshaw had with her gay friends.

Rodney, however, wasn't keen on togetherness – or *Sex and the City*. He seemed to like shopping, as long as he did it alone. He bought her great designer clothes and had exceptional taste. But she knew full well that the trousers, shoes or spectacular evening ensembles he bought weren't altruistic gifts – he was merely ensuring she didn't embarrass him. In fact, when he'd seen some of the things she'd purchased herself the other day, he'd advised her to sue the shop assistants for negligence.

And things would only get worse once they were married. The reality of her situation was really sinking in. She'd sold herself to the highest bidder and was no better than a high-class prostitute – worse, even, given she wasn't exactly high class. Once from Tooting always from Tooting, no matter how many facials and brazilians she got; no matter how many pairs of Jimmy Choos were stacked in the wardrobe; no matter how much she learned about politics and wealthy families and how to walk and talk and act like royalty. Despite her best efforts to change, Jools would always be a failed cleaner from the wrong side of town.

'Are you ready yet?' Rodney knocked on her door. 'We told Carlisle's we would be there by ten.'

As she bumped and grinded her way into the jeans, she decided she hated Rodney for having purchased them. It was most insensitive, given the proximity of Doughy Doughnuts to the house, to purchase skinny jeans for anyone who wasn't anorexic. Maybe he hadn't been serious when he suggested she wear them today.

'How do the jeans look?' Alright, he was serious.

'Give me a minute, will you?'

Rodney was obviously going to stand by her bedroom door and torment her until she was ready.

'The jeans, do they fit?'

Shit. 'A bit long, I might need to have them taken up.' How on earth was she supposed to tell him that she would certainly have to have them let out – by a whole leg's worth? Not that it was even possible. At this point, her best bet was to exchange them for a size that actually fit her and somehow fudge the tag so that if he ever peeked, he wouldn't be utterly disgusted by what a cow she'd become. The fact that they might not make them in a size 16 was an issue she chose to ignore.

She started rooting through her closet, looking for items that would hide her lower body, at least long enough to wean herself off Doughy Doughnuts and onto some sort of amazing diet. There was nothing, though. She could hardly wear a lizard-skin handbag, could she?

'Do you have anything else decent to wear?' Rodney was still staked out by the door.

'Of course.'

Not. In truth, Jools hadn't actually tried on much during her shopping trips. Most of the time, she'd see something on a mannequin, decide she was in love with it and tell the saleslady to ring it up in a size 12. She just assumed she'd be able to get herself into it when she needed to.

Tuesday's purchase, a sassy little top and skirt number by Stella McCartney. Fit fine on top, but her derriere appeared to be trying to make a break for it via the zip of the supposedly flouncy skirt.

She couldn't wear that.

'Jools! Come on, will you?'

Okay, maybe she could. She looked around for the light beige Burberry trench she had bought, again without trying it on. It was a little tight under the arms but it'd have to do. At least it hid the skirt.

The phone rang. Jools heard Rodney's booming voice telling someone something was not acceptable, then footsteps. He banged on her door.

'Half-wits at Carlisle's double-booked us. Told them to call you to rearrange. I'm too busy for bloody wedding-present lists anyway.'

Jools breathed a very large sigh of relief, and popped a button on her skirt.

Later that day, Jools headed out to try to exchange the jeans.

Too late, she realised where she was – in front of Doughy Doughnuts.

'Hey, politician's-wife-to-be! Come get your doughnut!'

Her mouth started to water but Jools looked down at the evil skinny jeans in her arms and reminded herself of the sight of her bum in the mirror.

'Not today, thank you.'

He gave her a look like she'd just offered to stab his mother with a beigel. 'No? You don't like them?'

Jools walked over to him. Being nice to everyone was part of the deal, according to Rodney. Annoying any potential voter was an absolute no-no.

'Please don't take it personally. I really do love your doughnuts. It's just, I'm getting married soon and I can't keep eating them or they'll ruin my figure.'

'You? Never! You are so slim. Like a waif.'

Wondering if the Doughy guy was classified legally blind, Jools insisted it was too soon after breakfast to eat doughnuts, so the Doughy guy bundled up some Chocolate Temptations and told her to take them home for later.

'You need to keep strength up, for marriage.'

He didn't know the half of it.

A few minutes later, she was unfortunate enough to run into Mrs Pho in the lingerie shop next to Doughy Doughnuts. Jools had stepped inside to try and find some of those magic 'suck your gut in' knickers she'd heard so much about.

'Well, well, *weeeell*. Fancy you here.' Mrs Pho's waxen face peered up at her. 'With behind that size you no fit anything here.'

'You should be more concerned with your own saggy butt, Mrs Pho.' Jools smiled sweetly.

Mrs Pho stuck her face up close to Jools. 'Take it from someone with plenty experience. Men like hot woman in bedroom. They don't want make love to lumpy sofa.' She eyed Jools' rump.

Jools was already mildly nauseated by the idea of Mrs Pho in a pair of lacy knickers. The thought of her bumping away in bed turned her stomach.

Trying to slide past Mrs Pho and out the door, Jools' Vuitton clutch caught on a hanger and Mrs Pho grabbed her arm. 'I tell you, lose those extra cushions, arsonist, or handsome husband look elsewhere for warm body.' She winked and preened in a nearby mirror. 'Maybe I apply. Maybe he fancy me?'

Jools wanted to tell Mrs Pho that Rodney was already looking elsewhere nearly every night of the week but she didn't. She couldn't. Mrs Pho would spread the word quicker than swine flu. If anyone knew there was no sex in her relationship because Rodney wasn't interested in her body – and never would be unless she spontaneously sprouted male genitalia and started wearing leather chaps around the house – the deal would be off.

So, she just let Mrs Pho think whatever she wanted, even though Mrs Pho's comments weren't entirely off-base. Even if there was no hope of sex with Rodney, she didn't want to look like a total cow when that hot American Brad finally showed up on the doorstep.

Chapter 16

FROM: ELVA RENDES
SUBJECT: RE: EXTRA MATERIAL FOR WEDDING DRESS

Dear Miss Grand,

Thank you for your email. Unfortunately, we cannot reschedule your dress fitting as the wedding is less than three weeks away, and we have much to do to get it ready by the deadline. Regarding your rather unusual enquiry about extra fabric, I can assure you that we did not purchase any additional materials because the metre cost is so high and we were reluctant to cause extra expense to Lady Wetherspone. However, having already had one fitting, which as I recall, was perfect, I envisage no problems in having enough material to complete the dress.

Yours faithfully,

Elva Rendes,
Chief Designer

NILES WAS SICK and tired of the cloak and dagger routine. He'd had no luck getting any dirt on Rodney and hadn't even managed to get Rodney's address. All he could do was wait for Jools to return.

Where the hell had she gone anyway? Who did she think she was, disappearing like that? Sure, she'd answered Brad, but the email was extremely noncommittal. Not what he'd expected at all. Even though the online auction had been put to bed, she'd still expressed interest in Brad and as far as she knew, he might be planning a trip to the UK any minute now. How was she planning on meeting him if she was never home?

Niles had to check himself from time to time to keep from becoming convinced that Brad was real. Although Brad was just a clever rouse to get Jools into his car and under his house in Slough, sometimes Niles would lose himself in fantasies where he was the handsome, charming American man sweeping Jools off her feet, making wild passionate love to her wherever and whenever he wanted.

Before locking her up for the night.

It was a soggy morning and Niles had been waiting in the tree outside Jools' flat for hours. Very few people had come and gone and Jools, of course, was nowhere to be seen.

Niles was just about to light up a fag when he caught sight of a tall man heading down the block. He wouldn't have thought anything more of it, but the man's elegant attire and graceful walk looked alien in these parts.

He wore a finely tailored wool suit under a grey mac, and he held a plaid umbrella. The umbrella itself probably cost £50, Niles thought as the man neared his spot in the tree. There was something oddly familiar about the face.

As the man approached, Niles jumped down from his hiding place and scurried to conceal himself near the mailboxes at the front of the building.

The man walked towards Jools' front door, then stopped, staring right at Niles, who was pretending to extract letters from number 4's box.

The two men locked eyes.

Feeling braver than he felt, Niles flicked his cigarette into the gutter and took a step towards the man, who, in turn, took a half step back.

'I know you?' Niles asked.

'No, I'm afraid you don't.' The well-dressed man backed away quickly and walked on.

'Bollocks.' Niles continued after the man, who promptly turned and rushed down the street. Niles followed but the guy was fast. He rounded the corner at the end of the block and when Niles finally made it to the same spot, panting and huffing from the exertion, his quarry had all but vanished into thin air. Couldn't have gone into the bus garage though – the gate to the front entrance was locked.

'Well, that's certainly strange.' Where had he seen

that guy before? But it wasn't long before Niles was thinking about Jools again, strange men in suits forgotten, and he hightailed it back to his tree in anticipation of her return.

After yesterday's run-in with Mrs Pho, Jools had lost her appetite for shopping but unfortunately not for doughnuts. Thoughts of the impending wedding dress fitting that afternoon drove her straight into the arms of the Chocolate Temptations that Doughy guy had given her. They'd been sitting in the fridge in the hope that Rodney might eat them.

Thankfully, he hadn't.

Was it possible to lose two dress sizes in four hours? She scoured the Internet looking for something, anything, to help but everything she found sounded potentially life threatening. She was desperate, yes, but not desperate enough to deliberately ingest a parasitic worm, inject saline in her bum, or have a couple of ribs removed. Not to mention that she didn't have the time.

Well, she'd just have to go to the bloody dress fitting and do her best interpretation of well-manicured hippo. She was getting pretty good at it now. Besides, it'd only be her and the dressmaker and who cared what the woman thought about her hip measurements.

Jools arrived at the studio at three. Elva, the chief

designer, appeared almost immediately, holding her near-priceless gown like a delicate jewel.

And behind her was Lady Margaret.

'I hope you don't mind, darling.' Lady Margaret sauntered into the studio like she owned it (which, as far as Jools knew, she might well do), wearing a houndstooth swing-coat, red felt cap and dark sunglasses. 'Rodney told me you had another fitting today and I decided to come along. Luckily there's no law that says the mother-of-the-groom can't see the bride in her dress before the ceremony.'

Jools was horrified Rodney's mother would see her belly rolls but the wedding designer seemed nonplussed by Lady Margaret's unannounced appearance. Jools looked down as she sucked in her gut, hoping it'd magically disappear. But no, the rolls refused to budge.

In the change room Jools hurriedly confessed. 'I might have put on a little weight.'

'Ah!' Elva's face betrayed the horror of Jools' flesh straining against the silk and organza.

'Lord in Heaven!' Lady Margaret said when Jools walked back into the room wearing the dress. She couldn't even get it buttoned in the back and the drop waist wasn't doing her belly any favours. 'What on earth happened to you?'

'I've just been a bit, er, stressed lately,' Jools told her future mother-in-law, finding it hard to speak and suck her gut in at the same time.

'I'm stressed, Julia,' Margaret Wetherspone said, still staring, boggle-eyed, at Jools' body, 'The whole world is stressed. That doesn't mean the whole world is eating itself to death.'

'But the wedding, the press… '

'You're a beautiful girl, Julia. Don't ruin it by becoming a morbidly-obese potato.'

Jools burst into tears, collapsing on the sofa in a heap of ill-fitting organza and silk. Lady Margaret sent Elva out of the room and passed over a tissue. She perched her rail-thin frame on the chair next to her.

'Oh dear,' she said awkwardly. 'Come now, Julia. It's only weight and you can control it. You can take it off as easily as you put it on.'

Jools imagined for Margaret Wetherspone it was something she controlled with an iron will. She couldn't imagine any errant bit of fat daring to defy her. 'I don't know, it was pretty easy to put on. A few doughnuts and here I am. I don't think losing all of this is going to be that simple, or that delicious!' Jools was close to hysteria.

Lady Margaret moved a little closer. She smelled like she'd fallen into a large vat of Obsession and Jools almost choked.

'I'm going to let you in on a little secret,' she said.

Jools raised her head.

'Blow.'

Uh, alright, Jools thought. She'd just blown her

nose, but maybe she didn't get it all. She covered her nose with the tissue again and honked.

'No!' Lady Margaret shook her head. 'Not that sort of blow. Cocaine.'

Was she insane? Next she'd be offering to score some heroin. Surely it was a joke.

Or not. 'Have I ever told you I was a muse for Yves Saint Laurent?' Lady Margaret stroked her hair. 'Well, have you ever heard of a fat muse? No. We could barely eat. So this was the solution. Still is, in fact.'

Jools stared.

'Just one tiny snort a day is enough to suppress my appetite. And it makes me feel powerful, a bonus considering I'm getting on in years. One does become invisible as the decades march on.'

'You're suggesting I develop a cocaine habit?' Jools asked, just to be clear. Maybe Lady Margaret had a terrible sense of humour. Or maybe this was some kind of test.

But no. She seemed to be deadly serious. 'Oh, just a little one. I tell you, it'll do the trick in no time.'

Jools considered it for a brief moment. But becoming hooked on drugs to cure an addiction to doughnuts was hardly admirable – even for someone like her.

'Thanks, Lady Margaret. But I should probably just try to diet or something. Maybe join a gym.'

'Suit yourself, dear,' Lady Margaret said airily. 'But do keep this between us. Langston or Rodney need not know.'

Jools nodded. At least one good thing had come out of her disastrous wedding dress fitting: she and Lady Margaret were now united by her dirty little secret.

Chapter 17

FROM: ALQUISIA KITCHEN
SUBJECT: TABLE RESERVATION

Dear Julia,

Thank you for your reservation request. Whilst we can certainly accommodate your request for a table of four, we cannot agree to your request to serve food containing nuts to a man called Michel, who may or may not have a nut allergy.

To ensure the safety of all the diners in your party, we will exclude nuts from the menu offered to you this evening.

Yours faithfully,

Matt LaAqua
Manager

JOOLS HAD DECIDED to go on a diet – just not tonight. Tonight, she and Rodney had dinner plans with Mel and Michel.

They'd be going to a new place known for its huge portions of red meat. As much as Jools was dreading spending more than two minutes with Michel, she'd also been hanging out for a giant juicy wagyu steak with fried onions.

On the way to the restaurant, Jools warned Rodney about Michel and told him not to expect much in the way of social graces, interesting conversation or personal hygiene. Sure, Michel was fit (if you liked the oily, greasy sort) but he was definitely not good enough for her friend. Maybe Rodney could find Mel a handsome, straight politician to treat her respectfully and give her all the love she truly deserved.

Michel and Mel were already seated when they arrived, and Jools couldn't help but notice Michel's eyes light up when he saw Rodney. Must sense the cash, Jools muttered to herself.

Worse still, after their second round of martinis, Rodney and Michel discovered they loved the same things: polo, tanning and Thai massage. It was as if they'd been separated at birth.

'You never told me you played polo,' Jools said to Rodney.

'Yes, well, there's still quite a bit you don't know about me, isn't there?'

As Rodney and Michel continued to chat, Jools felt a strange sense of betrayal. In less than an hour, Michel had managed to get more information out of Rodney than she'd been able to extract in a month.

The ease at which the two men conversed made Jools uneasy.

She cornered Mel in the loo and told her how she felt.

'So they're getting on. So what?' Mel asked, applying a fresh coat of lipstick.

'It's just not fair!' Jools whined. 'He's supposed to be my husband and Michel is getting to know him better than I probably ever will.'

'Jools, get a grip,' Mel commanded. 'You're starting to sound like a desperate girlfriend. Why do you care anyway? It's not as if your relationship is anything more than a business deal!'

Mel had no right to speak to her like that! Jools was just about to say so when it hit her – again – that Mel was right. She wasn't a real girlfriend and she wasn't going to be a real wife. She had no right to know what Rodney was up to. Her desire to do so only proved that somehow, despite all the facts, Jools hoped the marriage might morph into something real. She needed a reality check, and fast.

When they returned to the table, Michel and Rodney had made plans to play polo that weekend.

'But we have brunch with your parents on Saturday and Sunday we're tasting wedding cakes,' Jools protested.

'Jesus, Jools, we can taste wedding cakes any time,' Rodney responded, winking at Michel, who grinned back.

'No. We. Can't.' She tried to keep her voice at an acceptable volume even though she wanted to scream in frustration. 'We have an appointment. I can't just go cancelling appointments, can I? How would that look?'

'Of course you can,' Michel chimed in. 'Appointments are made to be cancelled. Tell them Rodney is ill, in bed.' He started laughing, as if he'd cracked a hysterical joke.

Reject. He absolutely oozed filth and lies. Even if *some* people were fooled into overlooking Michel's lack of moral fibre, Jools certainly wasn't. A lanky build and bright blue eyes might have that effect on the right person, but they did nothing for Jools who chose to focus instead on his greased-back hair and crooked teeth; his bad breath and cheap gold jewellery; his infidelity and his affinity for much older, wealthier women.

'Keep out of this, Michel,' Jools said.

'Christ, Rod, she's got you on a short lead, doesn't she?' Michel cackled.

Rodney shot Jools an icy glare and motioned to the waiter that their meal was over and he'd take the bill now.

Rodney ended up paying for everyone even though Mel offered to pay for what she and Michel owed. Jools was tempted to make a big scene by asking Michel why he wasn't offering to pay for his girlfriend, but thought it better to keep her mouth shut. She was already in trouble and she knew she'd get a talking-to once they arrived home.

She was right. The minute they walked through the front door, Rodney lost it.

'You made me look foolish tonight, Jools, and I absolutely refuse to be made to look foolish by you, of all people!'

'I don't understand,' Jools fought back. 'All I did was state a fact. We already have plans for the weekend so how are you going to play polo?'

'Get this straight,' Rodney told her, 'we don't have anything unless there are cameras on us or we're attending a public function. My nights and weekends are just that – mine – and I'll do with them what I want. That's what £76,000 – and your meals and accommodation – buys.'

'But don't you want to have a say in what cake we serve at our wedding?' Jools felt crushed.

'Quite frankly, we could serve sticky toffee pudding out of a wooden trough and I wouldn't give a rat's arse.'

Jools knew he didn't mean that. This wedding – or at least the appearance of this wedding – meant a lot to him. He did care about what they served, just as much as he cared about what she wore, who was there, and how many newspapers covered the event. In fact, Rodney's only care in the world right now — apart from, apparently, polo with Michel – was pulling off a convincing wedding.

So they bloody well wouldn't be serving anything out of a trough, be it sticky, sloppy or otherwise.

Rodney glanced down at the dining room table. The new edition of *WhatNOW!* sat on top of a stack of other magazines recently delivered. The minute he saw the cover, a huge grimace spread over his face.

'What? What is it? What's the matter now?' Jools asked, agitated and starting to feel the after-effects of too much wine at dinner. Rodney held up the magazine and turned it towards her, revealing the cover photo.

She raised her hand to her mouth. There, on the cover of *WhatNOW!* was a photo of Jools and Doughy guy. She'd willingly posed for it – he'd said he wanted to post it on the back of his doughnut booth. He was holding a tray of Original Glees in front of her and smiling like a clown; she had a Boston Crème literally stuffed into her mouth. The caption simply stated:

No Sugar Free for Wetherspone's Grand Wife-to-Be.

The photo was atrocious and although Jools knew the editors must have Photoshopped about three stones extra onto her, she still couldn't hide the shame she felt for letting herself go. She started to cry but Rodney was having none of it.

'This is great. Just great.' His face was frozen.

'It was a publicity shot. I had no idea he would sell it to a tabloid.'

'Are you completely thick in the head? I've explained to you a million times what goes on in my world.'

Jools was in dire need of a tissue and beat a hasty retreat to her bedroom as snot slid down her chin. Rodney followed her.

'I'm just supporting local business,' she sniffled.

'Looking like an overfed goose whilst doing it was not what I had in mind. And why not support a bloody health food store instead?'

'They added those pounds on, and you know it. Besides, I'm going to lose the extra weight.'

'You'd better,' he barked. 'Because you certainly can't go around looking like this.' He threw down the magazine in disgust.

'What about all publicity is good publicity?' Jools asked.

'Eating for eighteen is never going to spin well!' Rodney screamed.

Jools slammed the ensuite door in his face and locked it from the inside.

Chapter 18

Dear Miss Grand,

We refer to your letter in which you stated you planned to sue us for doctoring a photograph of you and your doughnut supplier. We assure you that we in no way altered the photograph to which you refer. We enclose an original print from your supplier's email for comparison. We hope that this puts your mind at ease and we hope to see you on our covers again very soon.

Percy Williams
Editor-in-Chief
WhatNOW!

JOOLS FIGURED THE only reason they were poking fun at her was because she actually was getting fat. If she was skinny and eating doughnuts, no one would care. Or if they did, it would be in admiration that she could manage a high-fat diet and still cavort about in bum-skimming skirts.

The 'fattie photo', as Rodney had so sensitively christened it, had now made its way onto the cover of nearly every tabloid in London. The headlines varied in their level of humiliation but they all said pretty much the same thing: Grand Big Doughnut Fan. Well, they weren't wrong; she loved them, which is why Rodney's lawyer said she couldn't sue for libel.

Even her father had seen it. He'd left a message on her voice mail to say she was looking a little plump and he hoped she wasn't going to risk her new, cushy life by becoming a blimp.

Rodney had demanded she stop eating doughnuts immediately.

'Just close your mouth and have some self-control. That's not too much to ask, is it?'

Problem was, self-control had always been the one thing Jools couldn't quite get the hang of.

But she promised him only lo-cal foods would pass her lips from now on.

At least when she was in public.

Mel called to meet up for coffee.

'Alright, but let's go to Mama Blue's.'

'Why? It's miles away! And I thought you were above that now.'

'I can't be seen near food outlets around here. The paps are all over me.'

Mel laughed.

'It's not funny.'

'It is ever-so-slightly humorous that you're famous for eating doughnuts, don't you think?'

'Yeah, I've been in hysterics ever since I first saw that shitty photo.'

'Mama Blue's it is then,' Mel conceded. 'I've got a client near there, so I'll meet you in the café at noon.'

Jools arrived at Mama Blue's clad in a ridiculous disguise straight out of a detective novel: beige trench coat (Rodney's, so at least it fit); oversized hat; dark glasses. The costume was so insane it actually had the opposite effect of what Jools had intended. She was drawing more attention to herself now than she would have if she'd just worn jeans and a T-shirt.

Mel burst out laughing the minute she clapped eyes on her.

'It's not funny!' Jools said in a harsh whisper, adjusting the dark shades she refused to remove. 'These people are maniacs. They're following me everywhere now. I can't leave the house without one of them trying to snap a picture of my big fat bum.'

'Jools, your backside is fine. You know they manipulate those pictures digitally. Come on, take off the glasses.'

Mel was laughing so hard Jools thought she might fall off of her chair.

Jools wasn't keen to share the news that the bum featured in the photo was all hers. 'It doesn't matter if they manipulate them. People believe what they read in the papers and now everyone in London thinks I'm fat. Which, let's be honest, I am. I'm the fattest I've ever been.'

Mel shook her head, a bit taken aback by her friend's heightened emotional state. 'Do you want anything? 'I'll go up and get it so you don't have to worry about being recognised.'

'That's sweet of you,' Jools said. 'I'll take a large mocha latte and one of those mini peanut butter and chocolate-chip Bundt cakes.' Mel paused for half a second, wondering if Jools was joking.

'One cake isn't going to kill me, is it?' Jools snapped, banging her hands down on the table.

'I didn't say a word, Jools. Have you finally gone insane?'

Jools removed her glasses and let her head fall flat onto the laminate table. Her horrible, low-pitch moaning quite unsettled Mel. She'd never seen her friend in such a state – not even when Jools had found out she wasn't pregnant and the government threatened to jail her over those illegal handouts.

'It's just not what I thought it would be,' Jools managed to say. 'I know you want to say you told me so. So go on. Say it. Tell me what a fool I've been.' Jools continued to moan and Mel shook her head.

'I'll go get the coffees – and your Bundt cake.'

She walked away towards the counter.

Niles needed a coffee.

It was extremely chilly and wet. Sitting in a tree all

day waiting for Jools – especially now that some pesky birds had decided to mate on the branches above him – was thirsty work.

He made his way down to Mama Blue's, the only café around for miles. The tables outside were full so he went inside and walked straight up to the counter, where a tiny dark-haired girl was placing an order.

Jools lifted her head and looked over at her friend. God, she was lucky to have Mel. Kind, level-headed Mel, who didn't know that she deserved so much better than that philandering Michel.

When Mel returned with the latte and the Bundt, Jools had (almost) lost her appetite. Once the cake was placed in front of her, though, she ripped off small portions of it and shoved them into her mouth at warp speed.

'The problem is,' she tried to explain, 'Rodney doesn't seem to want anything to do with me when we're not out in public.'

'Well, what did you expect, Jools? He's never going to sleep with you.'

'I don't *want* him to sleep with me. But I thought we might be friends, at least. Hang out at home, make dinners, go shopping. But he's never at home. He doesn't eat anything other than these stupid protein shakes and I shop by myself, all alone, every day!'

'Poor you.' Mel looked anything but sympathetic.

'It's terrible!' Jools whined, feeling very sorry for

herself. 'My fiancé doesn't even like me, let alone love me. And he's really a terrible snob – much worse than his mother and father put together! At least they talk to me.'

Jools sighed and swirled her latte with a wooden swizzle stick. The rain was still coming down outside and the day was starting to feel long and exhausting, like it would never end.

'He goes out every night,' she continued. 'I've no idea where he goes but wherever it is, he heads there right after work and he doesn't come home until well after midnight – sometimes three or four o'clock in the morning. We never talk unless he's having a go at me for something. I can't even remember the last time we had breakfast without fighting!'

'I said it at dinner the other night, Jools, and I'll say it again: what you're looking for is a real boyfriend. Someone to take you out and talk to you and make dinner at home with you and sleep with you. Someone you can share a real life with. As great as he is, Rodney's obviously not that guy.'

'But he's not great!' Jools blurted. 'Haven't you been listening to a word I've said?'

'Of course I have,' Mel said, trying to stay calm and compassionate, even though Jools was making it harder by the minute. She had, after all, gotten herself into this mess, ignoring all of Mel's sensible advice. Now Jools was begging for more and still refusing to heed it.

'What I'm saying is that outwardly, Rodney seems like a great guy. Michel certainly thought so.'

Jools made a rude noise and looked away.

'And you know,' Mel continued, 'I wasn't going to bring this up because nothing's confirmed but, well, Michel and I have started talking about marriage.'

Jools had to stifle her natural impulse, which, in this case, was to slap her friend hard across the face in hopes she'd come to her senses. Instead, she took a deep breath. 'Really? Well, that's different.'

'He was so cute about it after our dinner the other night, Jools. You should have seen him. He was like a little boy on Christmas morning. And you know what he was most excited about?'

'What's that?' Jools asked, not caring in the least.

'Hanging out with you and Rodney. You know, the four of us. Like those old married couples who go on trips together, retire together, get their families together for holidays . . .'

Jools started to laugh.

'What? What is it?'

'Maybe Michel could put in a good word for me with Rodney?' Jools erupted into fits of laughter. 'Him being a boy and all.'

Shaking her head, Mel joined in and the women sat at the familiar old table, giggling until the sad reality of the situation hit them both.

Mel watched as Jools consumed more Bundt cakes.

Niles ordered black tea with four sugars and some raisin toast and turned to find a seat. The place was crowded, but he spied a table way in the back. Sidling along, he eased himself into it, then sat back to observe the crowd. Loud laughter from a table near the window caught his attention.

Two girls.

One startlingly familiar.

'Say what you will about Michel . . .' Mel started.

'Oh, don't worry, I will,' interrupted Jools.

Now Mel worked hard not to smack *her*. 'Michel came back to me. He repented and we are totally committed to each other. He's changed. Grown up and come clean about every bad thing he's ever done, although he says that woman you saw him with wasn't my mother.'

'Come on, Mel, I know what your mother looks like.' Harriet Smythe-Brooks had thrown a drunk Jools out of Mel's place enough times for a positive ID.

'I can't believe I'm saying this, but not from that angle, you don't.'

Jools shook her head in annoyance. She wanted to tell Mel she'd seen Michel wandering around near Rodney's Knightsbridge terrace at night. She'd spotted him three times in as many days and had no idea what he might be doing over there – probably bonking some wealthy old grandma who was keeping him in tight jeans and hair gel.

She'd mentioned it to Rodney, who simply said London was a small place and Michel probably had friends or family in the street. He didn't seem concerned and told her not to upset Mel with rubbish stories she couldn't substantiate.

'He's hardly likely to choose the street where you live, is he?' Rodney asked, right before he questioned the wisdom of her teaming her new designer flip-flops with an Armani suit.

No, Jools would need hard proof that Michel was cheating again to convince Mel this time, so until then she decided to stay quiet.

But her friend had lost interest, and was staring over Jools' shoulder.

'Mel, did you hear me?'

'That's strange.'

'What?'

'That weedy little guy in the corner came in, ordered some food just after me, sat down for a moment, looked around, then jumped up and left.'

'Maybe it was the food?' Jools' Bundt cake had tasted a little off.

'Don't think so. He didn't taste it.'

'The clientele? I mean, look at the woman with the lycra fluro tights on. Not even I would dare to team those with a crop top. At least not in winter.'

Mel shook her head. 'No, not that.'

Jools sunk down in her seat. 'He wasn't one of those evil paps, was he?'

'I didn't see a camera.'

'Just some nutter, then.'

Mel shrugged. 'Must be. Something familiar about him though.'

'Let's just forget it, shall we?' Jools got up. 'Another latte then?'

Niles was breathing heavily. He'd finally found her. Now his plans for lifelong companionship and happiness could move forward. She was in his sights and this time, she wouldn't get away.

Waiting between a parked lorry and his white builder's van, Niles watched Mama Blue's until Jools and Mel exited. Walking across the road, they got into Mel's neat Mini and roared off down the street. Jumping in his van, Niles did a quick three-point turn and followed them along the high street, back towards the Royal Borough.

By the time Jools got back to the house, she'd had four lattes and eight Bundt cakes. The liquid hadn't fully worked its way through her system until she was halfway home and she'd been in desperate need of a toilet. But she hadn't wanted to risk being recognised so she'd decided to hold it. Making it back to the house just in time to avoid wetting herself, she raced down the hallway towards the downstairs loo.

As she did, she noticed that Rodney's bedroom door was ajar.

It was mid-afternoon and he was never home this early, even on weekends.

Maybe the maid had left it open?

But then Jools heard Rodney's voice. Maybe he wasn't feeling well, she thought, and he'd decided to work from home. He was probably on some important conference call. Another male voice joined Rodney's in the bedroom. A full bladder trumped Jools' curiosity, so she decided to do her investigating after the loo.

But by the time she'd finished, Rodney was already out in the kitchen, fixing himself a protein shake, and he was very much alone. Jools sauntered out, slightly on guard, and stood in the doorway. The blender was going full speed so she had to shout to be heard.

'Who were you with?' she asked.

'I can't hear you!' Rodney shouted back.

'I said: WHO WAS IN YOUR BEDROOM WITH YOU?'

Rodney stopped the blender and went to the cupboard for a large glass. He poured out the blender's thick, grey contents and took a sip before answering.

'What were you asking?' Rodney liked his lips slowly.

Jools was growing more and more suspicious by the second. 'Someone was with you when I got home. Who was it?'

'Oh,' Rodney started, continuing to take big, fat gulps of his drink. 'James Slattern.'

'Never heard of him,' Jools crossed her arms.

'Of course not. Why would you have heard of him? Do you move in City circles? Did you go to Eton?'

'You know I didn't,' she answered, moving fully into the kitchen.

'I do know that, yes.' He drained his glass and put it in the sink. 'James was a classmate of mine. He works way out in Kent so I don't see him much. Rang to ask if I was free for lunch.'

'So did you?'

'No, Jools, I told him to go screw himself. Of course we had lunch. We ate at the club. He hadn't seen the house so I invited him for a tour. He's thinking of getting a new stereo system so I showed him mine. Now, if you don't mind.' He tried to push past her.

There was something going on and Jools was determined to get to the bottom of it. She blocked the door. 'But if you had lunch at the club, then why are you having a protein shake now?'

'Jesus, Jools, I had a bloody salad and a bowl of consommé. You know how these places are with their portions. I'm still hungry. Is that all right by you?'

'Didn't he think it rude you didn't introduce your fiancée?'

'Not really,' Rodney responded, walking towards his bedroom. Jools trailed behind him. She'd never spent much time in Rodney's room (probably because she had never been invited in), and even standing in the doorway was a bold manoeuvre.

But Rodney didn't say anything, just started

changing right there in front of her. 'He's a bit dim, James. Most of the others don't bother with him, but me, well, you never know, there might be a donation for a political campaign in it.'

Rodney was lying for sure. Jools knew a liar when she saw one. She could thank her father for helping hone that skill. Rodney's very thorough explanation about James Slattern – who, she was convinced, did not even exist – meant he was trying to cover his tracks. And he'd only do that if he was afraid she'd find out something she could use to destroy him. Jools decided to use his fear to her advantage.

'Sounds like an interesting fellow,' she said.

'Good ol' James!' Rodney laced up his running shoes.

'So listen,' Jools said, 'I have a favour to ask of you. You and Michel seem to be best friends now . . .'

Rodney jumped. 'Who? Michel? Oh, well, yes, I suppose we've become friendly.'

'I've seen him around here again and so it can only be assumed he's met another woman and is cheating on Mel.'

'There you go again, jumping to nasty conclusions about people.' He was moving nervously around the room now.

'Yes, well, just the same, I was wondering if you might be able to persuade one of your policeman friends to keep an eye on him? Mel will never believe he's back to his old ways unless I have proof.'

'You're so sure he's cheating?' Rodney asked.

'Of course he's cheating. The sick bastard can't keep his hands off other women for more than thirty seconds.'

Rodney started laughing.

'What's so funny?' she asked.

'Nothing, Jools. Nothing.' He patted her on the back as he moved into the hall. 'I'll see what I can do.'

As Rodney made his way out of the apartment for an afternoon run, Jools realised she hadn't seen him do that since she'd first moved in.

Rodney was shaping up, she thought, but for whom?

Chapter 19

Dear Miss Grand,

As per your recent request in writing we have instructed Julio, our manager in Knightsbridge, to stop offering you free merchandise as you pass his store. We apologise if this has turned you into, and I quote, 'a rotund and unattractive excuse for a human being', however, with the greatest respect, all our customers have free will in regards to our doughnuts.

As a goodwill gesture we have enclosed a voucher for ten free boxes of Trophy Delight doughnuts from any of our 15 stores.

Kind regards,

Reginald Black
Public Relations
Doughy Doughnuts Ltd

JOOLS SWUNG OPEN the front door, expecting the delivery boy with breakfast. Instead, she was greeted with the angry flash of a very large, very expensive camera. Wearing pyjama bottoms and a too-tight tank top, her hair squashed down and her face dotted with spot cream, she was liable to break the lens. Serves them right, she thought angrily.

The pavement was teeming with paparazzi and the popping flashes nearly blinded her. What the hell had she done now? She slammed the door but it was too late. There were probably fifty paps out there and she was sure they'd all got ample shots of the rolls of soft flesh currently spilling over the elastic band of her flannel pyjamas. Ever since the *WhatNOW!* cover, she'd been like a sacrificial pig they all wanted a piece of. Well, she thought, there was certainly plenty to go around.

And according to Rodney, there was little she could do other than simply take the abuse – and lose the excess pounds, of course.

She hoped the delivery boy would be able to get through unscathed; all this stress was making her hungry. She had a standing breakfast order with the bakery around the corner. Every morning they delivered three cranberry scones, two apple turnovers, a Belgian waffle and a serving of apple crumble.

Naturally, Jools didn't eat everything all at once; it took her the better part of the day to make her way through the basket of delectable goodies. However, she had definitely got used to having scones and clotted cream with her coffee. That her breakfast had yet to arrive irked her even more than the knowledge that, at this very moment, there was a photographer trying to peer into the living room.

Part of her wanted to throw open the blinds and flash the bloke, to give him what he really wanted. But she knew Rodney would massacre her so she drew the blinds more tightly.

Rodney was just as fed up with the negative attention as Jools, but for a very different reason. He didn't care that his fiancée was being rubbished by every tabloid in London; he didn't care that her feelings were crushed; and he didn't even try to understand why she couldn't stop eating.

No, Rodney only cared about the pictures because they were starting to make him look bad, too. His party was beginning to complain. The men he answered to were now pulling him aside to discuss Jools' 'condition', telling him he could not succeed with a cow for a wife. Rodney believed they thought him less of a man because he couldn't control his wife-to-be – and the last thing he needed was anyone thinking he was less of a man. He was a man's man. Quite literally.

Jools knew Rodney was miffed about her weight and the resulting attention. But he didn't bring it up in conversation — he didn't bring anything up in conversation – because they had completely stopped talking. Jools wished he would say something, anything, but she didn't want to risk starting a dialogue. He seemed tense and on edge, and she was terrified he'd snap and call the whole thing off.

So she decided to wait it out. He would have to speak to her eventually, at least to say 'I do'. If there was one thing she could rely on, it was that Rodney would put on a good show when the big day finally arrived.

But for now, she'd have to be satisfied with the narky notes he left her and the silence that filled their sterile house.

The shrill ring of the phone echoed in the empty room. Jools grabbed the receiver.

'Good morning, Julia,' said Lady Margaret, in her throaty, cokey voice. 'Have we greeted the sun yet today?'

Jools smiled, happy to hear from her soon-to-be mother-in-law. She'd come to rely on the old woman as a means of comic relief, if nothing else. At least she was getting something out of her 'relationship' with Rodney.

'Oh, yes,' Jools said. 'Not only did I greet the sun but I greeted the blinding flash of the paparazzi. They're camped out in front of the building trying to get a look at my stomach.'

Lady Margaret laughed and Jools almost felt insulted. Was she providing comic relief to them, too? Sometimes she wanted to tell Lady Margaret the truth about her relationship with Rodney, just to spite the whole bloody family. She suspected Lady Margaret secretly enjoyed Jools' predicament because it meant that Rodney had failed once again by having a lard-arse for a wife.

'I don't think it's very funny,' Jools sniffed.

'Of course you don't,' Lady Margaret said, still chuckling softly. 'You're their target. Why would you think it's funny? But as I've said, dear, you have the power to change public opinion – and your dress size.'

Lady Margaret had made Jools' weight loss her mission. She called every day to tell Jools about the latest in body-modifying surgical procedures, or the hot new drug that was supposed to help you burn fat while you slept. This morning, she'd sunk to a new low by suggesting Jools try crystal meth. It was very big in America, she'd said, and highly effective for working mothers who had to juggle career, kids and housekeeping duties while staying thin enough so their husbands would still want to sleep with them.

Jools didn't particularly relish the idea of talking sex with Lady Margaret, nor did she have any desire to start taking crystal meth.

'I have to go,' Jools said, cutting her off. 'I have to eat breakfast. I'm starving.'

'I hope you're not waiting on your baked goods, dear, because I cancelled that little addiction this morning.'

Jools' face went red. How dare the old hag meddle in her breakfast affairs? As far as the wedding went, she could meddle in any way she wanted. But Jools would not sit idly by and let the woman make decisions about what Jools ate.

'You shouldn't have done that,' she said, trying to stay calm.

'It's for the best, dear. You'll thank me the next time they run your backside across the cover of *Hi!*'

Jools hung up. She knew she'd probably get in trouble for doing so but right now, she really didn't care. All she wanted was a bloody scone.

Niles was at work, wondering if he could tap Rodney Wetherspone's home phone. He did work at a call centre, but he suspected that asking questions about illegal phone tapping would have him hauled before a disciplinary committee faster than he could say Camillagate.

Still, things were looking up. He was enjoying a daily drive-by of Jools' new Knightsbridge home. At least twice in the last week he'd seen her entering the white Georgian terrace, running the gauntlet of crazed photographers. Poor girl was looking a little larger than life, but that didn't worry Niles. He would soon work it off her.

Checking his supervisor was otherwise engaged, Niles logged onto his private email account as Brad and sent Jools another message, this one a little more suggestive than the last. Looking the way she did, she was unlikely to be getting much attention from that slick fiancé of hers, so she might welcome the sexual advances of a handsome American, who, as he told Jools, was on his way to London to seal the deal.

When Rodney made a rare trip home for lunch that day, Jools figured he was going to haul her over the coals for hanging up on his mother. Instead, he hauled her over the coals for her fat bum. Again.

'I cannot have you looking like this anymore,' he told her. 'It's ruining everything. I can still call off the wedding, you know. What possessed you to write to the Doughy Doughnut people? Didn't it occur to you the first thing they would do is distribute your letter to the press?'

No, actually, it hadn't, or she wouldn't have written it, would she?

Jools thought fast. 'If you call off the wedding, people will know you dumped me because I'm fat. How will that make you look?'

Rodney walked over to the window. He pulled the blinds back just enough to see that the mass of photographers had thinned. There were only five or six of them out there now and they were all absent-mindedly texting or talking on their mobiles.

Rodney knew Jools was right. The publicity from a break-up (particularly since they were engaged and not simply dating) would be just as bad as any of the publicity Jools' bum was generating now.

'I suppose you're right,' he said, closing the blinds

and walking back to the couch. He sat, crossed his legs and folded his hands in his lap. There were dark circles under his eyes and his skin was pasty and grey. Jools wondered if he might be ill. She almost felt sorry for him, but she stopped herself short. Whatever was wrong with him, at least he was talking to her again.

'What can I do?' she asked.

'I don't know.' He seemed genuinely at a loss. 'But it's not my responsibility to figure that out. It's yours.' He was serious. She had gotten them into this big, fat mess and she was going to get them out.

'But I have no ideas,' her tone pleading. Or willpower, she added silently.

'You're a smart girl,' he said. 'Well, smart enough. You've certainly got the capacity for problem solving. We wouldn't be here if you didn't.'

Rodney's comment reminded her of another big problem that required sorting out – her father. If he wasn't removed from the picture fairly permanently, none of this would even matter. Fat or not, Rodney's public image would be ruined by his teenager-molesting father-in-law.

Jools' dad had been calling more and more. And it wasn't just her mobile; somehow he'd got the house number too. Luckily, Rodney was barely ever home so the chances of them actually having a conversation were slim. Still, the calls were starting to make her nervous. The last thing she needed was for her dad to hit Rodney up for cash.

Chapter 20

Dear Miss Grand,

Owing to your recent purchase of a vehicle, we regret to advise that your balance no longer meets the criteria for a Black account, which as you know included a higher rate of interest, free insurance for your car, travel and mobile phone, commission-free foreign exchange and a personal banker. Hence we have downgraded you to our basic account, which I trust will meet your current needs.

Yours sincerely,

Rutherford Smith
Imperial & Colonial Banking Corp.

THE NEXT MORNING, as if on cue, Jools got yet another phone call from her dear old dad.

'I told you, the money's being transferred. Three thousand Euro, just like you asked. The bank said it might take four to five working days.'

'That's the thing, Joolsy, I might need a little more.'

Jools felt sick. 'What have you done now?'

'Nothing,' her father said too quickly. 'Well, nothing new. The copper who arrested me somehow knows about your wedding. Said he was going to lock me up 'cause I'm a flight risk.'

'Dad!'

'Don't worry, Joolsy, I sorted it, didn't I? Gave him your three thousand big ones and he let me go. But I need another three thou, pronto.'

'Dad, there's no way I can give you that sort of money again.' Little did he know how true that actually was.

'I'll pay you back, Joolsy. You know my word is good.'

Jools rolled her eyes. 'I don't have it. Besides, I'm sick of having to bail you out.'

'Fine. Perhaps Rodney or his mum would feel more comfortable giving me a loan.'

Jools bit her lip. He'd been threatening and guilting her into things since she was a little girl. But now wasn't the time to stand up to him. She needed to keep her father quiet and out of the way just a little bit longer – and the only way to do it was with money.

The thing was, Jools really didn't have that much left. In fact, she'd almost run through the entire chunk Rodney had given her at the beginning of all of this. She wasn't sure how it'd happened – maybe buying that new BMW 1 Series convertible last week had something to do with it?

She needed a car, she'd reasoned, to make quick getaways when the paps were after her. And why not get one that was completely tricked out? She was going to be a politician's wife, after all. She needed to get around town in style.

All that was left in her bank account was the five thousand pounds she had earmarked as a gift to Skuttle. She was dead set on giving him the money as a thank you for his kindness. Now, though, she was forced to choose between the man who had (albeit accidentally) brought her into this world, and the man who had saved her from certain death. Although she hated to go back on her promise to Skuttle, she knew what she had to do. Give her dad the hobo's money.

Suddenly, a brilliant idea struck.

'Alright, Dad, I'll try to get you the money.'

She quickly hung up and ran into the foyer. There, sitting on a small table by the front door, was a pile of mail for Rodney. She leafed through the envelopes, looking for something she'd seen the other day. Tearing it open, she removed the contents.

MasterCard had been kind enough to send Rodney a stack of blank cheques. But Rodney never seemed to need the cheques and usually tore them up – when he actually spent enough time at home to bother looking through his mail.

Jools reckoned what she was about to do would

actually help Rodney. It was far better his wife-to-be used the cheques than some identity thief, wasn't it?

Making out one of the cheques to herself and forging Rodney's signature at the bottom, she considered her handiwork. Five thousand pounds would be enough to cover her dad's dodgy passport and provide a little cushion for unexpected expenses. Dressing in her best neo-noir disguise, she hopped into the shiny new BMW and sped past the hungry photographers – still parked out front and blissfully unaware of her new mode of transport – and drove to the bank.

Once the funds cleared, Jools would wire the money to Spain and that would be it. Charlie Grand wasn't getting another penny. And if he made it into the country, he could be stopped before he got to the wedding. (Rocco would no doubt be up for a little dad-napping for a quid or two.)

Jools drove back to the house. Rounding the corner onto her block, she was thrilled the photographers had left but surprised to see none other than Michel heading unsteadily down the street, smoking a cigarette and looking like a cat who just stocked up on a few dozen cartons of Irish cream.

Luckily, Jools was in her disguise of black sari and sunglasses. Michel hadn't seen her new car so there was little chance of being recognised. His lurking about the neighbourhood was really becoming unnerving. He had to be screwing that Spandex-loving geriatric, Mrs Plotrem, who lived in Number

51 and was always coming home with much younger men attached to various parts of her anatomy.

Jools was so certain of her theory that she pulled an illegal U-turn and headed for Mel's flat. What additional proof was needed? It was time to save Mel from Michel's dangerous and heavily after-shaved embrace. Besides, it gave her something to do – other than eat.

As Jools pulled her car into a metered spot on Mel's street – cursing as she realised she didn't have change for the meter – she spied a cupcake bakery up the road, just opposite the pub. It wouldn't do to show up at Mel's without a little something to have with coffee, would it? Anyway, maybe she'd be able to score some change for the meter at the same time.

Unfortunately, Cupcake Heaven wouldn't give her any change, so she left with only a dozen mixed gourmet treats and the very real risk of her car being towed.

Sloping back to the BMW, she stood there for a moment. Should she call Mel and ask for change, or should she turn around and head for home, where she could devour the delicious temptations in peace?

Come to think of it, she could devour them right now.

Just as she was about to tear open the box, Mel appeared. As happy as she was to see her friend, Jools was a tad annoyed she had to share.

Her friend began firing questions. 'What on earth

are you doing here at ten on a Friday morning? Why are you wearing that sari? And whose car is that?'

'Thought I might have breakfast with you!' Jools held up the brightly coloured box, ignoring all questions except the first. She was not eager to tell Mel about her hot new BMW. Mel didn't understand her compulsion to buy nice things – a luxury car to Mel was like a pub lunch to most people.

Her friend's serious little pixie face lit up. She held out her arms and gave Jools a tight, sincere hug. 'Well, it's so good to see you!' she said, a bit too enthusiastically for Jools' liking. Mel grabbed Jools' hand and pulled her towards the flat. 'I was actually about to call you. We're on the same wave length!'

'Yeah, must be,' Jools said, wondering what was up.

Mel made some decaf herbal tea but Jools was too fixated on the baked goods to complain. 'Dig in,' she said merrily, through a face full of cake.

Mel launched into a lecture straight out of the Lady Margaret Dietary Harassment Handbook. Grabbing a second cupcake, Jools wished she would shut up. She was completely ruining the cake's spongy goodness.

Jools grabbed Mel's arm with the hand that wasn't wrapped around cake. 'Listen, I've got some bad news. I'm sorry to have to be the one to tell you, but I figure better me than someone else, right?'

'Oh God,' Mel said, steeling herself. 'Well, all right, but let me tell you my good news first.'

Jools considered her friend quizzically. A little moment of sunshine before the clouds rolled in was probably a good idea.

Besides, it gave Jools more time to eat.

'Michel and I are engaged!' Mel screamed, shoving her left hand in Jools' face.

There it was, right where it was supposed to be, a big fat diamond ring that Jools was certain couldn't be real. There was no way Michel would be able to afford a diamond that big. He'd either stolen it or bought it for ten pence from one of those machines in the paper shop.

'Sweet Jesus,' Jools said, shaking her head. Surprisingly, the bad news hadn't put her off food. Her hand crept back towards the plate of goodies.

'I know, isn't it gorgeous?' Mel admired the ring.

'No, it's horrible,' Jools said through her cake.

'What did you say?'

Jools swallowed. 'I don't like it.'

Mel's face fell. 'You're not happy for me?'

'Of course I'm not happy for you, Mel!' Jools shrieked, cake spraying everywhere. 'He's cheating on you again.'

'Jools, of course he's not. You've always hated him. What's your story this time?'

'I've seen him in my neighbourhood. Several times, in fact.'

'So?

'But . . .'

'He's been in your neighbourhood. So what? That doesn't mean anything. You're in Knightsbridge, not Mars! It's just around the corner!'

'Why else would he be there? Early in the morning? Late at night?'

'I don't know. Maybe he's taking a walk.'

Jools had to laugh. 'Yeah, like the dog he is.'

'He likes to walk,' Mel continued, defending her man. 'He's extremely health conscious. Besides, have you actually seen him with a woman?'

Jools hated the fact that there wasn't harder evidence but she was completely sure that Michel was up to no good. Why couldn't Mel just give her the benefit of the doubt, instead of lobbing it in the direction of that sleazebag?

'Look, it's just something I feel in my gut,' Jools said. 'Even if he's not cheating, he's beneath you. If you marry him, you're throwing your life away.'

Mel shook her head and Jools saw her eyes narrow. Mel was angry now.

'That's just too much, Jools. Talk about the pot calling the kettle black.'

'My situation is completely different,' Jools said.

'Yeah, I know. Because your situation is a joke and mine is real and that just burns you up.'

'Are you saying I'm jealous?' Jools asked, incredulous.

'Yes. You're jealous that I've found what you can't: true love. With a heterosexual man!'

Jools couldn't listen any more. She grabbed her bag and stood up. 'You want to make the biggest mistake of your life, go ahead. But don't expect me to be there in some ugly taffeta dress holding your train as you walk down the aisle.'

'I wouldn't want you there anyway,' Mel stood too, meeting Jools' eyes. 'I don't want any photos of cows in my wedding album. Anyway, I doubt there are any lenses big enough to capture all of you.'

Jools smacked Mel across the face. The slap was loud and hard and when Mel turned to look at Jools there was a bright red hand mark where Jools had hit her. Tears were beginning to well in Mel's eyes and the only thing Jools could think to do was run away.

Well, walk as quickly as she could, considering the weight and the cakes.

Chapter 21

Dear Miss Grand,

We note that you have asked that your guests spend more money per item, rather than purchasing a single smaller item, or indeed a number of smaller items.

Unfortunately, our reputation here at Carlisle's of Sloane Square does not allow us to dictate the spending habits of our patrons, and we feel it most improper to raise your suggestion with your guests.

We hope you understand our position.

Finally, we wish to completely reassure you that we will never release details of correspondence between ourselves and our clients to the press. On that note, however, perhaps you would be interested in replacing the ice-cream machine on your wedding gift list with a lovely vegetable juicer? They are in stock and available in the latest fashion colours from only £99.

Jacinta Millani
Carlisle's of Sloane Square

WHEN JOOLS FINALLY got back to the house she collapsed on her bed, sobbing. How her life had become so rubbish? Only a month ago, things were looking up. Now, she was engaged to a man who seemed to hate her; she'd just assaulted her best friend; and she'd managed to burn through nearly all the money that was supposed to be her future nest-egg. Plus her bum was the size of France. Or even China.

She had no idea how to fix things. The miSell auction had really been a last-ditch effort to get her life back on track. What would happen to her now?

Over on her desk, her computer beeped indicating a new email had arrived. Well, at least *someone* wanted to talk to her, even if was that guy trying to sell her a penis enlarger. Dragging herself up off the mattress and wiping the tears from her eyes and the stream of snot from her nose, she sat down in the high-backed, ergonomic chair purchased online for a thousand pounds and clicked the touch pad of the Mac.

She had not one, not two, not even three, but five new messages from Brad. Poor man. He'd been emailing non-stop for a week and she hadn't responded yet. Jools just figured she'd get back to him when she had a firm plan; when she had some sense of how her life might look after the wedding. But at the rate things were going she'd probably never know and if she didn't sort things out soon, she'd end up blowing both the deal with Rodney and her chances of sexual happiness with Brad.

Reading Brad's most recent email only made her even more frustrated.

Hi Gorgeous. What gives? Did you get my last email re: coming to London on business? You've got to stop torturing me like this. Just tell me you're still out there and that maybe we've got a chance. I want to be with you, baby, and at this point, I'll do whatever it takes. What I can do to hold you in my arms?

Yours eternally, Brad.

Jools was shocked by how openly emotional and raw Brad sounded in his email. It was difficult to believe that anyone could be so smitten with her – though to be fair he hadn't actually clapped eyes on her yet, had he? She was certainly flattered, but Brad was starting to sound too good to be true. Jools was so disgusted with herself now that she wasn't sure if any man would ever want to be with her again, let alone a man as breathtakingly handsome as Brad.

What would happen if he saw her in the flesh – a lot of flesh – and was disappointed? It was a definite possibility, if not a sure thing. After all, the one picture Brad had seen of Jools was nearly a decade old. Brad was basing his affections on a version of Jools that no longer fit within the parameters of the original photograph.

Her new relationship with the paparazzi made things even more complex. If they were stalking her every move – and one of those moves involved a clandestine meeting with Brad – surely someone would be there to snap an incriminating picture.

Jools had to be extra careful. With the wedding day approaching faster than a toddler to an ice cream van, it was important to protect what was left of her and Rodney's image. She already had enough problems just trying to stay away from baked goods. Did she really need to get caught having an affair as well?

It was time to cut things off with Brad. Things were bad, sure, but they would be much, much worse for her if she lost Rodney. Brad was beautiful and he seemed ready to take the plunge, but could he provide for her? Could he really save her from her financial woes? It was too risky and Rodney was a sure thing.

Marking Brad's address as spam, she deleted all of his emails and snapped shut the lid of the stainless steel laptop.

Well, that was that.

Sighing, she went to take a hot shower, hoping to wash away all of the day's emotional dirt and grime.

Niles was at home in Slough, hoping Jools might finally answer Brad's email. The read receipt for his latest email to her sat in his inbox, but there was no other communication. He stared at the wavering screen of his decrepit old PC, waiting for a response.

Three hours later, he decided enough was enough. Clearly the girl was so intellectually disabled a handsome man begging for attention wasn't good enough. Girls like that needed to be taken in hand.

Niles got up. It was time to put the finishing touches on Jools' new home in his basement.

She'd be there soon enough.

Jools emerged from the shower feeling somewhat better about her lot in life (with a power shower like that – a definite improvement over the bus-station hose – who could stay sad?).

What she needed was fresh air. Staying around that computer meant she could backslide and email Brad with multiple apologies for her flakiness over the last few weeks.

Maybe go for a run? She'd heard rumours that exercise was good for your mental health, although she'd certainly never found it to be. Besides, at her size busting a kneecap or throwing her back out was a definite possibility, so she settled for a nice long fast-paced walk instead.

Jools still had the ratty old jogging suit she'd worn as a hobo (she managed to save it from the Terrible Trio at Percys). Misshapen and smelly, it would make a brilliant disguise when the paparazzi came a-calling. Adding a visor and a pair of sunglasses, the final touch was a rather pathetic, loose ponytail.

All traces of the posh politician's fiancée had vanished; she looked exactly as when living with Skuttle.

Leaving through the back door, she climbed over the rubbish bins and walked down the dark alley behind her building before hitting the pavement at a brisk pace.

To avoid Harrods and the Doughy guy, Jools decided to catch a bus back to the bus garage and pay Skuttle a visit. She had been meaning to give him his five thousand pound gift for ages now and today was as good a time as any. Besides, if she waited any longer, chances were she'd end up spending the money on sugar-laden treats or a too-small frock.

Heading for her bank, Jools kept the pace up so no-one could recognise her. It was a difficult task – she hadn't used any muscles (except those necessary for the consumption of food) in months, and the extra weight made it feel like she was dragging a spare tire behind her. She twisted to look at her backside. Well, really, it was more than a spare tyre for a lorry.

It felt good to get moving, but her throat was dry from all the huffing. She almost stopped to catch her breath but the desire to avoid detection was a great motivator and she pushed on, feeling the sweat start to drip down her back, between her now mountainous breasts and over her belly rolls.

At the bank, she glanced around in case an errant photographer had followed, then popped in to withdraw the remainder of her cash in one hundred pound notes for Skuttle. It was amazing how small a pile the money made.

Keep moving, Jools told herself. She walked past Burberry, forcing herself not to look in any of the windows in case she spent Skuttle's money on that amazing evening gown and those gorgeous strappy sandals calling out to her from the glossy window display.

The number 52 bus stop was just on the corner and luckily, the bus was just rounding Scotch House. She jumped on before the lure of plaid became too strong.

Despite her recent past as a homeless hobo, Jools was shocked at the quality of low-life on the bus that morning: a group of hoodies playing loud misogynistic gansta rap peppered with swear words that would make even Mel's boyfiend blush; the stinking drunk who had the sense to stay well away from the rap louts, harassing Jools and a young mum at the front of the bus instead.

Worried the drunk was about to lose his breakfast of vodka and cornflakes, Jools got off the stop before the bus station. She hadn't noticed it was pouring rain and when she finally arrived at Skuttle's squat she was soaking wet and short of breath. Leaning against a phone booth for a moment, she struggled to get her breath back. Her heart was racing a mile a minute and her thighs felt like they were on fire.

It was all good. The fact that she was in so much pain must mean she was losing weight.

Making her way to the tiny entrance, she moved

the cardboard and slid down the chute, knocking on the door with cheery rhythm. No answer. She waited a minute and then knocked again. Still no answer. Jools gave the door a little push and as usual, it opened without much resistance. Inside, the little squat was dark and empty. No Skuttle.

Jools sat down on Skuttle's bed and looked around. Not much had changed. The place still smelled of fumes and slightly-off prawn tandoori. The furniture was still haphazardly arranged around a large gaping hole in the concrete and bags of collected rubbish had been added to the mess, contents spilling out as if part of some esoteric art installation.

Seeing all the familiar junk, Jools felt strangely nostalgic. Surely she didn't miss this? But her short interlude with Skuttle had been relatively peaceful, and in retrospect, she had felt safe – in spite of the constant danger of being discovered living down a chute and/or gnawed by rats while she slept. It was easy being with Skuttle, who had a way of making her feel cared for. And that was more than she could say about Rodney.

Jools waited another twenty minutes before deciding that Skuttle was probably out skip-foraging. Sighing, she dug the cash out of her bag and stuffed it in the small tin box by his bed.

At first, she had assumed Scuttle kept all his valuable possessions in that box, only to discover it was filled with a natty little collection of buttons to clothing Skuttle didn't own. Well, counting money was better than counting buttons. Now Skuttle could to do something with his life. Maybe get a new place. Some snazzy clothes. A Vespa. Deodorant. A razor. After all, he'd always been a hobo with potential.

Replacing the cardboard that acted as a door to the chute, Jools glanced up and down the block to check that no one had seen her. Imagine the fallout if the paps caught her skulking around the back of a bus station, looking for hobos.

She headed for home, picking up pace in the vain hope that she might be about to burn off a dress size before dinner.

What Jools didn't know was that two men had, in fact, spotted her leaving Skuttle's place. They'd been sitting in the office at the bus garage for about two hours before she showed up, and watched her rather suspicious movements at the entrance to the chute with amusement.

After she'd descended into the basement, one of the men (short, balding, with a surprisingly lush ponytail and dark glasses), had asked the other (well-built, badly-dressed), if they ought to deal with the trespasser.

'Give her a scare, if you know what I mean.'

'Don't bother. She's not a thief.'

'I suppose so. What would someone steal from that cesspit anyway?' The balding man picked at his teeth and smoothed his ponytail simultaneously. 'I was thinking more terrorist. Or arsonist!'

'It's okay. I know her.'

Baldie laughed. 'You would. With all due respect, boss, you are fucking insane.'

'And revelling in it, my friend. Now, shall we get back to business?'

'Sure,' Baldie grinned. 'What's a tubby little trespasser when you have a multi-million pound empire to run?'

The well-built man raised his rather bushy eyebrows. 'Tubby? Really? I think she's perfect.'

'Yeah, but you ain't exactly normal, are you?'

Instead of reminding Baldie who paid his large wage, the boss just laughed. Truth be told he *was* as odd as a nun at a Sex Pistols reunion concert, but that's what came from having too much money and absolutely no need for it.

Niles worked away tiling the makeshift bathroom he had built for Jools — the fact he knew nothing about tiling having no impact on his completing the task.

As he cut tiles crookedly, he thought, of course, of Jools. She must be the pickiest chick in Britain to reject a looker like Brad. Even Niles was a little hot for him. And he was him!

Women were only drawn to attractive, wealthy men with fat wallets and large appendages. That's what his mother had told him when he was a teenager, right after suggesting he turn gay because there was less competition and that he could definitely attract at least a biker or prison escapee if he put a little lipstick on. He hated well-built, successful men as much as his old slapper of a mum. They ruined everything for normal, if slightly weedy, blokes like Niles.

Modern women, Niles reasoned, had grown far too accustomed to having their needs met. They'd become selfish and lazy. But Niles was determined to bring back the nice, quiet, subservient woman of yesteryear. The woman who only lived to serve her man; who didn't ask questions; didn't ask for equality; and didn't complain if her husband wanted to stuff a ball-gag in her mouth and probe her nether regions with household objects.

Yes, Jools could easily be moulded to fit the image perfectly. After some quality time in the basement, of course.

It was predictable that Rodney had managed to snag Jools. He was good-looking, successful and rich; came from a very well-established family and his future was brighter than Niles' face after twenty minutes in the sun.

No, what was intriguing was how Jools had managed to meet Rodney in the first place.

Seeing her for the first time at Mama Blue's, Jools seemed like an average, lower-middle-class bird with little going on upstairs. After all, she was selling herself online, wasn't she? Judging from her looks and social graces, any silver spoon she had grown up with was nicked from the local chippy.

So how did Jools, the failed cleaner from the wrong side of town, hook up with aristocratic Rodney Wetherspone?

Surely it couldn't have been via miSell? A wealthy, handsome politician didn't need to shop for women online. Five minutes in some posh joint in South Kensington would do the trick.

Besides which, Jools didn't seem the type to frequent nightclubs of the rich and royal. Homely and unkempt weren't attributes that would endear her to bouncers at ritzy West End clubs.

Niles broke yet another tile and grew hot with rage and jealousy and incompetence. Why was he doing all this anyway? How could he get close to her when she had abandoned communication with Brad? Approach her? No way. One word to that fiancé of hers and Niles would be banged up at Her Majesty's pleasure in a minute and a half. Plus, he needed to stay under the radar, because he wasn't daft enough to think what he was doing was entirely normal.

He could drive to central London and stake out Jools' house again, but he'd become bored with that. Wherever she went, hungry photographers followed. His stalking was already yielding poor results and it would be even worse now that she was on the verge of getting married. How to lure her into his car without a hundred paparazzi documenting it was quite a problem. Then Niles had a brainwave. The paparazzi! They had the best access to Jools, probably second only to Rodney Wetherspone. And you didn't need a press badge to be a scumbag photographer: all you needed was a camera and attitude.

Niles immediately got on the phone to his manager at the call centre and told him that he wouldn't be able to come in that night. He'd come down with a terrible flu and was worried that he might be infectious. Insect flu, or pond flu, or something of that sort. He certainly didn't want to run the risk of spreading his terrible virus to all of the operators at the centre. The manager, a dim-witted young graduate of about thirty, quickly agreed that he should stay home and rest until he was fully recovered and disease free.

'In that case, don't expect me before next week.' Niles promptly hung up.

Logging onto to Google, Niles searched 'high quality cameras'. One website, 'Professional Camera Barn' had exactly what he was looking for — used photographic equipment for the paparazzi. Scrolling quickly through the selection, he finally purchased the best second-hand camera they had. Overnight shipping promised that Niles could be on the street, snapping pictures of Jools, within twenty-four hours. He couldn't wait to get started.

There might even be a few pounds in it.

Chapter 22

Dear Miss Julia,

I used to work for you – Lopez, yes? I see you on cover of magazine looking big and fat and rich so I write to ask if you need cleaner. You no look like you do much yourself. I charge only little, and happy to go shopping for all your food so you no go outside and have photo taking.

Lopez Vasquez

RODNEY WAS HOME when Jools returned from her speed walk.

'Shit', she grumbled when she saw him at the kitchen table. She'd picked up some cupcakes on the way home as a reward for all the exercise and had been hoping to spend some quality time with them.

'Hello,' he said as she breezed through the kitchen. She responded with a grunt and a flick of the wrist.

'I said hello!' he shouted after her.

Still no response. Jools was hoping he would get the hint and trot off to whatever gay nightclub was in favour that week.

Rodney got up from the table and stormed down the hallway towards Jools' room. Hearing his heavy footsteps, Jools closed her door and locked it quickly. She really didn't want to deal with him right now. She didn't have the energy to deal with much – except her precious cupcakes – after her workout. The walk had been less the streamlined athlete she'd envisioned when she'd thrown on her tracksuit bottoms, especially when someone called out that the sea was 50 miles south. Besides, all exercise seemed to do was make her hungrier.

'Jools, we need to talk.' The familiar, narky voice filtered through the heavy door.

'No,' Jools barked. 'I'm not in the mood for any more abuse today, thank you. I'd like some time alone.'

'I have no intention of abusing you, Jools, but we do need to talk about the wedding for a moment.'

The wedding! Jools would call off the whole stupid affair – if only she still had that £76,000. Why parade around in a silly sausage-style white dress, trying to convince people she and Rodney were in love, when the truth was they could barely stand to look at each other? Jools could accept marrying a gay man and being celibate. She couldn't accept marrying a total control freak who failed to understand her weight issues.

Why on earth had she ever dreamed up this stupid plan to begin with?

'I don't want to talk about the wedding,' she said.

'Neither do I, quite frankly,' Rodney responded, 'but we need to. Come on, I'll be nice.'

He could be nice when he wanted to be, thought Jools. Maybe she'd give him a chance. And a cupcake, because she couldn't hold out much longer before she stuck her face right into the white box that was tempting her from the dressing table.

'Fine.' She unlocked the bedroom door and quickly hopped into bed, cake box in hand, covering her body and the cakes with a thick down comforter. Rodney entered and took in the sight of his fiancée doing a pretty impressive impersonation of an elephant in a blanket.

'What's wrong? Are you ill?'

'Like you care.' She hugged the cakes to her chest. Maybe she didn't want to share them after all.

'I care if you're contagious.'

'I'm not ill. I've just had a bad day. Another bad day,' she said, correcting herself.

Rodney didn't even bother to respond. 'Look, here's the thing. A few of my school mates rang today to ask if we were planning a pre-wedding party. When I told them no, they insisted. So we'll have to have one.'

'A party?' Jools perked up. A party might be just what she needed. There was lots of scrumptious food at parties, wasn't there?

'But you'll have to plan it. I'm far too busy to deal with such trivialities right now. I'm lobbying to help get a housing bill passed and it's taking all my time and energy.'

Jools sat up in bed. 'Me? You want me to organise it?'

The bastard obviously considered her time worthless. Okay, she didn't have that much going on, especially now that Mel wasn't talking to her, but it did take an inordinate amount of time sourcing baked goods without being caught by either the press or Rodney. Anyway, she had never been one for party planning and she had even less interest in planning an event for his friends, most of whom she'd never met. God knew *she* didn't have anyone to invite. As it was, she would probably be without a bridesmaid during the ceremony – unless she wanted to ask Mrs Pho (and she would have to be a size 8 and recovering from a recent lobotomy before that happened!).

'I'm not your PA Rodney,' Jools said, more boldly than she should, considering her financially-challenged condition. 'Hire a party planner if you want. I don't see why it has to fall to me.'

His handsome face turned an unfortunate shade of puce. It reminded Jools of the blueberry icing on one of her as yet undevoured cupcakes. 'It falls to you, Jools, because I say it falls to you. You do nothing all day but shop and eat. If we're to be believed as a couple, we've got to be on somewhat equal footing. At the very least, you need a few leisure activities. Entertaining is a wonderful hobby for a politician's wife. It's believable. It's credible. You *will* plan this party and you will plan it properly and if you don't, then we won't be getting married!'

'Fine,' she said, taking a chance. 'Then let's not get married.'

'Fine,' Rodney responded, 'give me back my seventy-six grand.'

Crappity crap. Jools was trapped. There was no possible way she could give him that money – she'd spent every last penny of it, and more. And Rodney still didn't know about the cheques Jools had forged and the additional five grand she'd, er, borrowed. It was far better he discovered *that* little detail when they were well and truly wedded to each other.

There was no escape from the mess she'd made. Especially if the whole truth was revealed.

'OK,' she said finally, 'I'll plan the party.'

'Of course you will,' Rodney smirked. 'It's not bloody difficult, even someone like you should be able to manage it relatively easily. Just make sure you do a good job.'

What was he insinuating? She had run her own business for years, hadn't she?

'Oh I'll do a spectacular job, just you watch. This will be the best party you've ever attended in your whole life. The best and most expensive.'

Rodney shrugged. 'Whatever. Mummy has agreed

to pay for it. I'll email you my address book. Oh, and Jools, I'd like to have the party next Saturday.'

'The day before the wedding?' He must be joking. How was she going to look on her wedding day without her usual 14 hour sleep? But before she could protest, Rodney turned on his handmade heels and left.

Shit. Double shit. Forgetting her cupcakes, Jools leaped out of bed and fired up her beloved laptop. What did she need? Think Jools. Remembering the cupcakes, Jools consumed four in a row, then began making her lists – caterers, DJs, maids and florists. Probably not as hard as it first seemed, especially with the aid of the Internet and Lady Wetherspone's unlimited funds.

Within an hour she and a kooky man called Chop Choi had decided on an Asian-themed menu with hot appetizers and an on-site chef to make dim sum to-order for all the guests. 'I have portable deep-fryer', he told Jools, who began salivating at the thought of crisp, freshly made spring rolls.

There would be a full bar with a special cocktail to celebrate the impending nuptials. Of course, the cocktail needed a name so Jools came up with 'Gay Abandon': vodka, creaming soda and Baileys with ice. An homage to their whirlwind romance, and an ironic 'up yours' at Rodney. Jools planned to drink at least eighteen of them.

By the second hour, she had a florist on board too.

A rasping young girl told Jools she needed to cover the entire house in white lilies and add a jungle-inspired vine to drape over the light fixtures. She also recommended loads of candles and white lights to be dotted around the foliage, but Jools was aiming for a dark and dreamy atmosphere that would hide her excess baggage so the lights were vetoed, but the candles got the nod.

Four cupcakes provided the strength to carry on, so she went online dress shopping and found the perfect outfit on a designer shopping site (courtesy of Rodney's credit card of course) and prayed it would fit. It was a black, kaftan-type ensemble with ruffles and sequins. Slightly over-the-top, but she hoped it would hide her many problem areas. Or, at least her large derriere.

Dress sorted, she moved onto the DJ, and a funky Aussie couple called Bazz and Jazz told her they could guarantee the 'tops bash' of the year. She instructed them to play the music as loudly as possible, so that she wouldn't have to talk to anyone and if she was lucky the cops would shut the whole thing down in the first hour and she and Chop Choi would be left alone to finish off the dim sum.

The only thing left was the invitations. Jools checked her email. Sure enough, Rodney had sent her his address book – only a hundred of his closest friends, co-workers, political cronies and family acquaintances.

A hundred people in their house would feel a bit cramped. Jools would need to open up the roof-deck and make it party-ready with heating lamps and tiki-torches. She'd have to call that florist girl with lung problems back but tomorrow would do. As long as Lady Wetherspone was paying whatever it took, the suppliers would comply.

It was strangely thrilling to be so extravagant, and although she did have a slight twinge of guilt at the exhorbitant costs she was being quoted, Jools decided that it was only what Rodney and his disfunctional family deserved.

Right. What's next? Ah, the all important invitation. Drafting an e-vite, she checked it over quickly. What date was Saturday? She clicked the calendar on the computer, typing in the date. There – done! Clicking 'Send', she sat back, feeling chuffed at getting everything finished so quickly. I might just become a great politician's wife after all, she thought smugly.

While Jools was busy planning their extravagant lie of a party, Rodney was on his way back to the office.

He, too, was fed up with the idea of marrying for his career and was considering throwing in the towel on the whole silly affair. It certainly didn't help that the sight of his future wife made him want to heave. Given her penchant for food, shopping and sleeping, he doubted she could pull off the role.

Maybe he should just come out of the closet. Even

that might be better than living with a fat lazy cow the rest of his life, or as long as it took to divorce her without recrimination.

He shook his head, sadly remembering his original hopes for Jools. He'd stupidly fancied himself as Professor Higgins; Jools his Eliza Doolittle. Take a lager-swilling, lower-class girl – obviously going through a rough patch – and transform her into an elegant, top-notch woman. But all he'd managed to do was create the human form of a saggy mattress.

Maybe one day she'd eat herself to death, he thought hopefully. The perfect ruse would be a grieving widower. If there was no chance of getting caught he might even do the deed himself.

Sitting in a queue of traffic at Knightsbridge, Rodney pondered the fact that if he didn't know any better, he'd almost think his parents had hired her to make his life even more miserable.

She repulsed him. Admittedly there wasn't any need to be attracted to a fake wife – to any woman for that matter – but it was impossible to fathom how believable she would be as a bride, wearing a hideous white concoction created by his mother. Worse, how was he going to make a public declaration of his love without laughing or crying or running for dear life?

Lost in thought, Rodney didn't even notice his assistant waving at him as he entered his office. Slamming the door shut, he slid into the massive leather deskchair and dropped his head to the table.

For the first time in a very long while, Rodney wanted to talk to his mother. Let's see what Mummy really thinks about all of this, he thought, dialling the number. She'd been surprisingly silent about the whole marriage, choosing only to speak to Jools about the arrangements.

Maybe there was still a way out. Mummy had a good way of making things, and people, disappear – without resorting to violence.

Rodney and his mother had never been close, but over the years their relationship had become strained to the breaking point. Desperate for grandchildren to boss about, she took Rodney's refusal to get married as a personal affront. Before he'd presented Jools to his parents, his mother had become convinced that Rodney would never settle down.

Rodney didn't waste any time coming to the point. 'Mummy, I'm thinking of ending it with Jools.'

Neither did his mother.

'Are you mad? The wedding is this week! What on earth has happened.'

'She's crass, materialistic and obese. She's changed since we first met. I don't think she was ever honest about who she really was.' As soon as the words were out, Rodney felt like a giant weight (something approximately the same size as Jools' backside) had been lifted from him.

His mother laughed, as if she found him hilarious. Not a first, Rodney thought petulantly, remembering report cards, football matches and excruciating attempts at school plays.

'I don't understand why you think this is funny,' he whined.

'Chin up, Rodney dear. Of course she's not the same person she was when you first met. People change, sometimes for better and sometimes for worse. If I'd left your father the first time he showed signs of change, we'd have separated soon after the honeymoon when he asked me to pick the fluff from between – '

'Mother!' Rodney shuddered. More information that any sane person required. Why defend her future daughter-in-law to this extent? She hated sloppiness – even fired a gardener after catching sight of his builder's cleavage.

'You're overreacting, as usual,' she told him. 'Julia is just as lovely now as she was when we first met her. Yes, she's put on a few pounds but she's the same girl on the inside.'

'Lovely?' Rodney asked, incredulous. 'Are you losing your sight?'

'Not at all. She's a fine match for you,' Lady Margaret responded. 'It's time you got serious and settled down. Yes, she may need some additional grooming but given time she will make an excellent wife. And mother.'

Rodney couldn't believe his mother was so taken with Jools. What did she see that Rodney didn't?

Grandchildren, obviously. She probably sensed Jools was her last hope.

Margaret Wetherspone would probably embrace Myra Hindley if it served her purposes.

As much as he wanted to shove Jools back onto the streets where she belonged, his mother's words did calm him slightly. She hadn't insulted him nearly as much as she usually did. If his family was actually on board – if they believed that the relationship was real – maybe, just maybe, they might eventually respect him.

The issue of producing a child with Jools could be addressed at some later stage. Clearly copious amounts of alcohol and male porn would be required.

'Maybe you're right,' Rodney sighed.

'Of course I'm right,' his mother said. 'I always am.'

When Friday night rolled around, Rodney stayed late at the office and waited until everyone had gone home.

His wedding was in two days and he needed some light relief, especially as tomorrow was the pre-wedding party Jools had better have organised to perfection.

It might have been advisable to check the details with her, but that would have meant bothering to speak to her, and he didn't much fancy doing that.

He changed into tight leather trousers, clinging

wife-beater and black cowboy boots, slapped on a wig and cap, and went out for a night on the town with his special friend.

Jools could fend for herself – as she had done nearly every night since she'd moved in.

Jools was used to spending her nights alone. When Rodney didn't show up for dinner the Friday before the pre-wedding bash, she assumed he'd gone out to do whatever it was he was so fond of doing at night. She settled in for a quiet, calorific evening by herself.

First, a calming tomato-peel mask which smelt a little like feet – or maybe that *was* her feet? Next, her favourite ratty pyjamas – about four sizes too small with burping pigs dotted on the front and behind (they didn't quite make it over her bum, but no one was around to see, were they?). Finally, a position right in the sofa with a box of Celebrations (oh, the irony!) in one hand, a bag of crisps in the other and a glass of Merlot at the ready on the coffee table.

Just as she was starting to get comfortable, the buzzer rang. Must be the pizza man with her extra-large ham-and-pineapple, she thought.

'Coming!' she called, grabbing some money from the housekeeping supply Rodney kept for the cleaner. She walked to the front door and threw it open. Her pyjamas gaping open at the front but what the hell, she thought. It's just the pizza man – they probably see that sort of thing all the time.

But there were no pizzas in sight.

Instead, she was greeted by the horrified faces of a group of people gathered on the doorstep.

Party guests – about fifteen of them, all bearing gifts and dressed to the fifty-nines in the latest designer garb.

Seeing Jools, one woman shrieked, turning away as if Jools' wayward breasts had burned her retinas.

Other guests began muttering about the right house, the right day, being in the *Twilight Zone*, or on *Little Britain* or something.

But the worst was yet to come.

Several photographers pushed their way to the front of the group, snapping wildly and elbowing people to get better shots.

Shit.

Jools did the only thing she could do.

She slammed the door fast and locked it behind her. Then she hightailed it to her bedroom and turned on the shiny laptop, clicking quickly on the e-vite for the pre-wedding party.

Double, triple, quadruple shit.

Friday! The invitation said Friday, not Saturday!

How could she have been so careless? Rodney was going to slay her when he found out.

And to make matters worse, it wasn't only the friends that had clocked her attire.

How many pictures had the paparazzi managed to snap of her looking like a fishwife on crack?

Once those photos hit the papers, it was most certainly all over between her and Rodney.

She needed to get out. Now. Okay, she probably should go down and face his friends and invent some excuse; she could hear them talking loudly on the front door step. But how? It was just too humiliating, particularly as she only had half a packet of Wotsits and a demolished box of Celebrations to offer them.

Instead, she washed her face and threw on some clothes, racing out the back door as if her Juicy tracksuit was on fire. Hopping into the BMW she sped off into the night.

Dire thoughts pounded her head. What to do? Where to go? Nowhere that had anything above a builder's dress code, that was for sure.

Then somewhere came to mind – the only place where she wouldn't be judged, wouldn't be harassed or mocked: Skuttle's squat.

Jools parked in an alley a few blocks away and walked, hood up, to the familiar, soot-encrusted chute. She slid down and saw light spilling out from under the door.

Please, please, please, she prayed, knocking loudly and jumping up and down on the spot because she had forgotten a coat (and underwear) and it was bloody cold.

The door opened and there he was.

Jools stared in surprise. Skuttle was clean-shaven, hair neatly clipped, looking like he'd taken one hell of a shower. His skin no longer looked leathery and worn but radiated youthfulness and health.

Had he been on some sort of life-changing reality show? Surely not. She'd watched so much TV lately she definitely would have seen him.

'Wow,' Jools said, taking him in. 'You look . . ., well, like a person.'

Skuttle grabbed Jools by the arm and pulled her into the flat. 'I've been, er, working,' he told her.

'Great! So the money helped, then?'

Scuttle mumbled something she couldn't decipher. Probably embarrassed, thought Jools, deciding not to press the issue.

'What about you,' he asked. 'Are you alright?'

There was no point beating around the bush. She sat down on the lumpy bed. 'God, I'm in real trouble.'

'What kind of trouble?' Skuttle's handsome brow crinkled with concern.

She told him everything: how her relationship with Rodney was becoming more and more strained as the days went on; how she'd messed up the party and the invitations; how the paparazzi just wouldn't leave her alone. Recounting the horror of the past few weeks, tears filled her eyes. Her chest heaved and sobs scratched at her throat. Scuttle put an arm around Jools and pulled her to him.

'Sounds awful,' Skuttle said.

'It is.' Jools wiped her eyes.

'So why not cancel the wedding?' he asked gently.

Jools didn't have the guts to tell Skuttle the whole truth. She couldn't tell him that the only way out would be to pay Rodney back. She couldn't tell him that she had blown through all that money. She was so ashamed of how low she'd sunk she couldn't even be honest with a career hobo. So she lied and told Skuttle that despite everything, she loved Rodney and wanted to do right by him.

'You're a good person, Jools,' Skuttle said, holding her face in his hands. She noticed that his nails were newly-manicured. Plus, he smelled wonderful.

'I don't know,' she told him. 'I doubt that more and more each day.'

'You're always welcome here. Stay here with me until the wedding on Sunday. I'll make sure the photographers leave you alone.'

'I don't know about that,' Jools said, even though it sounded like a great idea. It would be easy to give up her huge bed and amazing bathroom in exchange for avoiding Rodney's wrath.

'At least for tonight?' Skuttle looked hopeful.

Jools nodded and smiled, curling up into a little (okay large) ball on Scuttle's makeshift bed. For the first time in ages, she felt relaxed and safe. It didn't take long for her to fall into a deep and dreamless sleep.

Chapter 23

Dear Miss Grand,

Please find enclosed the 'BIG LIE' pants you ordered last week, with the additional elastication you requested. We do hope they help you fit into your wedding dress.

However we must caution that whilst they can indeed help you appear one dress size smaller, they obviously cannot perform miracles and there is no replacement for a healthy diet and regular exercise.

Yours faithfully,

Justin Case
THE BIG LIE COMPANY
'Your Big Problem is
Our Little Secret'

LOOKING AT HER new 'suck in' knickers, Jools thought it a good thing Rodney wouldn't see her undressed on their wedding night. These flesh-coloured beauties were enough to bring on impotence in a teenage boy marooned backstage at a Miss World pageant. They'd been on the kitchen table when she'd snuck in after spending the night at Skuttle's. (Discovering she couldn't give up on a warm shower, she'd left Scuttle sleeping and had driven back home at dawn.)

'What the fuck is this?'

Rodney threw the morning paper onto the table. There was Jools in her sleepwear outside the house last night, on the hunt for pizza. Her muffin top was the inspiration for that morning's headline: *Top of the Muffin, says MP's Grand Ol' Bride-to-Be.*

Far too early in the morning to fight. Jools hadn't even had a double espresso yet.

'That's it!' Rodney bellowed. 'You've finally managed to go too far. I didn't think it was possible. I'm a fair man. But you have proven yourself to be too much for even me to handle. What possessed you to send out invitations without checking them?'

He held up another tabloid. 'And as for this one, can't you remember to pull the bathroom blind?'

Jools looked up at the paper in Rodney's hand. There she was, mask on her face and chocolate smeared over her mouth. She couldn't even remember eating chocolate now and wondered if it were one of those clever computer tricks. It didn't matter. She looked monstrous.

'I'm sorry, Rodney,' Jools said. 'It was an honest mistake.'

'It was an honest mistake that could have been avoided had you just consulted a bloody calendar!' he barked. It was bad enough having a fat wife with no self-control, but there was no way he could stand a fat, disorganised wife. Jools' main responsibility as Rodney's other half was to keep his home clean and his social calendar orderly. Right now, Jools was completely incapable of not only looking the part but also acting it.

How long would he be able to convince the public that this sham marriage was the real thing? Maybe he could find another, more suitable woman; a woman who could at least keep herself under two hundred pounds, look somewhat decent in couture, and pose for the paparazzi without a doughnut hanging out of her mouth.

His friends and co-workers were starting to ask questions. 'For a pair about to be married, you two certainly spend enough time apart,' they were all saying.

Rodney tried to laugh it off, explaining that separation, as far as he was concerned, was the key to a happy relationship. It made the heart grow fonder. The time they spent together was richer for the time they spent apart, blah, blah, blah. It was all lies and deception and even though he was a politician and could lie with the best of them, this was starting to turn even his stomach.

At the start, he'd been able to put on a convincingly

happy face. Now, his mild disdain for Jools was becoming a full-blown hatred. He wasn't sure he'd be able to spend five more minutes in her presence, let alone any number of years.

And the money she had cost him didn't even bear thinking about.

'It's over,' he said harshly. 'I can't do this. I thought I could but I can't. You are a complete disappointment – nothing like what I imagined when we first agreed to this arrangement.'

Jools' eyes widened. A pain gripped her heart and her stomach started to churn. Could you have a heart-attack at 28? Swallowing desperately to stop herself from being sick right then and there, she tried to speak but couldn't. Questions clogged her mind. What will I do? Will he want the money back? Where will I go?

Finally, she managed to speak. 'You can't do this.' Her voice was so weak she barely recognised it.

'I can and I will,' Rodney said. 'You misrepresented yourself.'

Her fear changed to anger. She might not have been everything that he wanted, but Jools had been very up front about herself. He'd known what she looked like and where she came from; he'd found her foraging in a skip for God's sake. She'd never hid anything from him. Not completely. In fact, she'd gone out of her way to tell the truth! Well, mostly.

'I was completely honest with you!' she shouted. Sure, she hadn't told him about her father (admittedly a pretty big omission), but she'd told him everything else. Rodney wasn't going to get away with being so cruel. Not anymore.

She stood up now, her breath coming in quick gasps and her cheeks flushing red with anger. Jools forgot she was wearing just a T-shirt and knickers. Rodney recoiled.

That was it!

She charged towards him, backing him up across the kitchen cabinets. At least there's one advantage to being fat – I'm twice his size, she thought grimly. 'Believe me, I wanted to live up to your expectations. But no one can! It's just too much!' She jabbed a finger in his chest as she spoke.

'It's not about my expectations,' he choked out. 'It's about the public's expectations. My duty is to them, not myself.'

Jools' anger drained away and she laughed. Rodney really believed his own hype. It made her sick. He didn't care about people. If he cared, he'd be spending his nights helping them instead of shagging men at seedy gay clubs.

'Don't you dare laugh at me.' His eyes bulged. 'Don't you dare.'

'I'll do whatever I want,' Jools said, still laughing to spite him. 'If I'm not going to be your wife, I can say and do whatever I want now. I'm free.'

'You're not free,' he responded.

Jools went a rather unflattering shade of puce.

'Oh, no. You're not free until you've paid back every last penny of the money I gave you.'

Jools froze. Her chest tightened again and her breath came even faster. Hopefully she *was* having a heart attack. How else was she going to dig herself out of this one?

Maybe it was time to be honest with Rodney?

'Look,' she started. 'You and I both know that I've, um, spent most of the money.'

'I'm sure that's an understatement,' he said.

'Whatever,' she told him. 'The amount is not important. What's important is that the total is not, er, intact. And you know that I can't pay you back. At least not immediately.'

'How is any of this my problem?'

'It's your problem if you'd like me to go quietly.' Jools realised she was holding a trump card. Or two, for that matter. Rodney's sexual orientation – and his mother's coke habit.

'Are you threatening me?' Rodney's tone was like steel.

'No,' she said sweetly, 'I'm just suggesting that we give this a little time. The wedding is on Sunday. I can promise you that it will go smoothly.'

'How?' He should have seen this coming. Anyone who'd sell themselves on miSell was not above blackmail.

'Well for starters, your mother is organising it. Not me.'

Rodney was quiet for a moment.

'I don't know,' he said finally, 'if I can go through with it. To be frank, you repulse me.'

Jools flinched. 'Well, I don't feel much differently about you,' she said with spirit. 'Once we're married, you can divorce me and tell everyone how horrible I was. You'll be the hero and I can just go disappear somewhere. That way we both get what we want. You have a successful political career, and I have the £76,000.'

There was silence. Jools struggled to cross her fingers. Was it possible to put weight on your hands? They did look a bit chubbier than usual.

'I need to think about this,' Rodney said. 'I'll call you later, once I decide.'

He turned and left, and Jools promptly headed for the fridge.

Rodney headed to Barts, the private gentlemen's club, badly in need of a drink. He knew Jools would never be able to pay the marriage money back. He'd seen the receipts – the Harrods' purchases piling up in her closet and, of course, the car. She was spending like crazy and there was only one place that cash could have come from from. Him. She wasn't working and she certainly hadn't any money when he'd saved her from that roach-infested squat by the bus garage.

He didn't feel bad for Jools. No sympathy whatsoever. She was exactly the kind of person he'd grown to loathe over the years. Fat, lazy and dumb – with no discipline or will-power. He couldn't marry her because he had absolutely no respect for her.

Of course, if he didn't marry her, there was the very real possibility she'd tell the world he was gay. He'd just invested a lot of time and money in his newest male conquest – and he needed Jools for that to work.

As Rodney slugged back the rest of his drink, fellow party member and MP Martin Willoughby walked up and tapped him on the shoulder. Martin sat down next to Rodney and ordered a scotch and soda. He was a bit sweaty from his tennis lesson and Rodney had to stop himself from leaning over and taking a deeper sniff. He did love the way men smelled after a bout of intense exercise.

'Shame about the wedding party last night, yes?' Martin said.

'Yes, Julia isn't extremely well-organised. Not sure she is exactly what I need, to be honest.'

'Look, old chap,' Martin said, 'You need a wife. In politics, it's as simple as that. Nobody trusts a middle-aged bachelor, if you get my meaning.'

He most certainly did. Rodney's preselection would only translate to a seat if he got married, especially after all his promises to that effect.

So this was what it came down to. Jools, or his career. He snapped his fingers and downed the promptly-delivered drink before the bartender had even left the table.

Waving off Martin, Rodney cowered in the dark corner of the club to ring his special friend. Last week they'd agreed it would be best if they were both married. Hiding behind sham marriages would minimise the chances of detection. Without the façade, their relationship would be highly suspect. Two grown, nearly middle-aged, single men spending that much time together? They'd be discovered eventually.

'I don't know what to do,' Rodney whined into his mobile. 'I hate her.'

'I don't blame you,' his friend said. 'But at least give it a few months. She'll probably get so disgusted with herself she'll head for the nearest roof. If not, maybe you can get her a personal trainer.'

'Great,' Rodney said, 'more money. I've already spent too much on this woman. I can't waste anymore.'

'It's a matter of what's important,' the man said. 'If I'm important to you, it's a no-brainer.'

'Of course you're important to me. I love you and I want to be with you.'

'Then you have to stick it out.'

'Alright.' Rodney hung his head. 'Can I come over? I told her I'd be out all night.'

'Get that bad ass over here,' the man said in a sexy low voice, disconnecting with a soft click.

Rodney couldn't leave fast enough. He hopped into his Benz and sped off, roaring by a popular bakery along the way. And failing to notice Jools' car parked out front.

*

Jools however, definitely saw Rodney zoom past, mainly because he was driving much faster than his normal 'vote-for-me-I'm-responsible' speed. What the hell was he up to now? Where was he going?

Whatever it was, she should find out. Maybe it was something dodgy and she could use it as further ammunition. It never hurt to have a back-up plan.

Running to her BMW, Jools gunned it and managed to catch Rodney's car at one of the many traffic lights along the park. Tracking the Benz past Hyde Park and Kensington Gardens, she followed as he made a left into a very familiar street. Mel's street. And pulled into a spot right out front of her mansion block.

Surely he couldn't know someone else in Mel's building? He would have mentioned it?

But the alternatives were just as baffling. Was Rodney really straight? Could he possibly be sleeping with Mel? It didn't make sense.

Rodney got out of the car, mounted the stone stairs, looking carefully around him before buzzing.

Shit. Jools ducked down. The deal would definitely be off if she was discovered stalking him – particularly if she couldn't uncover anything worthwhile to support her position.

Pushing herself further towards the pedals she wedged her large frame under the dash, planning to hide long enough for Rodney to get inside. She munched a couple of cupcakes while she waited.

Finally, she poked her head above the rim of the driver's door window. All clear.

Struggling to free her bum from the small space under the wheel, she managed to get out of the car. Creeping cautiously to the side of the building, she snuck around to Mel's bedroom window.

Thank God Mel was on the ground floor. Jools was in no condition to climb walls. The blinds were drawn, but she peered through a narrow gap and tried to focus on the room's dim interior. At first nothing was visible. Then, Rodney entered the room, half-dressed and red-faced. Bloody hell, that was fast.

He was sporting a strange expression Jools had never seen before. She squinted, realising it was a smile. He was grinning and playfully beckoning to someone, exuding happiness.

Jools held her breath. Who was there with him? It must be Mel. How could she? Sure, he was only a fake, gay husband-to-be – but he was still hers.

Eyes glued to the window, she waited until the pertinent someone else entered the room.

No. Surely not.

It wasn't possible.

Michel. The *boyfiend*.

Michel was supposed to be getting it on with rich old women! Not her pretend fiancé.

Michel ran a slimy hand down Rodney's chest and Jools felt bile building at the back of her throat. Backing away from the window, she tried not to look but it was strangely fascinating, like watching a car accident in motion. Rodney was supposed to be sleeping with a bevy of anonymous blokes, which hadn't bothered her – much. But this was too close to home.

And too bloody confusing!

Mel really needed to know this particular home-truth about her fiancé. But after everything that had happened, Mel was unlikely to believe this. Even Jools didn't quite believe it after seeing it with her own eyes. It was almost too ridiculous to be true.

Rattled by the turn of events, Jools decided to head back to the house, get her head on straight and figure out a plan of attack. But a lorry carrying scaffolding decided to make a three point turn into a bus, and The Gore was blocked for what felt like hours. Traffic fumes combined with the horrific vision of Rodney and Michel grinding away turned her stomach. She got out of the car and threw up in the gutter.

'Hope you're not drink driving,' called the man in the Volvo behind her.

'I wish.' Jools dragged herself back to the BMW.

Fifteen minutes later she was home and not surprisingly, there was no sign of Rodney.

Unloading the three boxes of cupcakes and carrying them into the kitchen, she stared at them solemnly. A few hours ago they'd been the highlight of the day. Taking one from its bright box, she realised she had no appetite. For the first time in ages she did not want to eat.

Tossing the cakes into the rubbish, she made a massive pot of soothing camomile tea instead.

How had things gone from worse to even worse so quickly? The maid had been and for some reason had gathered the tabloids from Jools' room and re-stacked them on the kitchen table, showing her humiliation off to full effect. How very thoughtful of her.

Jools looked at the picture of her bulging belly and felt the nausea creeping up on her again. Even if Rodney agreed to continue their deal, would she even fit into that horrendous wedding dress? There was no more time for any more adjustments. She might have to settle for a bed-sheet.

Jools let her head hit the table. She had nothing left, not even tears. Just exhaustion. And possible sugar poisoning.

God, she was sick of pretending, sick of stuffing her face and sick of watching Mel fall for Michel's bullshit time and time again.

Wanting desperately to call Mel and tell her what she'd seen, that stern little voice inside her head curbed the idea. Even if she did manage to convince her friend that Michel was untrustworthy and apparently bisexual, Mel would be unlikely to let sleeping dogs lie (literally) and Rodney might decide Jools was too much hassle and demand his money back. Again.

She was definitely caught between a rock and a concrete-reinforced place.

The doorbell rang. Jools was tempted to ignore it.

Probably just photographers and she'd had enough of them. But it rang again, more insistently. Jools finally dragged herself up and went to answer it.

'Darling, you look dreadful.' Lady Margaret was smoking, with the aid of a ridiculously long cigarette holder, her yappy little dog cradled in her arms. Mercifully the dog was asleep and snoring softly. Jools gave her future mother-in-law a quick peck on the cheek and invited her in.

'After those hideous photographs in the papers this morning, I thought I'd come by for moral support. Looks like you need it. My dear, you're positively green.'

Understatement of the millennium. Jools stifled the impulse to tell the truth. Instead, she told Lady Margaret it was just cold feet.

'I'm not sure he wants me anymore,' she added, snuffling into her sleeve.

Lady Margaret patted Jools' hand and passed her a tissue. 'There, there. Of course he does. Getting married is very stressful. Lots of pressure, especially when you're in the public eye. You really need to give cocaine a chance, my dear.'

'The press are so cruel,' sniffed Jools. 'I think even Rodney is beginning to believe them.'

Lighting another cigarette off the existing one, Lady Margaret inhaled toxic chemicals and exhaled into Jools' face. 'Don't be ridiculous, dear. He loves you, he told me so.'

Jools could see where Rodney got his excellent skills of deception.

'You know, women are far superior to men when it comes to emotional strength. In a few years, you'll be used to your life, dear, and you will have found your own ways to cope. Especially once you've had a few children.'

Lady Margaret balanced her cigarette on a nearby ornamental relic and removed an antique snuffbox from her purse. She flipped it open and dipped her long pinky finger into the fine white power piled up within. She took a sniff, waited a moment, smiled and breathed a giant sigh.

'It's high time you got yourself a new vice, Julia dear.' She looked over and spied the cupcake box in the bin. 'After all, the current one won't get you anywhere.'

'I don't want anything right now, except to be left alone.'

Lady Margaret's well-Botoxed face strained to form a grin (she and Mrs Pho must go to the same shonky practitioner). 'Come, come, my dear. We all want something, no?'

Jools had the uncomfortable feeling Lady Margaret was subtly bribing her. And it was working. Who didn't want a nice place to live; money to buy life's little luxuries? And if Rodney would just agree to go through with this wedding, the deep pockets of the Wetherspones would be at her disposal.

*

Rodney finally rang a few hours later. 'Alright, I'll go through with it – on one condition. Any more nasty surprises or misbehaving on your part and that's it. I mean it this time.'

'Fine.'

'Do we understand each other?'

What did he think she was, stupid? 'Of course.' Jools could finally breathe properly again. She hung up the phone and felt her muscles relax.

There was only one more day until the wedding, anyway.

What could go wrong now?

Chapter 24

For the attention of Miss Julia Grand,

Please find enclosed the requested photographs pursuant to your threat of legal action over the article 'Doughnut MP Wife Wedding Party Faux Pas.'

As you can see, the originals, with written authentication from the Kodak professional laboratory, perfectly match those printed on our tabloid pages.

If you require any additional information about our publications, we ask you to contact our solicitors Bradford, Berry and Co.

Yours faithfully,

Samuel P. Wringer
Editor-in-Chief
The Daily London News Review

BEFORE SHE KNEW it, the big day had finally arrived. As nervous as she was, it was best to get it over with so that the next phase could begin – her new life with

Rodney (the man who loathed her and could barely look her in the eye without calling for a sick bag).

The good news was she hadn't eaten in sixteen hours, so at least the wedding dress might actually zip up. The thought of not fitting into it filled her with dread. She should have tried it on yesterday to be sure, but short of resorting to Lady Margaret's coke-filled snuff box in the hope of an overdose, there was nothing more she could do, then or now.

Rodney had enlisted Percys' Terrible Trio to work their torturous magic. They were practically pulling her hair out by the roots when her mobile rang. A glance at the local number on the screen caused mild panic. Her father! Bloody hell, obviously he'd managed to make it into the country.

She could choose to let the answering service take it, but then he might call Lady Margaret for directions to the church. And as coked-up as she was, the old bitch would definitely give them to him.

'Hi Dad,' Jools whispered.

'Hiya, darling! How's my little girl on her special day?'

Jools tried not to throw up all over her robe. 'Fine. Can't talk though. Having my hair done.'

'Alright, I won't keep you,' he said. 'Just need the lowdown on directions to the big event.'

Shit. There goes the vain hope that he had forgotten all about the wedding and had legged it to Topshop to trawl for a new girlfriend. Jools thought for a moment.

The only choice was to send him so far in the opposite direction, there would be no chance of his making the ceremony.

There was a church near Southend-on-Sea, wasn't there? At least a couple of hours away, one way. By the time he figured out where he was, she'd already have said 'I do' and be cutting cake at The Dorchester, where she'd have told the doorman he was a crazy on the run from the law and needed to be kept out at all costs.

'Really?' Charlie Grand queried as he took down the address. 'Kind of a long way out of town. Why would the Wetherspones change plans and have the wedding all the way over there?'

'We're trying to avoid the media attention,' she said.

'Oh, right. Well, that makes sense. Those photos were pretty gruesome. You should get that cellulite sorted, love. Anyways, see you at three, Joolsy. Can't wait.'

Jools hung up and took a deep breath. Thank God that was sorted. She'd have to face her father at some point, just not today.

The Trio finished with hair and moved on to makeup.

'Lots of spots,' said Tangy, shaking her head in disgust. Obviously, Jools was not yet forgiven for taking the precious Pradas.

'Forget that, look at the legs.'

'Pity Debonaire can't force you to give her your legs, too!'

The three of them poured over Jools' cellulite. But Jools was too worried and knackered to even resist.

Her nemesis, the ten thousand pound organza-and-silk white whale in size 12, hung from the top of her wardrobe. The stylist – a new one on loan from Harvey Nicks since Debonaire was somewhere in the Med styling Kylie – led her over to it, eyeing them both gloomily.

'Let's give it a go, shall we?' the stylist chirped, her tone at odds with the look of doom on her face.

She handed Jools an industrial-grade girdle, which she slipped on over her BIG LIE pants. Then Chirpy commanded her to suck her gut in as much as was humanly possible. Chirpy pulled and yanked and squished poor Jools' internal organs into an arrangement that couldn't be healthy and definitely wasn't natural.

It was massively uncomfortable, but when she got into the dress and the zipper actually went up, Jools was so relieved that the fact she couldn't breath or bend over was of little concern. At least, the paparazzi wouldn't see flesh oozing out of the dress like lava from a volcano.

The door swung open and Lady Margaret appeared.

'Oh, how lovely.' She sniffed. 'It does fit. See, Julia dear, all of that worry for nothing.'

Jools tried to answer but she couldn't catch her breath to speak and struggled to take in air.

In response, Lady Margaret removed a small camera from a miniscule Dior handbag, took a photo, and burst into tears.

'What's going on?' Jools asked worriedly. She'd never seen the woman cry. Maybe she'd forgotten her daily dose of coke. Or maybe Lady Margaret was having second thoughts and was planning on telling Rodney not to marry and to live a full and free life as a gay man?

'It's just, you look so lovely, dear.' Lady Margaret dabbed her eyes.

That wasn't possible, but she was touched just the same.

But Lady Margaret motioned for her to turn around. 'See for yourself.'

Obligingly, Jools swung about and looked at the image in the full-length mirror.

There stood a slightly overweight but glowing bride. Her loosely curled hair framed her face in a way that was actually flattering. She *did* look lovely. Well, about two stone overweight but aside from that, the Trio had done an exceptional job. She looked like a bride. Tears filled her eyes but she managed to stop them from spilling over. Tangy would stab her with her tweezers if the makeup got ruined.

Despite the transformation, Jools was melancholy as she considered her reflection. She'd never been the kind of girl to dream about weddings. But the few times she'd actually thought about it, this certainly wasn't how she imagined it – slathered in makeup, wearing a frothy white wedding gown two sizes too small; marrying a gay man she didn't love for money; and settling into a life of lies and deception.

Lady Margaret interrupted her thoughts. 'The car, dear. Try to suck in that huge stomach, and let's go.'

So much for the tears, then.

Her car pulled up in front of the church at quarter to two. What if Rodney failed to show? She definitely got to keep the money then, didn't she?

As it was early she stayed in the car, watching people flood through the massive ornate doors, protected from view by the car's tinted windows.

She'd specifically requested one of the Wetherspones cars instead of a wedding limo – wanting to remain anonymous until the last second. Rodney had decided to drive himself and was just now pulling up in his Mercedes, his best man (yet another balding MP – there must be a factory somewhere churning them out) beside him. The two of them got out and the paparazzi swarmed as they headed into the church. Some police officers did their best to keep the aggressive photographers away, but their diversionary tactics did little to curb the seasoned professionals.

But Rodney didn't seem to mind. He stopped at the top of the church steps and posed for a few shots, shook a few hands and smiled for the cameras.

Jools watched him, imagining what the faker was saying to people. 'So good of you to come. We're so happy to have you here on our special day. Yes, I am a lucky man to be so very much in love with my bride. We will be happy together, thank you for your kind wishes.'

It was enough to convince her to tell the driver to turn around and head for home.

Calm down, she told herself sternly. One throbbing vein and her horrid dress might split down the back.

Then someone caught her eye. She did a double take.

It couldn't be.

Oh shit. It was.

'Louis,' she said to the driver, 'do you see that man there? The one in the cheap suit holding the bouquet of red carnations?'

'Yes, miss.'

'Please go and get him. Bring him back here as quickly as possible.'

Louis nodded, walked briskly across the road and patted the man on the shoulder. He looked confused and Jools could see his mouth snap open and close in protest as Louis lead him back to the car. Louis opened the door and ushered him into the back seat.

'Joolsy!' He didn't look happy.

'Dad, what are you doing here?'

'That's a very good question, isn't it? I shouldn't be here, right? I should be all the way across town at a church that knows nothing about this wedding, shouldn't I?'

'Yes, fine, I lied. I didn't want you here. I don't want you here!' She was done tiptoeing around the subject. She'd been too nice for too long. It was time to reveal how she truly felt.

'But why, Joolsy? Why would you lie to me? Don't you want to have your dad by your side, walking you down the aisle?'

'I would, if my dad wasn't wanted by the police in connection with a statutory rape case.'

'I'm working it all out.'

She rolled her eyes. How many times had she heard that old chestnut?

'And you know, if things were different, if I weren't overseas, I would have been here for you the whole time. Helping plan, paying for things. You know.'

Jools laughed. 'Yeah, I'm sure. In a completely different world, as a completely different person, you might have been around to help me. But this is reality, so forgive me if I'm not entirely pleased to see you now.'

'I've just had a spot of bad luck . . .'

'A spot of bad luck that's lasted thirty years,' she yelled. The car was silent and for a moment Jools thought he might start to cry.

'I can't deal with this right now,' she said, trying to stay calm and keep her dress from ripping. 'You have to go.'

'I have nowhere to go,' he whined. 'I need your help, Joolsy. I need a bit more money.'

'There's no more money to give, Dad.'

'Come on. Soon all that juicy Wetherspone money will be at your fingertips. They adore you. I'm sure Rodney would do anything to make you happy.'

'Rodney hates me!' she yelled. One of the buttons on the back of her dress popped off and ricocheted off the window.

'Don't be ridiculous. He wouldn't marry you if he hated you.'

'He's gay, Dad!' The words just burst out and once she'd started, she couldn't stop. 'He's gay and he needs a foil and he paid me to go along with this sham.'

For once, her dear old dad was stunned into silence.

'I owed thousands to the bank and they were going to sue me for it. I could have gone to jail so I needed the money. But he hates me. More than anything. And I don't want to marry him, but I don't know what else to do.'

'Do, what can you do?' Her father was, as usual, no help at all. 'Run away?'

'No, Dad. This is my only option – at least until I get myself together and make a little money of my own. And I won't be able to do that if you're here.'

Charlie Grand opened his mouth to protest but Jools cut him off. 'What if they find out that you're back in the country? What if the cops show up at the reception? The Wetherspones can't know about you. It'd ruin everything. And really, you've ruined enough in my life already.'

Jools finally stopped talking and slumped back onto the car seat, exhausted. Keeping all of those secrets was really starting to eat away at her. It felt good to have released them to somebody, even if it was her shocker of a dad.

'Well. I'm a bit shocked, Jools. Shocked by your behaviour, truth be told.'

Jools would thump him if she had the energy. 'I'm sorry, Dad, but you need to go.'

'I don't know if I want to go,' he said. Jools knew what he meant. He wanted the money.

'I would go, if I had the means.' He cast a beady eye her way.

'Alright, alright, I'll find you more money,' she sighed. 'But only if you promise to vanish.'

He nodded and opened the car door. 'I really am shocked by your attitude, Jools. I never thought a daughter of mine could be so selfish. They say the apple never falls far from the tree, but you're in a different orchard all together.'

'Thanks, Dad.' She meant it. She wanted to be as far away from his tree as possible. She watched him cross the street and walk away from the church.

Taking a moment to collect herself, she informed Louis she was ready. He came around and opened the door and the paparazzi swooped down, flashes popping insanely. Hundreds of people had gathered outside the church and Jools was surrounded on all sides by the curious and rude, begging for pictures and autographs; telling her how lovely or horrible she looked; asking ridiculously personal questions like where she and Rodney would do it on their honeymoon; what size her dress was; did she enjoy all doughnuts or just those from Doughy?

Louis held them back as best as he could and with some help from the police, Jools made it safely into the church. At the start of the aisle, she glanced around and noticed that Rodney's side of the church was packed – people were even standing at the back – while hers held only a few cleaners she'd had to pay to show up, along with Mrs Pho, who shook her head and mouthed 'arsonist.'

Everyone on Rodney's side was extremely well dressed and had their noses so high into the air she doubted they could see what was going on. Jools' cleaners had come in their work overalls, and Mrs Pho was edging away from them towards Rodney's side.

The familiar first notes of the wedding procession filled the church and Jools started down the aisle. As she passed the rows and rows of Wetherspone guests, the power of their stares stung like nettles. They were judging her, clearly thinking that Rodney was making a terrible mistake.

Jools summoned the strength to keep going, even though she was missing a button and the strings of her corset were starting to unravel. Oh, to be out of this dress and back in a comfy Juicy tracksuit. Back in her room, away from the stares and sniggers; nestled warm and cosy in bed with a pint of ice cream and a few dozen gourmet cupcakes.

Rodney was waiting for her, another plastic smile stuck on his perfect, tanned face. The temptation to smack that smile right off was almost too strong, but she forced herself to focus on breathing instead.

Finally, she made it to the altar and turned to look him in the eyes, hoping desperately that no one could read her mind.

Louis the driver was sneaking a fag outside the church, leaning casually against the hood, when one of the paparazzi appeared.

'Nice day,' the pap said.

'That it is.'

'Good you get to take a break.'

'Can I help you with something, mate?' Louis flicked his cigarette in the man's general direction. The paparazzi made his job dangerous. Every time he had to swerve to avoid them, he risked his life. There had already been several near misses with trees and pedestrians. Once he'd nearly mowed down Amy Winehouse.

'Yes, you might just be able to help me,' the pap replied. 'Who was that old man in the car with Jools?'

Louis smiled. It wasn't the first time one of these fools had asked for information. He'd been a driver and bodyguard for twenty years and worked for all sorts of important people; people whose lives were of great interest to the public. He prided himself on being loyal and protective of his clients.

'You know I can't tell you anything about Miss Grand's private business,' he said, baiting the guy.

'Yeah, yeah,' the pap said, 'I know. But maybe you can tell *her*.' He held out a hundred pound note and pointed at the Queen's image. 'Maybe you can tell her all about that bloke, and what he and Jools were saying to each other. Maybe I can just listen in on the conversation.' He raised his eyebrows.

Louis licked his lips. With a mortgage and ex-wife draining him dry, a hundred quid would be extremely helpful – as long as the leak couldn't be traced back to him.

'You want me to betray Jools to the Queen?' Louis asked.

'She is the Queen, after all,' the pap said. 'She deserves to know.'

'I don't know,' Louis said, mulling it over. 'I might betray Jools to four Queens. In fact, I might tell five Queens every little detail.'

The photographer reached into his wallet and pulled out a stack of crisp hundred pound notes. He counted out five and handed them to over.

'Hiya, Your Highnesses,' Louis said. 'Want to hear

about Jools and her dad and how her marriage is a complete sham? Righty ho, pull up a chair.'

Louis told his five Queens the whole story. When he was done, he got into the car and locked the door. The pap was practically drooling.

Niles couldn't believe his luck. His photographer's disguise had finally paid off. It was worth spending a few hundred quid to pay off that dozy driver. Now he had everything he needed to get Jools right where he wanted her: his basement in Slough.

Given his newfound information, it was a sure bet that Jools and Rodney wouldn't be heading off for a romantic honeymoon anytime soon. Niles decided to go back to their house and wait. She wouldn't be able to run from him anymore.

After all, it was as he had suspected.

He was more man than Rodney would ever be.

Chapter 25

Dear Julia M. Grand,

We enclose a claim recently lodged with the County Court in your area. As the claimants stated in their letter before action, they seek the amount of £25,872.11 plus interest and costs. You are advised to pay this amount within the prescribed period, or defend the claim, to avoid recovery action by the County Court Sheriff.

This is an automated letter from the South and West County Court. If you are not the intended recipient, or wish to contest this claim, please contact us immediately.

AFTER THE RECEPTION, Jools and Rodney returned home. They chatted briefly in the kitchen about an up-and-coming appearance he needed her for, and then quickly made for their separate bedrooms. Jools couldn't wait to take off the terrible dress and crawl into bed, preferably with some tasty morsel.

Happy to be alone, she couldn't have cared less when she heard the front door open and close and voices coming from Rodney's bedroom. So what if he and that loser Michel were re-enacting a honeymoon? Let them. She was too exhausted to be grossed out.

Thoughts of Michel made her think of Mel, who hadn't come to the wedding. Jools had hoped she might at least show up to offer support, even if she hated Jools and knew the whole thing was fake.

Just as she was drifting off to sleep, there was a rap on her window. She tried her best to ignore it but it grew more violent and loud. Groaning, she forced herself to get up, thinking it was probably a rent boy Michel had hired courtesy of Rodney, or someone equally foul. She pushed the window open a crack.

A weedy guy appeared out of the darkness, looking about as sinister as an under-stuffed muppet in black, bride-napping attire.

Jumping back, Jools tried to recall where she had seen him. That's right. The ferret-like freak she'd met at the beginning of her miSell auction.

'What the hell are you doing here?' she asked in a loud whisper, opening the window a couple more inches.

'Just came to pay my respects to the bride,' he hissed, moving closer, camera in hand.

Jools hadn't seen Niles since that horrible day at the coffee shop. How could he know where she lived? And what was with the high-tech camera? Was he a pap? That was all she needed. Documented evidence of her humble beginnings as an miSell whore.

'You'd better go before I call the police,' she looked around the room for some kind of blunt object she could use if Niles tried to climb in. The best option was a rather heavy vase stationed on the bureau. It might not kill him but it would definitely knock him senseless. Not that he seemed to have much sense to begin with.

'Don't worry, Jools,' Niles said, pimply nose stuck against the window, enjoying her fear. 'I'm not here to harm you. I wouldn't dream of it. That would ruin my whole plan.'

'What plan?' Jools edged toward the vase.

'The plan where you spend eternity with me in my house in Slough. I've fixed it up for you real nice. You'll like what I've done with the concrete floor and cinderblock walls.'

'You're a nutter,' she spat at him. 'I'd never come anywhere near your place. I'd rather choke on my own vomit.'

'You'll end up in Slough eventually, baby,' he crooned, 'and when you do, I'll see to it you stay put. No more running away from Niles.'

Jools slammed the window shut, narrowly missing his hands, and drew the curtains.

'I know what's happening, Jools!' Niles screamed from outside. 'I know everything and you will submit to me!'

What the hell was he talking about? Jools stood behind the curtain, biting her nails. She hoped Michel was keeping Rodney aroused enough to ignore the noise.

'Your father! Your gay husband!' Niles' deranged shrieks pierced the windowpanes.

Shit. Double shit. Jools pulled up the window again. How the hell did he know about Dad and Rodney?

'So, I take it you reconsider?'

'Listen, Niles, your medication is clearly not working. You're delusional. My husband's not gay.'

'Really? Not what I heard.'

'Rubbish, you lunatic. Where did you hear that?'

'From you, my darling. Outside the church, talking to your father.'

How the hell had he overheard them? Maybe one of the car windows had been open? Or maybe her father had sold his story for the price of a hotel room and some Jack Daniel's? Jools' stomach dropped to her knees. In any event, the weasel knew the truth.

What was she going to do now?

'I'll give you money!'

'I don't want money. I want you.' Even from the window she could hear him licking his lips.

'A car?'

'You.'

'A holiday to the Caribbean? Nicer than Slough this time of year.'

'You.'

Jools sighed. 'Okay, a date, one date – but that's all.'

Niles thought for a moment. A date was better than nothing, but he suspected that the minute he left, she'd move house or get a bodyguard or an alarm or something, then tell him the date was off.

'Come and live with me in Slough or I tell all. That's the deal, my darling.'

Jools was exhausted and couldn't cope with anything else tonight. A paltry existence underneath the bus garage with Skuttle was looking pretty good right about now.

'Do what you want, you mentalist. I'm going to bed.'

She was about to shut the window when she heard Niles say quietly, 'I'll bring you down, and you'll be sorry.'

'You're blackmailing me and I'm calling the police,' Jools said, bluffing. Banging the window down again, she waited a moment, fully expecting Niles to try to break in. But after a few minutes everything was quiet.

Maybe she should tell the police? It wouldn't be difficult to make out that Niles was a psycho, given that he was, in fact, a huge one.

But she'd need Rodney's support.

Running from the room, she padded down the hall to Rodney's door. Some unpleasant sounds were emanating from the bedroom. No. It could wait until tomorrow. The thought of interrupting him in the middle of whatever he was doing with Michel did not appeal to her in the slightest.

Niles left Jools' place angry and frustrated. Her threat to call the police meant that even if he managed to spirit her away to Slough, the cops would probably be waiting on his front door step before he got her there.

If he couldn't have her, that homosexual toff wasn't getting her either. This time he had real ammunition. He could destroy her if he wanted to and – more than anything else – that was exactly what he wanted to do.

Taking a deep breath, Niles told himself to calm down. By tomorrow he would know if she had called the police. Leaking what he knew to the tabloids before then might lose him a trump card.

To fill the time, Niles decided to call the papers and explore the possibilities. He rang up *WhatNOW!* on his mobile and told them he had a hot story about a certain local politician and his new obese wife.

The young reporter was intrigued. 'What is it, then?'

'Let's not get ahead of ourselves,' Niles said. 'First, tell me what kind of money we're talking about.'

Reluctant to give Niles a hard number, the kid told

him they'd have to check him out before they reached a deal. 'But if it's a solid lead, we're talking somewhere in the realm of seventy-five grand.'

How ironic, Niles thought smugly – exactly what he would have paid for Jools. He grinned. If he couldn't have Jools, a fat wad of cash was the next best thing.

Feeling a whole lot better about the situation, Niles made his way home to wait for the reporter's call – and avoid one from the Old Bill.

Chapter 26

From: Studley@Grand.co.uk
Subject: Message for Joolsy

How come you don't answer your phone anymore? You promised me some cash and it's quite difficult to live in London without dosh in my pocket.

Call me, or I'll have to come round.

Your father, Charlie Grand.

WHEN MONDAY MORNING rolled around, Jools got up and squashed herself in her best Chanel suit. Scraping her hair into a conservative bun, she put on just enough makeup to avoid looking like death in the inevitable photos.

Rodney hated it when she layered on the blusher, so she tried to go easy. It was important to maintain Rodney's desired façade of dignified newlyweds.

She was already in enough hot water with her

father back in the country and Niles skulking about in the undergrowth; she didn't need any more trouble.

When Jools and Rodney arrived in Hampshire, Jools was horrified to discover that the meet-and-greet was at the head office of the Commercial Bank London – the same bank that had supplied her small-business loan and was taking her to court over non-payment. Shit. She'd meant to ring those court people and sort something out, using one of Rodney's cheques of course, but with all the wedding hoopla she'd completely forgotten.

Hoping desperately that Horace Fortescue wasn't around, it was extremely disappointing to find him standing right there at the front door, waiting to greet a very important guest and his new, spendthrift wife.

From the look on his face, it was obvious Horace had been waiting for this moment for a very long time. He didn't even pause for pleasantries.

'You owe this institution £25,872.11.'

Shutters were snapping happily now and several reporters, sensing a fresh kill, swarmed in like vultures. Jools didn't know which way to turn or what to say.

Luckily, Rodney knew what to say. 'I'm sure there's some mistake,' he pulled the banker aside. 'My wife is actually very good with money.'

'All our evidence points to the contrary,' Horace Fortescue replied cynically. 'Our claim is now a matter for the courts.'

Rodney shot an evil look at Jools. Yet another tidbit of information she'd failed to mention over the past few weeks.

'Can we settle this like civilised people?' Rodney whispered, still holding the banker's arm tightly, his back to the press.

They all trooped inside.

'Certainly. Just pay this institution every last penny of the money she owes and instruct her never to set foot through our doors again.'

Rodney struggled to keep himself in check when all he wanted to do was turn around and berate Jools. He reached into an inside pocket and pulled out a long, leather wallet. Walking over to a desk, Rodney wrote out a cheque for nearly twenty-six thousand pounds. Jools cringed as the tab she'd been keeping in her head grew to an unfathomable number.

On the ride home, Rodney didn't utter a word despite her feeble attempts at conversation. He just stared out the window, trying to convince himself that the whole thing was a horrible nightmare and tomorrow morning he'd wake up wrapped in Michel's firm, hairy arms.

This was the final nail in her already tightly sealed coffin. There was no way he'd win the election now. Not when the press ran their stories tomorrow morning about Rodney Wetherspone's failed entrepreneur wife and how she'd almost gone to jail over a bank loan.

Rodney's credit card statement was waiting for him

when they got home. In need of a distraction, he tore open the bill. Jools watched his eyes grow wide when he saw the cash advances. Immediately assuming he'd been a victim of identity theft, he informed Jools he was going to the bank to have the cheques traced.

'This day couldn't possibly get any worse,' Rodney shouted as he stormed out of the house, slamming the door.

But Jools knew it could. It was about to get much worse. Once Rodney found out about the cheques, she was a goner. Unable to think, she did the only thing that gave her any comfort: she opened the fridge and started eating. But the first bite of Gouda made her queasy, so she threw the cheese in the bin and went to her bedroom, pondering her very dismal future.

Niles was sharpening his knives in the kitchen when his mobile rang. It was the reporter.

'Well, Niles, we've checked out your leads and it's looking good. I'm ready to have my assistant make out a cheque. But you've got to come down here and tell us the rest of the story. And we want every little detail.'

A smile grew across Niles' face. He didn't even say goodbye to the reporter; just dropped the phone, grabbed his jacket and flew out the door.

Chapter 27

<u>By hand.</u>

Dear Mrs Julia Wetherspone (nee Grand),

We called today to discuss our investigation regarding the unauthorised use of credit card cheques.

We notice that cheque 004839 was deposited into an account in your name. As the cheques relate to your husband's account we wish to contact you to confirm that you did, in fact, make these deposits with his knowledge.

Please call me on the number below at your earliest convenience.

John Blunting
Fraud Services
International Bank Ltd

THE NEXT MORNING, Jools was pretty sure that life as she knew it was over. Rodney's bank was onto her, and to top it off, she and Rodney were all over the papers once again – only this time the heat was on him, as well.

As usual, her husband was awake long before her and he'd read every last article in every single paper that had been delivered. He was sitting at the kitchen table when she walked out in her pink La Perla gown and designer bunny slippers. Face white as a sheet, eyes red-rimmed and puffy, Rodney was still in his robe, unshaven. He looked terrible.

He held out one of the papers, the headline visible from Mars: ALL IN THE FAMILY: THE POLITICIAN AND THE PERV! Poster-sized photos of Rodney and her dad were plastered underneath.

Jools froze. If she moved, she might fall over. And she wasn't wearing any underpants.

'Happy now?' Rodney choked out. 'You've officially ruined my reputation, political aspirations, social standing – my life, in fact!'

The paper landed at her feet.

'I'm sorry,' she said, meaning it. None of this was meant to happen.

Rodney laughed manically. Sorry? She was sorry? 'You listen to me, you pathetic woman.' Pushing back his chair he headed towards her, a muscle twitching in his jaw. Jools backed away, terrified. 'I want every penny of that money back and I want it back within one week. If I don't have it in a week, I'll have you arrested for blackmail and fraud. And that's not all. A few phone calls to the right men, and there'll be nothing left of you. Nothing. And considering the size of you, that will take a lot of force.'

'I don't understand!' she said in a last-ditch effort to turn the situation around. 'Maybe we can say I converted you?'

'No one is going to believe a lump like you turned me straight!' Rodney screamed.

'So deny it!' said Jools desperately, 'Just tell them it's all false. Tabloids lie all the time.'

'You're so naïve. I can't fucking deny this. It's too big. Denying it would just make me seem guiltier. I'm going to have to come clean.' Rodney slumped over, looking spent. 'I was only doing this whole political thing, hiding the truth, for my parents. They're the only people whose opinions mean anything to me. Now that they know, what's the point in lying?'

Jools looked at Rodney. For a second, she felt a pang of sympathy for him. Even though he'd been awful to her, she really had destroyed his life. Then she remembered that he was threatening to sue and maim her and the sympathy disappeared.

Rodney pointed at the door. 'I want you out of here. Now!'

She ran from the kitchen and started throwing everything she owned into whatever bags she could find. Luggage, shopping bags, bin liners.

Meanwhile, Rodney got straight on the phone, no doubt to gloat over her eviction with that creep Michel.

Jools climbed into her BMW and was about to turn the key in the ignition when Rodney appeared at the back door, looking reasonably calm. Maybe he'd reconsidered and she could unpack and go back to their marriage of deception?

She waited for Rodney to cross the courtyard, noticing his tight jeans – usually reserved for nights on the town. A black tank top hugged his taut body and leather sandals showed off his perfectly manicured toes. His hair was no longer stiff and starched; instead, it was spiky and dishevelled. He was like a completely different person.

'Wow,' she said as he approached. 'That's a new look for you.'

He didn't answer.

'I like it,' she said, 'It works.'

'I really don't care what you like,' he sneered. 'All I care about is getting what I'm owed.'

'You gave me a week, didn't you? It's been an hour. I'll have your money.'

'I'm sure you will,' he said, 'but until you do, I'll be keeping the car as collateral. I'll also be keeping all the clothes, shoes and beauty products.'

Jools stared at him with her mouth open. This couldn't be happening. She was planning to sleep (upright) in that car! Without it, she was truly homeless.

Again.

'Rodney, please . . .'

'So if you don't mind leaving everything you've just loaded into the boot . . .'

'But what am I supposed to do without a car?' Not to mention eyecreams and designer clothes?

'The same thing you did before you came here. Take the bus,' he held out his hand for the keys.

'You're a real bastard.'

'And you, my dear, are something dragged up from the gutter. So why don't you crawl your rotund backside back there and get the hell out of my life?'

Jools gathered up everything she could hold, cramming as much as possible into various bags and a single carryall and walked away with her head held high, trying to muster a smile for the waiting paps.

Chapter 28

Dearest Julia,

I was horrified to hear that Rodney left you over those nasty little newspaper revelations. However, I do have every faith the two of you will reconcile. A good wife can always bring a man back to his senses, even if he has professed a desire for buggery.

As a woman of great character, I know you would like to receive the attached invoice for that little mishap over the pre-wedding party. Given what has transpired, I am sure you agree neither I nor Langston need bear the brunt of your debacle with Rodney. We hope to have payment of the £19,500 within the week.

All the very best wishes,

Lady Margaret Wetherspone

HAVING MANAGED to lose the press by escaping into the loo at Caffe Nero, Jools wandered aimlessly, wondering where to go. There was really only one option: Skuttle's. A finger of guilt nudged her. Sure she'd given him money, but certainly couldn't be described as a great friend – never inviting him round to Rodney's, or even made a proper effort to see him, except when she'd been desperate.

But right now there was little choice but to head to Willesden Green or camp out in the streets of SW7 in the vain hope that Rodney might take pity on her – and that seemed about as likely as her being voted Miss Thinnest Thighs UK.

Heading west towards the bus station, the extent of her predicament hit home. It had just started to pour and although having managed to hold on to the Chanel suit and a few other designer bits and bobs , she hadn't thought to take an umbrella. Or underwear.

The rain soaked through the thin, dryclean only clothing and lay cold and wet on her skin. Shivering, she picked up the pace.

The last thing she felt like doing was walking, but there was no money for a bus, let alone a cab. Glancing back, she prayed the paparazzi, or worse, that nutter Niles, weren't following. But there was no movement in the rear-facing shadows.

Up ahead, the glow of a slow-moving bus caught her eye, its cosy warmth tantalisingly close. Christ, just yesterday she was driving around town in a brand new BMW. Now, even standing room on a clapped-out bus was thoroughly appealing.

A crowd of eager commuters was gathering by

the bus stop. Maybe I can just slip on with them, Jools thought. When the bus pulled up, she wedged between a very tall man in a dark suit and a very fat woman in a red dress and tried to make herself as small as possible – not easy considering the spare tyre and numerous bags (some of which were perilously close to bursting open).

Jools made it onto the bus and past the driver without being spotted. But as she eased into a seat at the rear, the fat woman in the red dress shot her a nasty glance. At first, Jools thought the woman might have recognised her from the tabloids, until it became apparent she was simply irked at being an unwitting accomplice to a crime.

'I pay my way,' the woman hissed at Jools from across the aisle. 'Why can't you?'

Jools didn't have the strength to argue. Her toes were frozen and dripping wet hair was plastered to her head. Even the warmth of the bus couldn't stop her teeth from chattering.

Staring at the woman like a zombie, she said: 'No speak English,' in a strange Chinese-sounding accent. The woman observed her with disgust, then looked away and huffing loudly, got a packet of carrot cake slices out of a duffle bag.

'Ooh, can I have some?' Jools asked before she could stop herself. The sight of a frosted cake had a hypnotic effect.

The woman turned, daggers in her eyes. 'I thought

you didn't speak English?' Crumbs flew from her mouth.

Shit. 'No understand.' The Chinese accent was back again.

'Humph.' With a snort, the rotund woman manoeuvred her bulk into another seat as far away from Jools as possible.

Finally, a calm, automated voice announced they were approaching Willesden Green bus garage, where the bus terminated. Something about the familiar sight made Jools feel better. but climbing off the bus, reality hit. Willesden Green was hardly Knightsbridge; her business debtors and Rodney were still after her for money; and that weirdo Niles might be planning to kidnap and/or torture and murder her.

Jools made her way to the chute that led to Skuttle's squat, threw her belongings in first, then slid down. But Skuttle's door was shut and padlocked. The small windows that once allowed a dirty glimpse of the pavement above were boarded up and a sign tacked to the door read: 'Condemned Property. Trespassers will be sued.'

It was the final slap to her rather spotty face.

Jools knocked anyway, just in case the boards, the lock and the sign were some sort of elaborate ruse on Skuttle's part to keep away unwanted guests. She waited for a response. Nothing. Knocking again, even harder this time, she prayed for a miracle. If Skuttle really was gone, there was absolutely no way of finding him. Which meant she was completely alone in the world.

No joy. Rubbing her red knuckles, she made her way back up the chute. The rain was tapering off now but the day was so dark it felt like the end of everything, like she was the last person left on Earth. The streets were deserted and all was quiet save the soft tapping of intermittent rain drops on the bus station's tin roof.

She was so wet now there really wasn't any point in scrambling for shelter. Too tired to move, she sank down onto the grimy concrete and dropped her bags beside her. Pulling frozen fingers through her mucky hair, she contemplated possible options. Maybe launching herself off a cliff, but that would mean finding one first. Throwing herself in front of a bus had a certain poignancy, given the past, but was rather messy for all concerned. No. Right now, she needed to toughen up and get serious.

'Well, well, well, would you look at who it is.' A horrifyingly familiar voice. Jools whipped around. Rocco Martucci was standing above her, flashing his big, gold teeth, arms full of kebabs.

Jools scrambled to her feet. No way was she going to give him the satisfaction of looking down on her. Anyway, she was already dirty enough without adding kebab drippings to the mix. Grabbing her bags, she slung them over her shoulder, and stood toe to toe with her ex-landlord.

'To what do we owe the honour?' He tapped a cigarette out of a crisp new pack and popped it between his lips, skillfully balancing the kebabs.

'Just came back to see an old friend.' Not that she owed him an explanation.

'That old wino don't live here no more, innit.' Rocco lit the cigarette. 'Owner came and boarded the place up a week ago. Aint seen him around since.'

'Good to know,' Jools said, and not wanting to show how upset she was, she turned to walk away.

'I seen the papers, Jools,' Rocco called after her. 'Everyone's seen those papers, innit? I know your luck's run out.'

Jools stopped but didn't turn around. Why torture herself with the smile that must be plastered on his smarmy, greasy mug. It'd be the last straw – she wouldn't be able to stop herself from trying to batter him to death with those kebabs. Not a good move, because he'd retaliate with more force than her. Still, death by kebab didn't sound that bad, Jools thought, her mouth watering.

'It's not my luck that's run out, Rocco,' she said, 'It's my money.' Rocco walked towards her, the squeak of his rubber-soled shoes making ugly music on the wet pavement.

'Sounds like a familiar story,' he said. 'When you gonna learn, Jools?' A puff of stale, white smoke reached her nostrils.

She didn't answer because she had no idea.

'You need some help? Happy to oblige. For old times' sake.'

'I'll bet.' If Rocco was offering help there must be something in it for him.

'Come on. What you got to lose? You got nothing left, innit?'

Absolutely nothing. 'Maybe,' she told him. 'Maybe not. Depends on the offer.'

'Joolsy,' he snorted, 'good to see you haven't changed. You're paranoid, you are.'

'Yeah, and you're about as trustworthy as a fox at a petting zoo.'

Rocco smiled. 'Why, thank you! He leaned in closer still – so close she could smell the mix of stale body odour and the garlic kebab sauce. 'Happy to help, innit?'

Rocco ran his eyes over Jools, as if she was a wrapped meat selection at Whole Foods. She needed a shower from just being beside him.

'Work for me. I'll give you a place to stay – rent free – until you get back on your feet.'

That was priceless. Jools could only imagine what type of work Rocco had in mind. 'I'm not breaking anyone's knee caps. Or streetwalking!'

Rocco looked up at the sky and made a loud hiccupping noise Jools identified as laughing. Rocking back on his heels as he enjoyed his private joke, Jools thought he might fall over backwards (the kebab gut *was* rather large) but somehow he stayed upright.

'Oh Joolsy, Joolsy. You've always been my favourite non-payer. I don't need you to do nothin' like that. I'm thinkin' cleaning. You got the skills, innit? I need someone to make sure the flats are in top condition.'

Jools was bemused. The only way Rocco's rat-infested flats could ever be considered 'top condition' would if they were knocked town and rebuilt. Why was he suddenly so concerned with cleanliness anyway? Certainly never seemed to care when she lived there. Still, Rocco's offer might be her only hope for survival.

'I suppose I can do that,' she said slowly, 'as long as that is all there is to it. Just clean and maintain the flats?'

There had to be a catch.

'That's it,' he told her, 'swear on my kebab.' He held one hairy hand over his heart before passing it over for Jools to shake. She paused, then shook the greasy palm, trying to keep from looking too disgusted.

'Alright. But I'll need a new key to the front door, since you changed the locks on me.'

Rocco raised an eyebrow. 'What do you mean? You never had a key to that front door.'

'Of course I did. I lived there, didn't I?'

'Oh Jools,' Rocco shook his head with mirth. 'You got the wrong end of the stick again, innit? I don't need you to clean your *old* building. I need you to clean that.'

Rocco pointed down the street towards the massive

stone and concrete monstrosity that was sitting solid and heavy, looking like the structure that time forgot. Great. The local council block. It had at least forty units, instead of the eight that she thought she'd be cleaning. On top of that, it was probably filled with some of the most depraved and shocking examples of humankind she'd ever seen. Besides Rocco, of course.

'That? You want me to clean *that*?'

'Not all of it. Just the communal areas and the tenants who pay extra.'

Well, that was a little better. Surely, only a few residents could afford a cleaner? Besides, there wasn't really a choice. It was getting dark and she was homeless. Again.

She followed Rocco to the building. He led her to a small, dank flat off a long hallway in the basement. Unlocking a dented metal door, he pulled a cord on the single light hanging from the peeling ceiling.

Jools looked around, horrified. It was little better than a prison cell, with a stained toilet and sink in the corner and a small fridge that hummed louder than a lorry stuck in an uncharacteristic heatwave on the M25. A soiled mattress lay on the floor in one corner. In the other, a scarred wooden desk tried valiantly to remain upright. Jools knew how it felt.

'Home sweet home!' Rocco dropped a massive set of keys on the desk. 'Here are the keys for the flats that need cleaning. Numbers are on the tags. Don't forget the front hall and path.'

'When do you want me to start?'

'Now's good.' He rocked back and forth on his toes as he waited for her to get started.

'Now?' Jools could barely move.

Rocco's bruised features betrayed slight understanding. Or maybe the kebab was just repeating on him. 'Alright, Joolsy. Tomorrow, then. But you better toughen up. This ain't no easy ride.'

With that he left.

Jools collapsed onto the horrid stinky bed. The springs bit into her back as she rolled into the middle of the sagging, smelly heap. It was about as comfortable as sleeping on the boot of a car, but she was so exhausted from the intrigue of the last twenty-four hours she was asleep in two minutes flat.

The next morning she awoke, turned her knickers inside out (well, one had to have some standards, after all), splashed some cold water on her face and under her armpits and headed upstairs for a day of work.

The building could have easily won a competition for Most Festering Location in London. The elevator, which made horrible noises as it ascended through the narrow shaft up the middle of the building, smelled of urine and was covered in graffiti. The front hall was covered in some substance that required a nose peg to get close enough to clean.

She propped open the front door to air out the small room and set about mopping the floor and washing the walls.

Finished in the hall, she headed outside for some fresh air. A passed-out drunk blocked the front entrance. She kicked him a couple of times to make sure he wasn't dead. Or Skuttle. He came to, cursed at her through black teeth, and went back to sleep.

And it only got worse. In a flat on the third floor, she found several dead rats piled on top of each other, like some sort of surreal sculpture. All the furniture had been eaten through and the linoleum was covered in rat faeces and rubbish. The rats had been dead for some time. They looked hollowed out and dusty – much like Jools felt.

She swept the rat pile into a heavy-duty bin liner and headed down to the basement to throw it into the incinerator. On her way, she almost collided with a tall, gaunt man. Although he looked young, he was missing several teeth. In his arms was a tiny old dog covered in scabs. The animal's eyes were clouded and it barked and growled like crazy. She was tempted to toss the mutt into the incinerator along with the rats.

The man found his voice. 'I have a fucking leak in my fucking apartment. It's been fucking running for fucking days and days. It's right over my fucking bed, which makes sleeping very fucking unpleasant,' the man growled for emphasis, sounding remarkably like his feral pet.

Jools wanted to tell him to fuck off but given his familiarity with that particular expletive it was hardly worth it.

'I'll look into it,' she told him, still holding the bag of dead rats. Covered in grease and soot, she was knackered, her back was killing her and all she wanted was to crawl into bed and go back to sleep, even though her bed was so putrid it could hardly be classified as a place of rest.

Dumping the rat bag into the incinerator, she headed upstairs to see about the water problem.

Standing in front of the leak-causing abode, she knocked on the door. There was no answer at first, but soon Jools heard the sound of unsteady feet heading towards the door.

'Hang on.' The voice was old and scratchy. The door creaked open and an ancient woman wearing a floral print bathrobe appeared. The stench coming from inside the flat was unbearable. It was the worst thing that Jools had smelled yet — a mixture of decaying animal matter, urine and something sweet she couldn't quite place. She thought she might vomit right there on the old woman's fuzzy pink slippers but luckily managed to hold it together.

'The man downstairs says he's got a leak and we think it might be coming from your flat,' she told the woman, trying desperately to breathe through her mouth so as not to inhale the vile odours.

'Rubbish,' the old woman barked. 'He's a lunatic, that one. There's nothing leaking up here.' Just then, Jools heard a pained howl coming from the flat. It could have been animal or human. Jools wasn't sure.

'Don't you pay no attention to Henry,' the old woman said. 'He howls for attention. Been doing that for forty years. Since our wedding night.'

'Would you mind if I come in and take a look at your loo?' Jools asked.

'I told you there's nothing wrong with our pipes!' the old woman yelled, stamping her fuzzy foot at the same time.

'Madame,' Jools began, trying to stay professional, 'I have been hired to keep this building clean and orderly. I can't do my job if you don't let me in.'

'Fine, come inside. But watch where you step. We got traps set for the vermin.'

The old woman opened the door and Jools stepped backwards in horror. The entire flat was covered in rat-traps, many of which had already achieved their purpose. Dead rats lay scattered about the small two-bedroom flat, roaches scurried up walls and the entire apartment seemed coated in a fine sheen of urine.

Jools immediately spied the old woman's husband. He was hard to miss. Tied into his wheelchair with what looked like fishing line, he held an oxygen tank on his lap and shrieked as she approached. He held the mask up and took a deep breath of oxygen. Jools almost snatched the mask to use the fresh air herself, but managed to exercise restraint.

Where the floors weren't covered in rats, yellowed newspapers served as makeshift carpeting. The old woman had seated herself on a filthy sofa and was sifting through more papers when Jools spotted herself on the cover of one of them. She shook her head and headed quickly for the loo, hoping that the old woman wouldn't recognise her. But it was too late.

'You! It's you!' Jools heard the old woman shout from the lounge. Then she started cackling like crazy.

Jools closed the loo door. The bathtub was filled with rust-coloured water. Lord knew how long it had been standing in there. The old woman started banging on the door.

'You're the fat doughnut girl who was to marry that politician! Let me in, I want to talk to you!' The old woman pounded manically on the door.

'You're wrong. I'm a cleaner. Just a cleaner.'

'Bullshit. Come out, I want to take a photo, it might be worth something.'

God, enough was enough. Jools sprang out of the bathroom like a crazy person.

'Listen you pathetic old bag, my life is none of your business, and given how you live, I have absolutely nothing to be ashamed of. So you can take your leak, and your rats and your nasty little hovel and shove them.'

And with that, she stormed out.

The next morning, Jools headed straight for Rocco's office and told him she wouldn't be cleaning the building any longer.

'That's too bad, Joolsy,' he said to her. 'Obviously, you'll have to leave your flat then. Or pay rent.'

'Rent?' she asked, disgusted. 'That room is barely fit for human presence. And you want rent for it?'

'Better than the streets, isn't it?' he snarled.

Jools had to admit that it was a *minute* step up from sleeping in the gutter. But she wasn't going to sit back and let some thug manipulate her.

'Here's the thing, Rocco. I need a few days to get some money. And you know, if that building really is for council flats, it shouldn't be in that condition.'

Rocco yawned. 'Yeah, yeah.'

She flashed him what she hoped was a respectable glare. You wouldn't want anyone to find out about it, would you?'

'Just who would care?'

Thinking fast, Jools replied that the local council probably would. 'If you are being paid to look after those cesspit council flats, you might be in a load of trouble about the state they're in.'

'You threatening me, Joolsy?'

'No, just suggesting you give me a few days to come up with some rent, Rocco. Nothing more.'

And Jools flounced out of Rocco's office without another word.

She headed straight for the nearest Internet café, but as cash was a problem, a bout of lurking was necessary. Finally a guy in the corner seemed to be finishing up.

'I don't suppose you have any time left on your computer? That you could spare, I mean?'

'Sure, what the hell.'

Then he looked more closely. 'Wait a minute, aren't you the girl ...'

Oh for God's sake.

'No,' said Jools quickly. 'I just look a lot like her. Nightmare!'

Jools sat down and logged onto miSell with her old username. Thankfully it still worked. Setting up accounts was time consuming, time she definitely couldn't afford. Next to her a half-filled cup of still-hot coffee beckoned temptingly, but she resisted the temptation. Knowing her luck, an errant pap was sitting nearby googling long-range lenses.

The Chanel suit and Dior handbag she'd managed to extract from Rodney's clutches were in near-perfect condition. They might just fetch enough to keep her going until she found a job that didn't involve rats or urine.

With no time for a long, drawn-out auction she opted for 'Buy Now' and set a fair price for the items.

After conning the café operator for a credit for the remaining 15 minutes, she left the café and managed to sneak into a local cinema to watch some guys try to blow up other guys.

Or more accurately, to sleep in relative comfort.

A few hours later, she logged on again and was shocked to discover that both items had already been purchased by someone called **MysteriousSSSS.** That was remarkably quick.

Then again, high-end designer at high-street prices was always in demand, wasn't it?

At last, something was going right.

Jools wasted no more time wondering about the identity of the buyer. There was enough to pay Rocco three months' rent in advance – hopefully on something a tad more salubrious than the pit she was in now.

Maybe her old flat was still available?

If so, she would be right back where she started. Oddly, the thought was more comforting than depressing.

Chapter 29

Dear Lady Margaret,

With reference to your letter that Rodney was kind enough to throw at me on my departure, I respond as follows.

I will not be paying the £19,500 because I don't have it and can't afford it. If, however, you insist, I will sell the story of your ongoing coke habit to the highest bidder, allowing me to pay your invoice, and in all probability giving me plenty to live on for the next year.

If I don't hear from you, I will assume the debt is wiped.

Julia M. Grand

THE BUYER had used PayPal, so Jools went straight to Rocco and said she could transfer money from her account to his immediately, as long as he had a place to rent in her old building, not Rat Villas.

Rocco had been slightly surprised – no doubt fully expecting her to submit to his will (and slave-labour cleaning) again. Well, that was over. Jools was taking control of her life, and no one was going to push her around or threaten her again.

'Dare I ask what you had to do for it?' he asked, handing over new keys to her old flat.

'None of your business,' she said.

'Three months ain't long, Joolsy. You got some dosh in your pocket now, sure, but what will you do when it runs out? You'll be back to your same old routine, eh. Desperate, penniless and begging me for mercy.'

Jools didn't even respond. Turning and walking out of Rocco's office, she heard him snort through a mouthful of kebab. What if the bastard was right? Having just sold the last of her high-priced belongings, she'd better find another way to make money soon, or in three months she'd be scrambling about in rubbish bins again.

It's good to be home, she thought, swinging open the door to the old flat to be greeted by a familiar, dusty smell. She breathed it in deeply, happily realising she'd never been totally comfortable in Rodney's place. Like being an intruder marking time until the real occupants appeared and evicted her.

The suit and bag fetched quite a tidy sum and even after paying her rent, Jools had enough left over to stock up on some essentials at Sainsbury's. Walking the floodlit aisles, she paused in front of the cupcakes, chocolates and doughnuts, saliva pooling in her mouth. No. She forced herself to walk away.

No more junk food, ever again. Well, maybe on special occasions. Or once a week. Perhaps just one packet of HobNobs today if there was a pound or two left.

No. No. No. Jools was determined to stick to her new plan of sensible behaviour.

Surprisingly, it felt good to stock up on lo-cal canned goods and non-perishable items. When the unpacking and restocking was completed, there was barely room to edge past the breakfast bar into the kitchen. At least I'm ready for a nuclear holocaust, she thought. It did sort of feel like she was preparing for something, but had no idea what.

Never mind, with a roof over her head and enough food for a month, everything was under control. And this time, she was going to make it on her own.

Well, she kind of had to, didn't she?

She bought a small microwave from the pawn shop and was pleased to find that it worked. Preparing a treat of frozen fish fingers and green peas, she sat on the floor and declared to thin air it was good to be home.

Sure, her new place was a total pigsty but at least it was *her* pigsty. Nobody was going to kick her out – well, not for three months anyway. She could come and go as she pleased, keep things as messy or as clean as she wanted them and eat whatever she desired without the worry of someone, anyone, noting she was starting to look like a heifer in denim.

As happy as she was to be back in her old life, two staples were missing: Mel – and Skuttle. She couldn't shake the sad truth that she was completely alone. She missed her best friend, and it seemed Skuttle had vanished. No Hunk of No Fixed Abode to perv at from her little window anymore. It was tragic.

All by myself, she crooned tunelessly at the scarred walls, *a la* Bridget Jones, *Don't wanna be . . .*

Wait a minute!

She sat up. There was no reason to be alone. Skuttle might be gone, but she and Mel could make up. They couldn't let a man (if you could call Michel a man) keep them apart. They were better friends than that, weren't they?

The next morning, full of determination, Jools got up off the blanket on the floor that doubled as a bed, dressed in her Juicy Couture tracksuit, and headed for Mel's.

It wasn't an easy task given the bus had been cancelled and there were roadworks at Notting Hill, but finally she got to Kensington.

Eagerly, she raced up the stone steps to Mel's flat, but to no avail. No one was home.

She waited, pressing the buzzer intermittently for an hour before finally conceding defeat – and being told to 'piss off or I'll hose you down' by the porter.

So much for the tearful reunion she'd been expecting.

Jools dragged herself back to her flat, *All By Myself* playing on a never-ending loop in her head.

Somehow, she'd always thought she and Mel would get through this, like they'd got through everything in the past. Mel had always been there for Jools, through thick and thin, and the thought of spending the rest of her life without her best friend took away even Jools' appetite. She walked in her front door, looked with dismay at the fallen stack of bean tins in front of her (just something else to clean) before turning away and flopping on the floor.

A little while later she paid a visit to the Internet café, where more bad news greeted her.

Her father. Emailing to say he was leaving the country – again. Full of curses and blame, his lengthy message made it clear Jools had ruined his chances of living as a free person in his homeland. But Jools was beyond caring. She had no desire to see him ever again. Even living in Rocco's concrete rat hotel was preferable.

I'm leaving with a group of Ukrainians I met at a hostel I had to go when my own daughter told me to bugger off from her wedding.

From what she could decipher, he was going to an ex-Soviet Union state in the back of a biscuit lorry, where the law was of no consequence and he could live freely with whomever he wanted. He would not be bound by the laws of so-called civilised society any longer and if she chose to pass this email along to the authorities, she would surely rot in hell for betraying the man who had given her life and supported her emotionally and financially much longer than she deserved.

The nerve! Dear old Dad definitely had to be locked up, in an insane asylum if not jail.

With him and Mel out of the picture, Jools wondered if Skuttle was truly lost to her. There had to be a hobo registry or something, surely? Skuttle was the only friend she'd ever had who loved (okay liked) her no matter what. He'd always seemed to put Jools' needs above his own, and in the person-eat-dog world of the streets, that meant a lot.

Jools racked her brain to think of something but decided there was no way to find her Hunk of No Fixed Abode.

She was alone. No choice but to accept it. Taking a deep breath she decided Rocco was right. Time to get real, to find a real way of living, instead of relying on get-rich quick schemes and online sales.

A job was what was required. Immediately. Something that didn't involve rodents or excrement.

As she wasn't about to go back to cleaning, a new career path was required. But with no office experience, a corporate job was out of the question. She'd never waited tables or worked at a bar. Her computer skills were limited to the most basic of tasks and to top it all off, the only 'suitable for job interview' suit she had left was in the boot of the BMW confiscated by Rodney.

Suddenly, a large sign on one of the buses outside caught her eye.

Wanted: competent drivers. Good rates of pay. Immediate start. Apply now.

Brilliant! How hard could it be to drive a bus? Should be easy enough to convince the bus company she could handle an oversize vehicle. After all, she could steer herself around well enough, couldn't she?

Getting dressed in the best skirt and top that she could find in her bags, she swung out of the window and down into the bus station, heading for the sign that said 'OFFICE'.

'Yes, love, can I help?' The bloke in the office considered her with the interest of a bargain shopper at a penny bazaar. He had a bulbous nose and bloodshot eyes and was almost completely bald save a circle of fine black hair that wound its way over his ears and to the back of his head where it was tied into a loose ponytail. And he was more overweight than her.

A good sign.

'The sign out front says you're hiring.'

He sat back and folded his arms behind his round head. 'You? Can you drive a bus?'

'Don't I look like I can?' Dodging difficult questions seemed the best option.

'I don't know, but your heavy vehicle licence will prove it one way or the other.'

Shit. Double shit. Jools hadn't thought this thing through, had she?

'Look, can't you train me and then I take that test? You always hear about bus driver shortages. I have a valid licence and I'm a good driver, so I'm sure I could get whatever other licence I need to drive a bus.'

'It's not just about driving. It's so, so much more than driving.' He shook his head solemnly.

'Well, what's it about then?' she asked. 'Steering? Opening the doors? Swearing at passengers? It can't be all that complicated.'

His mouth plopped open and his eye twitched as if he was stunned by her ignorance.

'I just don't know,' he said, eyelid fluttering and head shaking. He lit a cigarette and began to puff. Jools thought it was illegal to smoke in offices, but didn't want to risk being set on fire by saying so.

'Please? Give me a shot? I promise to impress you.'

'Save the big-eyed routine for the boss,' the man said, mellowing slightly. 'He's the one you need to impress.'

'Fine.' Wishing she had worn her busty Topshop dress instead of the solemn shirt and skirt ensemble, Jools leaned over the table.

'Just give me five minutes. I'm sure I can convince him.'

Pushing her off his paperwork, the man stood up

and walked over to a door at the back of the office. He rapped sharply and waited.

Finally, a well-spoken voice answered 'Yes?' and the man went inside. Jools held her breath.

'He'll see you in an hour,' the man said, emerging a few moments later. 'You can wait here. Help yourself to some food and so on, if you like.'

Jools liked. She headed for the garage canteen and got herself a cup of coffee and a couple of donuts. But the coffee's tinny taste made her grimace. She'd got used to the special blend Rodney imported directly from Kenya. And after one bite of the donut she felt sick. Far too much sugar, given she had been sticking to more filling, savoury foods like beans.

Time to get real, she reminded herself as she flipped through the pages of a tatty old Penthouse. She was going to get this job and make a new start. Maybe Rodney would let her pay back the money week by week, with interest. Okay, it would take about 2000 years on a bus driver's salary, but if he refused the deal, well, he would have to sue her, wouldn't he?

Happy there was at least one magazine whose cover she hadn't graced, she skimmed the salacious tale of a buxom school teacher and a mailman as she waited.

'Jools?'

She looked up and her eyes widened.

It couldn't be.

It was.

'Skuttle!' She jumped out of her seat and wrapped her arms around him. God, he smelled good.

'Easy, Jools,' he said softly, although his arms were around her too. Neither of them let go for the longest time.

Finally, Jools pulled away. 'I've been looking everywhere for you!' She eyed the packet of crisps and the bottle of fizzy drink in his hands. 'Skuttle, you need to be careful nicking things from here.'

She cast a furtive glance rearwards to make sure no one had seen. 'Put those under your coat so no one sees you leaving with them.'

Skuttle smiled and did as he was told. 'I've been worried about you, Jools,' he said. 'The press have been sniffing around. It was worse last week but they're still popping up every now and again.'

'I'm not too worried. I'll be old news soon enough?'

'You look brilliant,' he said, changing the subject.

Jools giggled. She looked mismatched and unkempt.

'I mean it!' he continued. 'I like you with a little meat on your bones. You look healthy.'

Jools' cheeks went red. She didn't believe a word of it but it was certainly good to hear. 'You're very sweet. But come on. I'm a cow, as Rodney says. Used to say.'

A quick flash of anger flickered over Skuttle's handsome, hairy face. 'Some people don't know what they're on about.'

Eager to catch up, Jools asked Skuttle where he'd been and what he'd been doing.

'This and that,' he replied, looking away.

'But where have you been living?'

'Oh, here and there.'

Jools didn't want to pry; he was probably too embarrassed to tell her where he'd ended up. Maybe he was staying at a men's shelter or in some dodgy wino skip somewhere. The bus people must have discovered his hidey hole and evicted him.

'And you?' Skuttle asked. 'Where are you living?'

Jools decided to be just as cagey with Skuttle. She really didn't want him to know she was living in one of Rocco's flats – right back where she had started.

'Oh, here and there,' she said, smiling.

But Skuttle wasn't as quick to drop the subject as she had been.

'I care about you, Jools,' he said. 'I want to make sure you're safe.'

'Don't worry, Skuttle. I've got a place. My old place. Not much better than the one we shared together, but it's big enough for two. If you need somewhere to stay, you're always welcome.'

Blushing a deep red, Skuttle mumbled his thanks. As she glanced at the clock on the canteen wall, Jools realised she needed to get ready for her interview.

'Good luck,' Skuttle said when informed of her future as a bus driver. He even looked impressed.

'I mean it about staying with me,' she said again.

'Whenever you need anything, you know where to find me.'

Jools headed to the loo and splashed some cold water on her face. She hadn't managed to extract any of the expensive makeup from Rodney's, so hopefully freezing water would add a little colour to her cheeks. After a few minutes, she stood back. Her size 16 body was as lumpy as ever, but at least her face looked alright. Definitely pass for a twenty-seven-year-old.

A quick fluffing of hair and adjustment of bra (including undoing one more button on her stripey shirt) and she was ready. At least being obese gave you good cleavage. She'd do anything to land this job.

Well, just about anything.

New leaf, Jools, remember?

Making her way back to the garage office, she smiled winningly at the gruff man with the ponytail. Eyes fixed on her newly-revealed assets, he knocked over the potted fern as he stumbled to the other end of the office and knocked on the boss's door.

'You can go in now,' the man said to her boobs.

Jools strode into the office, all set to make a good first impression. But the boss wasn't even facing her.

Positioned behind a large metal desk at the far end of the room, all she could see was the strong profile of his shoulders and the hairy curve of his neck.

She felt a bit like Dorothy in *The Wizard of Oz* – a fat Dorothy with the beginnings of a dowager's hump.

'Take a seat,' he ordered.

Jools sat down in a hard-backed wooden chair about five feet away from the desk.

'Thank you for seeing me, sir,' she began but was interrupted before she had the chance to say another word.

'I wasn't going to. I've looked at your CV and you certainly aren't qualified for this position.'

Jools' heart sank. The man was right. She'd done it again – buried her head in the sand and stupidly hoped that, despite all logic, everything would be fine. Still, desperation kept her from walking out.

'I know, sir,' she said. 'You're right. On paper, I don't appear to be the best candidate for this job.'

'So why should I hire you?'

'I'm a hard worker and a decent person. I'm just a bit down on my luck.'

She wished he would turn around. It was hard enough begging, let alone begging someone's back!

The man didn't even answer.

Jools stood. She was hard up but there was only so much that could be achieved when you couldn't even see a person's face. 'I'm sorry to have wasted your time.' She choked back tears and started for the door.

'Wait,' the man said, just as she reached for the handle. 'Sit down for a second.'

Hope fluttered in her chest as she sank back onto the hard wooden chair. God, this chair was tiny. If he ever did turn around Jools prayed he wouldn't notice how her bum oozed over the edges.

'Yes,' he said thoughtfully, still facing the other way. 'I might have something else for you.'

Hope banged hard against her ribs now. 'Really? You'll give me a job?'

A proper job, one without rats and poo? Everything would be alright if she could get one of those.

'No,' the boss said and Jools felt her face fall. 'I don't think so.'

Christ, maybe she shouldn't have unbuttoned as far as she had. But no, he couldn't even see her.

'But why did you call me back if you're not going to give me a job?'

'Because,' he said, 'I just like hearing your voice.'

What? Was he insane? Or a sexual deviant?

Then the chair spun around and Jools gasped.

There, in the large, expensive leather recliner, sat the Hunk of No Fixed Abode – Skuttle.

Chapter 30

Dear Miss Grand,

Thank you for your email providing information on your father's whereabouts. Due to your public-spirited notification, we have arrested Charlie Grand and extradited him to Spain, where as you know charges are pending.

It must have been difficult for you to come forward, and in recognition of this, we have reinstated your eligibility for future benefits from the government, should you need them.

Yours sincerely,
Inspector Edwards Muffon
UK Border Agency

SKUTTLE GRINNED WIDELY but all Jools could do was sit and stare. Had Skuttle broken into the office? Had he knocked out the real boss with his bottle of Stumpy? Was said boss bound and gagged in the corner closet?

'What the hell are you doing?' she said when she could finally speak. 'You'll get arrested!'

Skuttle got up and walked around to where she was sitting. He positioned his well-formed backside on the edge of the metal desk and folded his hands in his lap. He really did look a treat in those combats!

'Just listen for a minute, Jools,' he said. 'There's something I really need to tell you.'

God, she'd never seen his face so serious. She hoped he hadn't murdered the real boss or something. Her heart raced. Maybe he wanted her to help hide the body? As much as she liked Skuttle, no way was she getting involved in something like that. Besides, she couldn't stand the sight of blood.

'Skuttle, this isn't funny. What have you done with the man who was supposed to interview me? Did you hurt him?'

'I'm that man,' Skuttle said calmly.

'Stop fooling,' she demanded, fear growing inside of her. Did just knowing him make her an accomplice?

A knock interrupted the tension in the room. The door swung open before Skuttle had a chance to respond.

'What on earth did you mean, dragging me all the way to this shithole, Skuttle, when we very easily could have met at your office in the City?'

Jools knew that voice. But she couldn't figure out why the hell its owner would be at the bus station. She whipped around.

Rodney was standing by the door. When he saw her, his eyes widened. He seemed just as surprised to see her as she was to see him.

'What is this? Have you gone completely insane?' Rodney asked Skuttle.

'I know you're angry,' Skuttle said, looking at Jools. 'But let me explain.'

Jools felt weak. Had Rodney drafted Skuttle into his plan to totally discredit and humiliate her? After all, hobos could be bought and sold if they were desperate enough. Look at what she'd done.

Thoughts clogged her mind. She opened and closed her mouth, but nothing came out. Finally she waved a hand in Skuttle's direction. 'Go on.' She needed to know what Skuttle's role was in all of this. And what had Rodney meant by 'City office'?

'Just wait one minute,' Skuttle said and as if on cue, Mel sauntered in.

'Hello Mr Ryan, I'm terribly sorry to have kept you waiting but I ran into a spot of traffic on the way over,' she said, before she realised who else was in the room with her. And that Mr Ryan was Skuttle the hobo.

'Not at all, Miss Smythe-Brooks. I was just entertaining some friends with whom I believe you are acquainted.' Skuttle stood and held out a chair for her.

Mel looked around the office. Her eyes went from Jools to Rodney and then back to Skuttle.

'Is this some kind of horrible joke?' Mel asked.

'Not at all. It's quite serious and now that we're all here, I'll explain,' Skuttle said.

'Too bloody right you'll explain, Skuttle,' Rodney shouted.

'Stop!' Jools said, breaking in. 'How do you know his name? Do you two know each other?' She couldn't imagine how plastic Rodney might have crossed paths with grotty Skuttle.

Skuttle nodded. 'We went to boarding school together, Jools. Rodney came up with my nickname himself.'

'The old boy was a master at skittles,' Rodney said. 'And as you know, 'skuttle' is the past tense of 'skittle', very clever, I thought . . .'

Jools rolled her eyes. 'And Mel? How do you know Mel?' she asked Skuttle, interrupting Rodney's reverie.

'I saw her with you at that coffee shop you're both so fond of, found out she was a lawyer and retained her services (by phone, of course) for help with some of my, er, new homeless pals.'

Jools looked around at the faces in front of her. Tears pushed at her eyes. 'You all think this is funny, don't you? This is a conspiracy, isn't it? To make me feel worse than I already do. Is that it? You're all in this together?'

'I had no idea you were acquainted with Skuttle,' Rodney said. 'I'm just as much in the dark as you are, Jools.'

'Me too,' Mel said. 'This is the last time I accept a brief over the phone.'

Skuttle sighed. 'I didn't want to make you angry, Jools. I just wanted to help.' He put a soft hand on her arm and looked around the room. 'Let me shed some light on this for all of you. The first thing you need to know is that I'm actually quite wealthy.'

'You're a bit more than 'wealthy'.' Rodney sank onto a grotty sofa and looked around with distaste. 'More money than Bill Gates, on a good day.'

Jools' head was spinning. 'Then why the hell did you pretend to be a hobo?'

'I wanted to find someone to love me for me,' he said, as if it were the most natural answer in the world.

Mel and Rodney laughed meanly.

'Come off it, old boy, you just like to drink,' said Rodney. 'At school, you put vodka in your ink pens and sucked them dry in Ancient Greek.'

Mel added: 'Besides, there are dating services for rich men like you. Plenty of psychiatrists too.'

But Skuttle wasn't laughing. 'Do you have any idea how many of those I've tried? Not the shrinks, the dating agencies.'

Mel shrugged.

'I don't have any trouble meeting women, Mel; I have trouble meeting women who are interested in me for anything other than my money. Online dating hasn't helped me. As soon as they find out who I am and what I'm worth it's the same thing. I can smell a gold digger from a mile away and I'm simply not interested in a loveless marriage.'

His words stung. Jools was suddenly ashamed of her willingness to engage in a sham marriage in exchange for a comfortable existence.

'Poor Skuttle. You've never been the best-looking bloke, have you? I guess with looks like yours, you need to do what you can.' Rodney preened, proud of his own good sharp features and smooth skin.

Jools turned and shot him an angry glance. 'I've always thought he was gorgeous,' she said, forgetting for a moment her Skuttle wasn't the same man she thought he was.

'Yeah, she has. She's crazy.' Mel looked over at her client. 'No offense.'

But Skuttle was beaming. 'You did?' he asked, his blue-grey eyes searching Jools'.

Transfixed by Skuttle's eyes, she could only nod.

'But why a hobo?' asked Rodney. 'Why not just pretend to be an ordinary guy? Did you really need to sink so low?' He shuddered just thinking about living anywhere other than Zone 1.

Jools would have loved to slap Rodney for being so condescending, but how could she expect him to understand given his own dysfunctional past?

Even so, she admired Skuttle's brave move to leave all his riches and comforts behind to find love.

'I just needed to get away,' Skuttle said, 'away from

money and privilege. To disappear, and see if I could manage without the cushion of wealth that's been there all my life. To see if there was a woman out there who liked the real me. If I could find someone who cared about Skuttle the hobo, I'd know I'd found a real gem.' He smiled gently at Jools.

Rodney and Mel sat, baffled, as if Skuttle had just told them he wanted to start an ant colony on the moon. The expressions on their faces said that on a scale of one to mad, they thought he was insane.

'So when I met Jools . . . ' Skuttle smiled again and raised an eyebrow.

Jools felt her neck get hot and she started to sweat. This couldn't be happening. Where were the hidden cameramen? When would the white-toothed host pop out and scream 'Gotcha!'? She was starting to think poor Skuttle really was nuts.

'Jools,' Skuttle said, 'I fell in love with you instantly. You're so down-to-earth, so open and generous. I know you've made a few mistakes, but we're all human, right?'

'Yeah, but mine were huge,' Jools said, still unable to believe Skuttle was serious.

'That's for sure,' mumbled Rodney.

'I don't care.' Skuttle's eyes were trained on her. 'I love you anyway. When you came to live with me, I wondered if you'd turn out to be crazy after all. But the more I saw, the more I liked – loved. I just loved you more and more.'

The pieces started clicking into place in Jools' mind. The laptops, the phone line . . . the Hermes handkerchief.

Skuttle was telling the truth.

He laughed. 'That computer was brand new, but I had to scuff it up so that you wouldn't wonder where I'd got the money to buy it. I made sure the squat, as dingy as it was, had everything you'd need to feel comfortable. I did it all for you. And then you left.

'I knew you were up to something online. When I saw the newspapers and how they were making your life hell, I wanted to go and get you. And when you came to me, all upset, you told me you loved Rodney. I didn't want to press you to leave.'

'You always were a gentleman, Skuttle,' Rodney said sarcastically.

Skuttle ignored him. 'But when you showed up at the bus station today and you offered to help me even though you don't have much yourself, I knew I had to be honest with you. You seemed so happy to see me again.'

'I was,' Jools said. 'I mean, I am.'

'I'm sorry I wasn't honest with you, Jools. I just needed to feel certain that you were the one.' As he leaned in closer, she took a deep breath of that delicious-smelling aftershave. 'And you are, Jools. You are the one.'

'Oh, come on!' Mel shook her head, arms folded across her chest. 'You can't be serious. First of all, you can never be sure someone is 'the one'.' Mel had her lawyer voice on again. 'Furthermore, you've spent the past few weeks lying to Jools about your true identity. Why should she believe you now?'

She grabbed Jools' arm. 'You're not buying any of this, are you? For God's sake, grow up.'

Jools leaped up. 'Why shouldn't I believe him? How is this any different to you believing everything that comes out of that fake Frenchie's mouth? Even over your own best friend!'

'Michel strayed once, Jools! Once. And we're working through it.'

Rodney let out a puff of air. 'Yeah, right,' he muttered.

Mel turned toward him. 'What was that?' Her voice was like steel.

Rodney's face twitched with anger. 'I said, yeah, right! That man is a born and bred cheater.' His cheeks were red.

'How would you know?' Mel matched the anger in his voice.

'Because he cheated on me, too!' Rodney screamed.

'What?'

'He's gay, or bi, or . . . I'm so sorry,' Jools tried to say the words (as gross as they were), gently.

'I don't believe you!'

'I've got a number of DVDs you could borrow,' said Rodney helpfully.

Mel collapsed into the chair and covered her face with her hands. Jools went over and threw her arms around her, whilst Rodney continued his tale of woe.

'He cheated on me with the owner of some restaurant in Islington. Apparently, he has a yacht and a flat at Sandbanks.' Rodney looked furious at the thought of anyone matching his wealth.

'I'm so sorry,' Mel tear-stained pixie face looked up at Jools. 'I should have listened to you. I just didn't want to.'

'It's alright,' Jools said. 'I just want you to be with someone who deserves you.'

Skuttle reached into his desk and pulled out a large cheque book. He sat down and started writing.

'I have a rough estimate of what Jools owes you, Rod. The tabloids have been very thorough with their details. But please, if the amount is not sufficient, do let me know.' Skuttle ripped the cheque out of the book and handed it to Rodney.

'Yes, that looks about right,' Rodney said.

'How much has he given you?' Jools leaned over and Rodney tried to hide the amount, but she saw the six figures.

'£100,000! Skuttle, that's way too much!'

But Skuttle just shrugged. 'It's nothing to me. Let him have it.'

'Sporting of you, mate.' Rodney tucked the cheque into his pocket, dreaming of all the leather accoutrements he would treat himself to. 'Now, if you don't mind, I'm off. There's a meeting with the council. If I'm late Mrs Pho will have my head on a platter.'

'Goodbye, Jools.' Rodney held out his hand formally. 'I certainly won't forget you.' A mirthless grin twisted his lips.

Jools touched his cold fingers with distaste. God, she was glad that chapter in her life was closed. She wouldn't even miss the doughnuts and cupcakes. No, she was a tried and true HobNobs girl, and she wouldn't forget it.

Skuttle shifted in his chair to be closer to Jools.

'Would you like me to give you two some time alone?' Mel asked, edging towards the door.

'No, stay, please,' Skuttle said. 'You're one of the most important people in Jools' life. Whatever I say to her, I can say in front of you.'

Mel smiled. 'Thank you, Skuttle.' She turned to Jools. 'I think you may have finally found a good one here. About time.'

'I told you so,' Jools said, smiling.

Skuttle reached out and took Jools' hands in his. She couldn't quite work up the nerve to make eye contact with him so she stared at her feet, which were encased in the only decent shoes she had managed to get past Rodney, peep toe Manolos.

'I love you, Jools. I want to be with you, by your side, and in your life.'

It was what she'd longed to hear from, well, anyone. But now that she'd heard it, she wasn't sure. 'I don't know, Skuttle. I think I might love you. But I need to get my life together. And I need to do it on my own this time.'

'Jools, I understand that. I'll give you whatever space you need to do it.'

Jools raised her eyes to meet his. 'It's not just that. I need to be sure who you really are. I've been so wrong before,' she added, remembering how she'd thought Rodney was such a nice guy.

This time she was going to do things right.

'How do I know that the Skuttle I've fallen for is the real Skuttle? I mean, Skuttle with money is bound to be completely different.'

'I think you'd be surprised,' he said, smiling. 'I still like hanging about in parks at night.'

Jools was silent. It was a lot to process.

'How about we start with dinner? No need to worry about all the big stuff now. We'll figure it out.'

Oddly, Jools wasn't hungry. Instead, her stomach was full of butterflies. 'Yes,' she said anyway. 'Dinner sounds good.'

Skuttle beamed. 'Brilliant. Do you have your passport handy?'

'Why on earth would I need my passport for dinner?' Jools asked, chuckling.

He *was* still the same. Crazy.

'We're having dinner in New York. I made reservations at Nobu and my private jet is standing by at Heathrow.'

'You want to fly to New York? Right now?'

'Well, yes. But only if you want to.' For a second, Skuttle looked nervous.

'Actually, do you mind if we just go to Mama Blue's?' asked Jools. She'd had enough of fancy dinners, or fancy anything, for a while. Just the thought of the familiar grotty café comforted her, and that whipped cream on toast combo had been surprisingly good.

Skuttle nodded. 'Whatever you like. New York will always be there for you when you're ready.'

Besides, as she looked over at her rather forlorn friend, Jools realised that she couldn't abandon Mel, not even for Skuttle. 'Could Mel come?' she asked.

'Of course. Wouldn't dream of heading to your favourite hangout without her!' He turned to Mel. 'Do us a favour and go tell my man Harry to have the car pulled around. He's right out front.'

'He might be a looker,' added Jools, but Mel just sighed and marched briskly to the door.

'So you don't hate me for lying?' Skuttle asked once Mel had gone.

'No. How could I? You know what they say about people in glass houses . . .'

Skuttle grinned. 'They pay a fortune in curtains?'

She punched him playfully.

'But there *is* one more thing we need to discuss before we head out.'

Jools was immediately despondent. It had seemed too good to be true.

Maybe this was the part where the hidden cameraman leaped out?

'I just want you to know that you'll never hear from that sicko Niles again.'

'You've met him?'

'Had him followed the moment I caught him in a tree outside your apartment.'

Jools breathed a huge sigh of relief. 'What happened to him?' Hopefully someone had tied him to a tree and graffitied him with Marmite at the very least.

Skuttle shook his head. 'You don't need to know. All that's important is he'll never bother you again. Or that guy he pretended to be. Brad Brown?'

'Niles was Brad Brown?' Jools felt more than a little disappointed that the hunky American who had kept her spirits alive all that time was nasty little Niles.

'He needs medication of some sort, that's for sure.'

'Car's here!' Mel called.

'Wait a minute.' Jools looked down at herself. 'Maybe I should get changed? I can't go in your fancy car looking like this!'

'Jools, I think you look beautiful no matter what you're wearing. But I have these just in case.' And he pulled out her suit and bag from miSell.

'You bought them?' Jools couldn't believe it.

'I was worried about you, especially when you went to work for Rocco.'

Jools looked at him sternly. 'I hope you're not some crazy stalker like Niles, Skuttle.'

'No, Jools, I am just a hobo. And no one notices a hobo. No one but you.'

Jools smiled shyly and took his hand. 'And I'm so glad you did.'

As they stared into each other's eyes, Mel made fake puking noises behind them. 'Come on, I'm going to be sick if you two don't stop it!'

Jools reached out and grabbed Mel's hand and the three of them walked out of the office, through the bus garage and to the large black Bentley that was idling at the curb.

Mel crawled into the front seat beside Skuttle's handsome driver. 'Why, hello there!' she crooned, turning to wink at Jools. The spell of Michel Matthews might have finally been broken.

Skuttle and Jools climbed into the back. He put his arm around Jools and pulled her close. She leaned her head on his chest. The fabric felt strange and foreign, but as soon as he touched her cheek she felt at ease.

No more lying. No more pretending. Jools would face life head on, make her own luck. Taking short-cuts was never worth it – as she'd discovered the hard way.

She smiled up at Skuttle and sighed in contentment as he stroked her hair. Right now, she wanted to savour every delicious moment.

Even HobNobs couldn't compare to this.

THE END

Look out for the new Nicky Schmidt novel
due out in early 2010

NICKY SCHMIDT

Marrying out of money